Battlesh[illegible]

Battleship RAIDER

OUTLAWS OF THE GALAXY #1

PAUL TOMLINSON

For country of manufacture, please see final page.

ISBN: 978-1-69914-859-4

First published April 2021
Publisher: Paul Tomlinson

www.paultomlinson.org/outlaws

This book is dedicated to the original intergalactic thief and conman Slippery Jim diGriz and his creator Harry Harrison

Prologue

I was beginning to miss the desert. The jungle was hot and humid and the flying insects were bigger than my head. Much bigger. They buzzed around like a gyrocopter stunt team. And anyone who tells you green is calming never saw a snake with a big flat head the colour of a leaf. The only thing that kept me hacking through the undergrowth was the promise of hidden treasure. That and the fact that I was bursting for a swazz and I was afraid to unzip in case something locked its nasty mandibles on my man-thing.

Did I mention the humidity? Every part of me was running with sweat and my clothes were soaked through. I was going to end up with all-over diaper rash. I'd always taken feeling dry for granted but now I was thinking of it as one of the must-have features of Paradise.

I paused to catch my breath and silently curse the old fool that had offered me this crazy 'opportunity'. And the young fool who accepted it. That would be me, Quincy Randall. Thief, conman and part-time idiot. If I'd known what this expedition would be like, well, I'd probably still have come. I needed the cash. But I'd have brought more changes of underwear.

I heard something incoming and swung the machete – then watched one of the giant insects spiral down towards the damp black soil. A long pink tongue snatched the wounded flyer out of the air. I couldn't see the mouth it belonged to, but I could hear the crunching. I shuddered, reminded of the hidden dangers the jungle was home to. Including creatures that were big enough to eat me.

The umbrella-sized leaves ahead of me stirred as a little yellow frog launched itself into the unknown and beyond them I saw... what? Dappled sunlight on tarnished metal? I hoped that's what it was. That's what the old man had promised I would find. I ducked another dive-bombing insect and hacked away at the foliage with renewed vigour, trying to catch another glimpse. If this *was* the wreck I'd been told about, maybe the treasure was here too.

Chapter One

The old man told me his name was Jack Sterling though I suspect that, like me, he'd had a few different names during his time. I met him in the prison in Margotsville, a desert town that lay almost two hundred miles north of the equatorial jungle. Old Jack had been found guilty of killing a man in a bar fight, or so he told me, and seemed content to live out his remaining days within the prison's walls. I had been arrested as a result of a misunderstanding regarding ownership of a sand yacht that I had won in a card game.

The old man had been in prison long enough to know how things worked and he somehow managed to get jugs of the local moonshine smuggled into the cell we shared. Dragon's Tears the locals called it. Dragon swazz more like. Old Jack liked to drink and talk, and I was happy to drink and listen.

"You stole a sand yacht?" he said, looking at me in a way that said 'What the heck would you want a sand yacht for?' Or maybe he was just squinting because he was soused.

"*Technically* I only sort of stole it," I said. "There was a misunderstanding."

"You'd better come up with a better story than that when you go up before the judge."

"It was a beautiful ship," I said. "You ever seen paintings of those old paddle steamers? It looked like one of those. Layered like a wedding cake... just floating over the desert like a mirage."

"How do you steal something that big?"

"I didn't *steal* it. Not exactly. I won it fair and square. Or so I thought. I had the registration document in my hand."

"I don't understand."

"I was playing poker with this guy. People called him One-Eyed Jack on account of his eyepatch, but his real name was Marmaduke – or was it Maurice? Doesn't matter. He had a 'tell'. When he had a good hand he'd touch his eyepatch – as if he wanted to show it to his missing eye."

Old Jack smiled. "You cleaned him out! Got everything, including his yacht."

I smiled too . Until I remembered what happened next.

"Turns out it was registered to the guy's wife. He didn't have a penny to his name. Gambled it all away." I don't usually drink much and this hooch was making my brain feel spongey. "To save himself, Maurice told his wife I'd stolen the papers. I saw his wife and I know why he'd feel the need to do that. I felt sorry for him, so I took the rap."

"That story's so crazy the judge might just believe it," Old Jack said. He took another long pull from the dirty stone jug.

"I told my whacky story, now you tell me one," I said. "You've been around – you must have seen some things."

Old Jack's eyes did the squinting thing again and I thought that perhaps he wasn't as drunk as he was pretending to be. I expected him to tell me about the man he killed, but he had an even better tale than that. Crazier than mine.

"There's a lot of men would like to learn what I know," he said, slurring his words. "There's a fortune to be had by the man who knows where to look."

Tales of hidden treasure were common in the years after the end of the War. Not gold and silver or pilfered works of art but tons and tons of salvage. Military hardware – either floating dead in space or lying on the surface of planets scattered across the warzone. Not the alien stuff, of course, that was mostly biological and decayed quickly. But the human stuff was still out there. Weapons and machinery brought a good price but the greatest prize of all was a ship's Navigator – the artificial sentience that controlled a battleship's systems and directed the movement of its fighter craft. A bounty had been offered by the Alliance for the return of a Navigator and even now, almost forty years later, you could collect the prize and never need to work another day in your life.

"My ship came down and she's never been found," Old Jack said, "but I knows where she's hid." There was a twinkle in his eye when he said it, but I got the feeling he was telling the truth. Or believed he was.

"You were a soldier?" I asked, taking another swig of the harsh liquor.

Jack Sterling shook his head. "Engineer," he said. "I used to service the Warbirds, kept 'em flying."

"What ship were you on?"

"The *Celestia*," he said. He noted my lack of recognition and explained. "Dreadnought class. Not the biggest warship we had, but by that stage we were sending everything we had to the frontline. And this is where we came down."

It took me a minute to realise what he was saying. I blame the moonshine. "You mean the *Celestia* came down here?"

Old Jack nodded.

"It crashed down on *this* planet? On Saphira?" I said.

He nodded again and smiled a crooked smile.

"And you walked away from the wreckage?"

"Don't be a doof, nobody walked away from the wreckage. I got away in a lifeship – came down after her. Our *Celestia* lies but a stone's throw from where we are tonight."

I made a wet farting noise with my lips and reached for the moonshine. Old Jack didn't seem offended by my scepticism, he just sat smiling, that twinkle still in his eyes. He passed me the jug and reached inside his stained and tattered shirt, pulling something out. He tossed it to me.

I caught the cloth-wrapped object and looked down at it. It lay heavy in my palm. I carefully peeled away the bandage-like covering.

"You know what that is, Quin?" he asked.

I nodded. The smooth sphere in my hand was part metal and part crystal. "It's one of the eyes," I said.

Old Jack nodded. "One of the tracking eyes from a cannon – a big one."

"Dreadnought class," I muttered.

"And the rest of the *Celestia* lies in the jungle a couple of hundred miles south of here, untouched by man since the night she came down."

I stared down at the eye. The metal was warm from Jack's body heat but the crystal was ice-cold under my fingers. "But surely she was salvaged," I said. "Her position would have been reported."

Old Jack shook his head, his eyes still glittering in the gloom. "We never reported it," he said. "There was maybe two dozen of us survived, coming down in three life ships. After we touched down, we stood in the desert and looked up at the stars, and all of us decided we'd had enough of war. We made a pact that we'd never tell a soul where the ship had come down and we'd live out the rest of our days as civilians. I'm the only one of us left."

He watched me, probably trying to see if I believed his story.

"That was forty years ago," I said.

"Give or take," he said, nodding.

I wrapped the eye back in the cloth and passed it back to the old man. There was every chance he'd stolen it or won it in a card game. It was an unlikely story. But it *might* be true. And if the *Celestia* was lying out there untouched, then there really was a fortune to be had by the man who knew where to look.

"And in forty years, you've never been back to the crash site?" I asked.

"I never said that, now, did I?" He tucked the eye back into his shirt. "I went there once on my own, just to see her again. And then a few years ago I went with some friends to see what we could get from her. But all we got was trouble. Salvage is a young man's game, Quin."

"And she's still out there..." I mused.

"She broke into pieces as she came down and nose-dived into the trees. Wreckage must have stretched in a line for twenty miles or more. Everything was burned when she hit, but the jungle grew back around her and over her and now no one can see she's there. But her belly's intact, Quin, waiting for the right man to open her up and relieve her of her riches."

It was one of those stories that you *want* to be true. Everyone loves a story of hidden treasure. But even with the 'evidence' Old Jack had shown me, and even in my drink-fuddled state, I knew it was just a story. He had almost certainly never been close to a battleship and that oblong scar on his arm wasn't a war wound, he'd probably burned himself stealing bread from an oven. That's what I was thinking as I went to sleep that night in that dusty prison cell. But it wasn't long until I came to change my mind.

Chapter Two

Desert architecture doesn't vary much from planet to planet. Buildings are low with thick walls made of concrete or mud or whatever. They're usually painted white to try and reflect the heat away. And roofs are either flat or made of heavy clay tiles. The buildings in Margotsville were all like this, including the prison. It was a squat two-storey structure with a yard at the back and a high wall around it, topped with coils of razor-wire. There were signs hung from the wire that warned of the danger of electrocution. I suspected that the fried rats and pigeons hanging from the wire were placed there to make us believe it was electrified, but that was a theory I wasn't in a hurry to test.

A wooden watchtower stood at one corner of the yard, manned at all times by a guard with a rifle. In another corner was a raised platform with a big searchlight on it at, manned only after dark. The prison warden's office looked out into the yard and there was a small section of the yard under his window marked off with white painted pebbles – a little garden filled with sickly-looking desert plants.

The yard itself was hard-packed dirt like the town's roads. You probably couldn't have dug your way out if you had a pneumatic drill or dynamite. The only way out was up and over the wall. Not that I was thinking of escape. Not at that moment. I wasn't up to thinking much of anything.

I'd heard it said that you couldn't get a hangover from alcohol distilled from fermented cactus. I can tell you now that this is a myth. That morning it felt like someone was driving a big spike into my skull and the sunlight hurt my eyes. Old Jack, sitting next to me, thought this was amusing. He seemed totally unaffected.

Being outside during the day was preferable to sitting in a cell trying to breathe the dry dead air. And the heat meant no one wanted to move, so we were unlikely to cause any problems for the guards. The assembled prisoners huddled in whatever part of the yard was currently in shadow, moving around during the course of the day as the sun arced through the sky. At midday everyone went inside for a meal and a siesta. There were only about a dozen prisoners in total.

It was a small prison but Maggotsville itself wasn't much of a place. Other than Old Jack, my fellow inmates were a handful of locals: a kid on a drunk-driving charge who flew an air-bike in through the mayor's front window and out through the back where there wasn't a window. A couple of vagrants there for the free food and water. And a man accused of scracking his neighbour's goat, brought into custody for his own protection. That's what Old Jack told me, though he may have had the story from an unreliable source. None of these men were real desperadoes. The closest we had to that were a couple of crooks that were straight out of a comic book.

The little one was Paulie Pickles, which was probably an alias. Or maybe his pappy had been an onion farmer. He looked like he'd spent a lot of time on high-gravity planets. It wasn't just that he was short and squat, he looked like he'd been squashed. His head was a sideways oval and he had no neck. If his legs had been any shorter he'd have been able to scratch his toes without bending. Dark hair sprouted from every bit of his skin, sticking out like spines on a cactus. He was like a hedgehog that someone had sat on. Prickly described him in other ways too. His brow was set in a permanent scowl and his lips had only one setting – sneer. Paulie's eyes were permanently shadowed and he always looked like he was up to no good. Maybe no one had told him that it was a bad idea for a crook to *look* like a crook. Though his career options must have been limited by his appearance. His high school counsellor had probably hinted that 'children's entertainer' wasn't really an option.

Paulie's partner was Augie 'The Axeman' Allsop. Again, I'm thinking the name was a bit of a giveaway. Augie was the muscle and he obviously took this role literally. Even in the blistering heat he was over in a corner loading all the cast-iron weights he could find onto a single bar for lifting. His head was shaved smooth and shiny and he had a thick dark moustache. He pretended not to see me watching him and pulled off his shirt and stood flexing. I like a man who looks like a man, but that bulging muscles thing doesn't really do it for me. He looked like an orange condom stuffed with walnuts. His tattoos had been done by someone who knew what they were doing – a talented artist or maybe a robot. There was a dragon with its wings spread across his chest – and there was enough space for them to be spread wide.

Augie was vain and he was watching us to make sure we were looking at him. But Paulie was watching us too and that made me uncomfortable.

"Something's going on," I said. "He's watching us."

"He's been watching you ever since you got in here," Jack said, nodding towards Augie and grinning. "I think he likes you."

I nodded towards Paulie Pickles. "I don't reckon much to yours."

"I've had worse," Jack said and cackled.

"Randall!" I looked up as my name was called. Grainger, the head guard, was standing by the little cactus garden, the door open behind him. "Warden wants a word with you." He tried to make it sound threatening, but even without the hangover I could have cared less. I pulled myself to my feet.

"Be careful today," I said to Jack, still uneasy.

"I always am."

Grainger tucked his thumbs in his belt and swaggered across the yard, squinting his eyes at me as we passed each other. I resisted the urge to blow him a kiss. The warden appeared in the doorway of his office as I approached.

"Macready," I said.

He turned and disappeared into his office without acknowledging me. We were supposed to call him *Mister* Macready as a sign of respect – maybe he noticed my omission. I followed him into the office, not closing the door behind me. I wanted to be able to see what was happening in the yard.

Macready was sitting on the corner of the desk. There was a chair off to the left and I wanted to slump into it, but that would be a display of weakness. I didn't want to show my hand too soon. It took a moment for my eyes to adjust to the gloom. The office had a dry dusty smell. The role of prison warden apparently didn't merit air-conditioning. Keeping my eyes down I shuffled sideways so that I could see out through the open door.

Warden Macready had skinny arms and legs and a potbelly. He looked like a thin kid trying to shoplift a bowling ball. His bushy eyebrows were a natural sandy brown but his thinning hair was a flat orange colour out of a bottle. The white shirt and tan slacks he wore were clean and freshly pressed every day but by mid-morning they had that wilted and dusty look.

"Judge will be here day next Thursday," he said.

I nodded. I knew this already. It wasn't why he had asked me into his office. He waited for me to say something but I chose to disappoint him. I wasn't worried about going up before the judge. Either I'd talk my way out of it or I'd escape after he'd sentenced me. This wasn't my first small-town rodeo.

"Got a message for you over the interstat," Macready said. He was pretending disinterest but he was obviously curious. Who was I to be getting messages from off-world?

"Yeah?" I said. I was pretending disinterest too, but in reality he had me worried. No one was supposed to know I was on this squit-hole planet.

"Old friend of yours asking to be remembered to you. Says he's planning to visit. O'Keefe. You know who that is?"

It must have been obvious from my reaction that this was bad news. I saw a flicker of a smile on his lips. But the warden evidently had no idea who O'Keefe was and I wasn't about to tell him.

"Like the message says, just an old friend," I said.

The warden watched me, wanting to know the truth. But what could he do? He couldn't have the guards beat it out of me. Not until I'd been up before the judge.

A movement in the yard drew my attention towards the open door. The warden couldn't see it from where he was. I made it look as though I was eager to make my exit. I saw Paulie Pickles approach Officer Grainger. They carried out a brief muttered conversation and the little man surreptitiously pressed something into Grainger's hand. Either a message or a bribe, I couldn't see which.

"That'll be all, Randall," the warden said, still dissatisfied.

I walked back across the yard and Grainger came from the opposite direction. As we passed, I stumbled and bumped into him. “Sorry, boss,” I said.

“Shouldn’t drink if you can’t handle it,” Grainger said, his lips twisted in a sneer.

Moving away, I looked down at the folded paper I had lifted from Grainger. A hundred dollar bill. That was quite a bribe. I wondered what it had paid for. I could have taken Grainger’s pistol when I’d ‘accidentally’ collided with him, but that would have been spotted quickly and we’d all have been lined up and strip-searched while the guard in the tower pointed his big gun at us. Sometimes you have to take a subtler approach.

I turned and watched Grainger disappear into the warden’s office and close the door behind him. Perhaps he had been paid for his absence. That meant something unpleasant was about to happen. Paulie Pickles was up to something. I’d have to keep a close watch on him until he made his move.

I didn’t have to wait long.

There was a flash of sunlight on metal and Paulie was standing behind Jack and had a shiv pressed against his throat. The little prickly man was standing on tiptoe.

“You and me is going to have a little chat, Jackie boy,” Paulie said.

I hadn’t seen how he managed to get the jump on Old Jack, I was over at the water barrel near the warden’s office. Augie was standing behind Paulie, making sure no one thought about coming to Old Jack’s rescue. I sat down with my back against the barrel trying to come up with a plan that didn’t involve me facing off against a thug with biceps bigger than my head. I came up with nothing. I should have taken Grainger’s gun. I pulled off a boot and tugged at my slightly damp sock, making sure there wasn’t a hole in the toe. Then I reached for one of the white-painted pebbles from the cactus garden. I looked down at it and then swapped it for a bigger one. There was no way this was going to work.

“Augie and me heard you and your bed-mate last night,” Paulie rasped. “That was some mighty interesting pillow talk.”

Paulie Pickles and Augie were in the cell next to ours. With the drink taken, it was possible that Old Jack and I had spoken more loudly than we thought.

"It was just talk," Jack said, "just a made-up story to pass the time."

"I don't think so," Paulie said, pressing the improvised blade into Jack's weathered skin. "You're going to tell me where that wreck of yours lies – or I'm going to start cutting bits off you with this... this..."

"It's a spoon," Jack croaked, looking down cross-eyed at it.

"I spent a long time sharpening it for you," Paulie said. He slashed a thin red line across Jack's neck to prove it.

"You don't have to hurt me," Jack wailed. He was looking in my direction, hoping I'd intervene. I should have told him I wasn't the hero type. "I'll tell you, I'll tell you!" Jack said. "Just don't hurt me."

Maybe someone *had* told him and he was now appealing to my criminal nature. I'd have to rescue him if I wanted to stop him giving away the secret of the hidden treasure. I cursed him, pulling my boot back on. It felt clammy against my bare foot.

I hurled one of the white pebbles towards Augie, sending it over his left shoulder and just missing his head. While he was distracted by this, I started whirling the pebble in the sock round and round over my head and giving the sort of scream I imagined a suicidal warrior might give. I ran towards the big man.

The pebble hit Augie in the side of the head with a loud hollow *thok!* Everyone in the prison yard winced. Apart from Augie. He hardly seemed aware that he'd been hit. As I started swinging the sock again, he reached for it and clasped it in one of his massive hands. Before I knew what had happened, he pulled me towards him and wrapped an arm like a tree trunk around my neck and the sky started to go dark.

Up close, he smelled like a horse. I had a better view of his tattoos. On one arm was a harsh-looking woman in a provocative pose – his mother maybe. But the best image was on his right arm: a highly detailed skull with a snake threaded into its eye socket and out of its mouth. The work on the serpent's scales was some of the best I'd seen. If I didn't do something soon, it might be the last thing I ever saw.

"Hey, gorgeous, don't hug me so tight," I croaked.

"I'm going to kill you and scrack you while you're still warm," he growled.

"You're a silver-tongued devil," I said.

"I'm your worst nightmare." His breath was warm in my ear.

"Actually, I *have* been dreaming about you," I said, "ever since I saw you in the shower." The arm around my throat relaxed – just a little.

"What's that supposed to mean?" he asked.

"It means I've been wondering how it would feel to have your arms wrapped around me."

"That so?" His grip relaxed a little more and I managed to squirm around and look up into his face. He was frowning. "You hit me with a rock." His lower lip stuck out, big and wet and pink.

"A love tap to get your attention."

"You already had that," he said. He leaned down and planted a wet kiss on my forehead.

"He's pretty – can I keep him, Paulie? Can I?" Augie mocked.

"Have you two lovebirds finished?" Paulie snapped.

Augie ignored him. "I bet you've never been with a *real* man."

"I never met anyone quite like you." I stroked the front of his sweatpants.

"I'm not wearing anything under them," he whispered.

Under different circumstances this might have been fun. I grabbed his scronies, squeezed hard and twisted. Augie cried out in surprise and it became a bellow of pain. He went down on his knees and I went down too, not daring to let go. If he got free, he'd break my neck.

"Don't move," I warned. I held a knife close to the bulge of cloth and scronies that I was holding on to. It was a big hunting knife, bright and with a sharp edge. I'd lifted it from Grainger when I took his money.

Augie had tears in his eyes and he was looking at me like I had betrayed him. He was lying on his back now with his arms above his head in surrender.

"Sorry, handsome," I said. I looked over to Paulie Pickles. "Drop the blade or Augie sings castrato."

Paulie hesitated.

"Drop it," Augie squeaked.

There was another moment's hesitation, then Paulie dropped the shiv. Old Jack bent and snatched it up, grinning triumphantly.

"You shouldn't bring a spoon to a knife fight," I said.

Paulie spat at me.

I looked at Augie. Sweat streamed down his face and he looked like he was on the verge of puking. I didn't think he'd give me any trouble if I released him. At least for a little while. I let go and backed away, still keeping the knife ready. Augie just lay in the dirt clutching his groin and making weak groaning noises. I felt for him, every man in the yard did.

"Maybe you can bribe Grainger to bring him some ice for the swelling," I said to Paulie.

"My eggs hurt," Augie wailed, "I think he broke them."

Paulie scowled. "You know what you are?"

"A smart guy with a big knife?"

"You're a dead man!"

"Say something nice at my funeral." I turned my back on him and walked away. Old Jack scurried after me.

"You never said he'd *hurt* me," Augie whined.

"They'll kill you for this," Jack said, "the first chance they get. You'll have to watch your back. And I'll watch it for you. I won't forget what you done for me, Quin. You're a good man."

"I'm not worried about them," I said. "But O'Keefe is a different matter."

"Who's O'Keefe?" Jack asked, confused.

"Trouble." If O'Keefe arrived I'd be facing worse than a charge of taking a sand yacht without consent. I found myself scanning the layout of the prison. "I'm going over the wall. Tonight," I said.

"That's crazy!" Jack protested. "The guards will shoot you before you're half over. And even if you make it, they'll hunt you down with dogs."

"They have dogs?" I asked.

"They always have dogs."

There were no hounds at the prison, we would have heard them. Maybe they called in a hunter from outside. I'd worry about that if – when – I got that far.

"I have to go," I said.

"O'Keefe?"

"A bounty hunter. There's a price on my head. A big one." Old Jack didn't seem surprised by this, which was flattering in a way. "You coming with me?" I asked.

Jack thought about this and then shook his head. "I'll take my chances in here. But I'll help you. Tonight you and me will be drinking and talking and singing like we did last night – only this time I'll be playing both parts. I'll give you as much time as I can."

"Thanks, Jack."

"You're a good man, Quin," he said again, nodding to where Paulie and Augie were huddled against the prison wall watching us.

"Just helping out a friend," I said.

"If O'Keefe is coming for you, you've got to get away," Jack said. "Off the planet."

"If I had money for passage off this rock, I'd have been gone long before now."

"Maybe I can help you with that," Jack said. "I'll give you my map."

"Hidden treasure?"

"Lots of it!"

Chapter Three

This wasn't my first prison escape. I've broken out of some pretty high-tech jails in my time. But this place was distinctly old-school. Old-school as in bars at the windows, human guards, and big rusty locks. This didn't necessarily make escape easier, but it did require different skills.

Technically I wasn't a convict. I was being held pending an appearance before the circuit judge and he might decide that I had no case to answer and let me go free. But he wouldn't. One look at my record and he'd have me extradited back to civilisation to answer for my many crimes. Once there, I wouldn't live long enough to see trial. There were people I'd upset who would have me killed within hours of learning my location. And it wasn't likely to be a quick death. It's a long story but the moral of it is never steal from the big bad guys. I'd done it by mistake but they don't take mitigating circumstances into account.

The judge's arrival in Margotsville was still a few days away, so I had believed I had plenty of time to plan my escape. During the seven days I'd been behind bars I'd already gathered some of the equipment I might need. I had an old torch and some batteries; I'd made a set of crude lockpicks, and accumulated some bits of wire and tinfoil. I'd also managed to make a couple of skeleton keys; one from a flattened spoon and the other from a piece of iron I took from the shower block. I didn't have a laser cutter so I had to file the metal the old-fashioned way. The way that gives you blisters on your fingers and rust under your nails.

I had been making slow progress, but I hadn't felt any need to hurry. Until the warden told me O'Keefe was on his way. This was bad. Very bad. How had he found me? The reason you hide out in the ass crack of the universe is so no one can find you. I needed to escape – and quickly.

But before I could break out, I needed to break *in*. I had to get into the warden's office to retrieve my gun, my computer, and my leather jacket. I don't usually get sentimental about possessions, but these three things were important to me. And I didn't want to leave them behind for anyone else to find.

It was twilight when I slid my home-made key into the lock of our cell door. I turned it slowly. I'd tested it before so I knew it worked, but I also knew the lock made a grinding noise and a loud click when it was opened. I muffled the sound as best I could and then waited a few minutes to see if it had alerted any of the guards. Hearing nothing, I pushed the cell door open.

"Last chance to change your mind," I whispered.

Old Jack lay on his bunk. He shook his head. "Thanks, lad, but I'll take my chances here."

I've heard that some prisoners spend so long behind bars that they're afraid to leave, even when their sentence is served. Had Old Jack been here that long? I had tried all day to persuade him to come with me, but he said he'd only slow me down. "Come back and buy me out of here when you have the money," he said. And he pressed the map into my hand. I told him I would come back for him. I liked the fact that he trusted me when I said that. And I liked the fact that I was actually telling the truth. You don't make many friends in our business. I waved goodbye and locked the door behind me.

The setting sun was turning the sky the colours of flames and the breeze still felt warm on my face. This was the best time to break-out, I had decided, because it was dark enough for the shadows to conceal my movements but not so dark that the guards turned on the searchlights and set them to automatically sweep their beams around the prison buildings and along tops of the walls. The guards would also be more interested in their supper and with sneaking an evening drink than in patrolling the grounds. If I did run into any of them, I would rely on the element of surprise and a swift blow to the head from the sock full of sand I was carrying.

Although Old Jack was covering for me, there was still a slim chance that one of the guards would discover that I wasn't in my cell. I didn't want them searching the prison building for me, so the first thing I did was lay a false trail for them to follow.

I had a piece of wood that I'd pried from the top of a doorframe. I planned to use it to lift up the wire on top of the wall, high enough that I could crawl under it and not get zapped. But when I got up onto the wall on the east side, I could tell that I wasn't in any danger from high-voltage electricity. There were no insulators separating the wire from the metal posts that held it up. And there was also no buzzing sound from the wire. Another giveaway was the dead animals hanging on the wire. Saphira is home to some odd critters, but I know for sure that none of them are knitted. Maybe the warden's wife made them. Heck, maybe he buys the wool and knits them himself.

I lifted the wire, propping it up with the wood and then dropped a knotted rope down on the outside. I climbed down the rope and walked away from the wall, leaving clear footprints in the dirt to a point where the dust was disturbed by lots of other prints from passers-by. The street was deserted at this hour. Then I walked backwards in my own footprints, back to the wall. I climbed back up the rope and into the prison. I left the rope dangling there.

I had expected to have at least one near-miss with a prison guard, but I saw no one. Maybe it was someone's birthday and they had cake. Keeping to the shadows, I made my way across the prison yard to the warden's office. I used the spoon to unlock the door.

It was dark in the office and it smelled of warm dust and cheap aftershave. I found my old leather jacket hanging in the warden's closet. When I slid my arms into the sleeves the familiar weight of it felt good. My gun-belt was hanging on the same hook and I spun the chamber to check that the pistol was still loaded. I buckled the belt and settled it into place – and I felt like myself again. I'd never killed a man, but the mere presence of a heavy revolver loaded with explosive rounds serves to ward off all sorts of trouble. Everyone wears a gun on Saphira, it's that sort of planet.

My computer was in its slot on the left shoulder of the jacket. I brushed my thumb across the computer's casing to activate it and popped the earpiece into my ear. I called it my box of tricks – Trixie for short – even though it was more of a stubby cigar shape than a box. Trixie played a jolly start-up jingle – because she knew it annoyed me.

"It took you long enough," her voice said in my ear. She had a sort of sexy schoolmarm voice. I'm not sure what that choice of persona reveals about me.

"I was thinking of leaving you behind," I said.

"Hah! You'd never get out of here without me."

"I've already been over the wall," I said, "but I came back to rescue you. I'm your knight in shining armour."

"One day a real hero will come and rescue me from you. Someone's coming."

"What?"

The door handle rattled and I wished I'd relocked it behind me. I was going to be caught red-handed. If it was one of the regular guards, they'd know who I was and I'd be escorted back to my cell. In leg-irons. But if it was the night-watchman who came through the door I might go unrecognised. You can't predict the night-watchman's routine because sometimes he patrols the corridors and other times he can't be bothered. I flipped on the lamp and dropped into the warden's chair, putting my feet up on his desk and hoping for the best.

It was Curly Benson, the night-watchman. He squinted at me.

Quincy's First Law is 'Always have a Plan B.' But you can't plan for every eventuality. Sometimes you just have to improvise.

"Where have you been?" I asked sternly, not giving Benson chance to open his mouth.

"Doing my rounds," he said. "Who...?"

I jumped to my feet, pulling one of the fake IDs out of my jacket pocket. The little wallet contained an official-looking card with my picture on it and a shiny badge that said 'Junior Detective.' I flashed it quickly so that he couldn't read any of it. "Inspector Joe Blondell, Prison Inspection Service," I said. "I'm here to conduct a surprise evaluation."

"We... we didn't know you were coming," Benson said, running the palm of his hand over his bald skull.

"That's the 'surprise' part of a surprise inspection," I said. "And I have to tell you that I have already discovered some serious lapses in security."

Like any long-serving prison employee, he took offence at this and frowned. "What lapses in security?" he asked.

"I'm here, aren't I?" I said. "How did I get in, tell me that?"

"Well, I... you must have..."

"Did you let me in?"

"No."

"No. And if I can get in here without you knowing, then it's obvious that prisoners can get out the same way – isn't it?"

"Well, I... I suppose so."

"This will reflect very badly on you, Mr. Macready."

I saw him visibly relax as he realised my anger wasn't really directed at him.

"I'm not..." he said, but I cut him off.

"Don't bother trying to make excuses. As warden of this facility, it is your sworn duty..."

"I'm not the warden!"

"You're not?"

"No, sir. I'm the night-watchman."

"Then why am I wasting my time with you? Take me to the warden. Immediately!"

"He's not here, sir."

"Where is he?"

"Well, sir, it being after sundown, I'd say he'll be having a drink – in O'Casey's Saloon, sir."

"Take me to him. Right away."

"I can't leave my post, sir. You know that. *Regulations*."

"Very good. I'm glad someone here knows what they're doing. I shall make a note of this. What's your name?" I activated the screen on my watch and poked at it like I was making a written note.

"Benson, your honour, Barnabus Benson."

"Excellent work, Benson. Keep it up and there'll be a commendation in it for you."

"Thank you, sir."

"Now, I want you to take me to the side gate and point me in the direction of this O'Casey's Saloon. I'm going to give

Warden Macready a piece of my mind, you can be sure of that."

Eager to be rid of the prison inspector, Curly Benson led me to the small gate in the west wall. When he got there he made no move to unlock it.

I pretended to examine the gate. "This appears secure enough. Are the locks well-maintained?"

"Oh, yes, sir. Locks and hinges are oiled regularly."

I peered more closely at the lock. "Do you have your key with you?"

"Yes, sir." He showed me the large ring on his belt. Men like him are usually proud of this symbol of their status. The more keys they have, the more important they feel.

"You know which key opens the lock?" I asked.

"Of course. This one." He showed me the key but didn't put it anywhere near the lock. I was starting to feel uneasy. Every minute I wasted here increased the risk of the guards discovering my absence.

"Excellent!" I said. "And you're certain the lock has been properly lubricated?"

Benson cast a quick nervous glance towards the lock. "I don't oil it myself, you understand..."

"Of course," I said, "much too lowly a job for a man of your position. Let's check if it *has* been done properly, shall we? We'll use your key since you have it to hand."

The night-watchman slid his key into the big old lock and crossed his fingers as he turned it. The mechanism opened without a sound and the relief was obvious on his face.

"Very good." I patted him on the shoulder. "This all looks very good for you, I must say. I think I shall put your name forward for a bonus."

"Thank you, sir."

"It'll have to be approved by the department, but that's just a formality."

"I'm very grateful to you, sir."

"It's only right that good work is rewarded. I'm always glad to see men like you recognised," I said. "Men like Warden Macready, unfortunately, are another matter."

"They are?"

"It will be my sad duty to deal with him personally," I said. "O'Casey's Saloon, you said?"

"That's right, sir."

"I've taken up enough of your time, Mr. Benson, I should let you return to your duties. If I could just ask you to point the way to this saloon?"

Benson pulled the gate open and stepped out into the dusty street. I followed him, feeling an immense weight lifted from my shoulders as I passed through the gate.

"It's that way, sir," Benson said, pointing.

"Close to the marketplace?" I asked, knowing it wasn't.

"Two streets to the east of that, sir."

"Thank you, Benson. I'll leave you to lock up. Don't want any of the prisoners wandering out, do we?"

"No, sir, we don't." He turned back to the gate.

"Oh, and Benson? You won't call ahead and warn the warden I'm coming, will you?"

"Thought never crossed my mind, sir."

"Good man." I walked away as nonchalantly as I could, knowing he was watching me. Only when I heard the gate slam shut did I begin to run.

I was tempted to head to O'Casey's for a celebratory drink – and have the barman pour a drink for Warden Macready. But only a fool takes that sort of risk. I'd learned that from experience.

The Trekker was sitting where I had parked it over a week ago. An all-terrain vehicle with big knobbly tyres was a bit over the top for the dirt streets in town, but once you got out into open countryside, this was the sort of vehicle you wanted. The layer of dust on it was thicker but other than that it was untouched. The lack of vandalism or theft was probably due to the large yellow clamp that had been affixed to the rear wheel and the police notice that said the vehicle had been seized as evidence in a criminal investigation. The police hadn't yet impounded it and taken it apart because they needed authorisation from the judge. I'd bought the Trekker when I first arrived on this horrible little planet – it was another one of those things I didn't want to be without.

I found my stash of emergency cash in its hiding place behind the dashboard. Then I took out the tool roll, ready to tackle the wheel clamp.

"You want me to take that off for you?" A voice behind me. I turned. The boy looked about seven years old.

"I can do it quicker myself," I said.

"Want to bet?" The boy held up a key. He grinned.

"Where'd you get that?"

"Copied it," he said. "My mom's ex was a cop."

I liked this kid. "How much?" I asked.

"Twenty."

"You'll never get rich at that," I said.

"I'll get another twenty when I report you for stealing it."

"How about I give you forty and you don't tell anyone anything?"

"Fifty," he said.

I shook his hand and the deal was done. He spent longer than he needed to unlocking it, wanting to make it seem worth fifty dollars. I handed over five tens. Alliance dollars. His face lit up, he'd been expecting local currency.

"A pleasure doing business with you," he said and gave me a cheeky salute. Then he disappeared into the shadows.

I needed to move quickly. The kid was a born crook so there was still a good chance he'd turn me in for the extra twenty. I gave the car a quick once-over. Trixie's sensors didn't detect any tracking devices.

I had to drive with the windows down to get rid of the smell coming from the week-old burrito wrappers on the back seat. I stayed off the main streets, parking the Trekker in the shadows when I went to make my purchases. Luckily I was buying equipment from the sort of people who are open for business after midnight. I only bought the bare minimum. I wasn't exactly laden down with currency and I wanted to be well away from Maggotsville before the sun came up.

I called up the satellite navigation program on the Trekker's dashboard screen.

"Trixie, plot me a route out of town to the north-west that will get us picked up on a couple of security cameras, but nothing too high resolution." I wanted to be seen leaving town but

I didn't want automatic recognition programs picking up my vehicles registration markings and alerting the local cops. The nearest spaceport was north-west of Margotsville, so hopefully the authorities would waste lots of time checking for me there. "Then find us a wide circular route that will take us south – ideally over terrain where we won't leave too many tracks." The jungle lay south of us and that's where Old Jack said I'd find his treasure.

"Do you want me to highlight places of interest along the route?" Trixie asked. She was being sarcastic. Saphira doesn't have places of interest.

"No, but if you spot a place that buys second-hand computers, let me know."

It turned out that there wasn't a treasure map as such. It was co-ordinates tattooed on a piece of skin. Human skin. Old Jack Sterling had removed the skin from his own forearm.

"Took it off myself with a razor, before anyone in here decided to take my whole arm. I told folks I'd sold it but that was a lie. I kept it hid. Even when the guards strip-searched me, they never found it."

I hoped he'd rolled it up and stuffed it in his ear, but I wouldn't bet money on the fact. It smelled bad when I unrolled it to read off the co-ordinates to Trixie. And it smelled worse when I burned it afterwards. I'd have liked to have taken a hot bath in disinfectant then, but there wasn't time. It was entirely possible that Old Jack had memorised the co-ordinates and might be 'persuaded,' by application of pain or alcohol, to pass them on to Paulie Pickles. I needed to stay ahead of any competition. There was also the fact that I was an escaped prisoner, a fugitive with a bounty on my head. And then, of course, there was O'Keefe. I headed south in the Trekker and didn't slow down until I saw jungle.

"Hey, you're famous," Trixie said. "Again."

She flashed an image up on the dashboard screen. It was a wanted poster issued by the Saphira Central Policing Unit. I scrolled through the text.

Officers are hunting an inmate who has escaped from Margotsville Prison. The prisoner, thirty-two-year-old Quincy A.

Randall, fled after climbing over the prison wall. Officers have said that he is not considered dangerous and is still believed to be planetside.

Randall is described as having black skin, brown eyes, and close-cropped black hair. He is five feet nine inches tall and of slim build. When last seen, he was wearing an old brown leather jacket, dark red shirt, jeans and boots. He was arrested last month on suspicion of theft and held pending an appearance before the judge.

Anyone sighting the fugitive should contact Margotsville sheriff's office. A reward of five thousand dollars is offered for information leading to his capture and ten thousand will be paid to anyone who apprehends Randall alive.

Chapter Four

No one would ever find me here. Even *I* didn't know where I was. I'd hidden the Trekker just inside the tree line. There was no way you could drive into the jungle, there were no roads. Or tracks to walk on. You had to slash your way through the leaves with a machete and make your own path. After five hours my arms ached and I had to keep stopping to catch my breath. I wanted to hurry, to reach the 'X' on the map before the sun went down. I was also worried by a note that had been scrawled on the bottom of Old Jack's little piece of human parchment.

Here be dragons. This wasn't just a bit of old pirate humour, Saphira really did have dragons. And I thought they probably came out after dark. If I could have, I would have started running as soon as I spotted the wreckage through the trees, but lack of oxygen was slowing me down. It wasn't the altitude, I was barely above sea-level, but since crossing the equator the air had been thick and damp so you almost had to swallow it down.

To my left was a tree that was filled with some sort of pale yellowish fruit. They looked like big juicy grapefruit but they were probably hard, leathery and poisonous. I was going to lean against the tree for a moment, but backed off quickly when I was attacked by something that looked like a small lime-coloured turkey. Huge boiled egg eyes stared out of a face made from scrotum skin and it squawked angrily, defending a clutch of eggs in a scraggy nest built in the centre of a flower that looked like a fluorescent-orange toilet bowl. With renewed enthusiasm I hacked away at the foliage blocking my way.

'Tropical rainforest' sounds like a nice place for a vacation and I'm sure it looks great in the brochure. The trees are two or three hundred feet high and their leaves form a canopy overhead that blocks much of the sunlight and keeps you in a greenish twilight. The older trees were twisted, covered in vines and large eye-like wounds that oozed blackish ichor.

Stringy moss hung down from the branches like hair and some trees held clumps of foliage that I thought were nests but are actually some kind of parasitic plant. Its fat purple berries looked delicious, which probably meant they were deadly.

The undergrowth I was hacking my way through was made up of smaller trees, palms, and ferns. Some of the plants had huge brightly coloured flowers with waxy flesh-like petals. You could easily imagine that they were carnivorous. As my blade sliced through the leaves they gave off scents like mown-grass, chopped cabbage, and something very like marijuana. The ground was mostly wet leaves and rotting vegetation and gave off a smell like compost as my boots disturbed it. No plants grew down there, there was no light for them, but fungi seemed to thrive, standing out starkly white or burnt orange or red.

I've walked in forests before, up near the mountains, and found them to be quiet, tranquil places where a man can gather his thoughts. The jungle, in contrast, seemed to have a nightclub sound system installed. The trees creaked loudly as they swayed and their foliage created an ocean-like whooshing sound way above me. Over this were layered the echoing whoops, squawks and screeches of unseen birds and warring tribes of monkey-like creatures shouting about some distant danger or bellowing that this was their territory. It took a while for your ears to become accustomed to the din and begin filtering it out.

I consulted the screen on my watch. It told me I was close. I looked around me but there was just more jungle. No indication of anything out of the ordinary. No weathered signs pointing 'This way to buried treasure.' And then it was there again, the unmistakable glint of sunlight on metal.

The expanse of metal in front of me was scarred and pitted and the jungle had done its best to cover it with moss and vines, but it was obviously manmade and part of something immense. It disappeared back into the trees so that I could only see perhaps a hundred yards of it in either direction. The canopy of trees overhead was leaning over to shield it so that it would be invisible from the air. Perhaps Old Jack had been right and it had lain undisturbed for the best part of forty years. And if he was right about that, maybe he had also told the truth about the main part of the *Celestia* still being sealed, protecting her contents.

"Show me the *Celestia*," I said.

Trixie projected an image into the air in front of me. The battleship *Celesta*. To get all of her into the frame, the photographer must have been miles away from her. From that distance, her hull looked smooth and sleek. Floating through space like a great grey whale. Zooming in, you could see that she was formed from thousands of boxy structures, her skin uneven like a whale covered in barnacles. The battleship wasn't a sleek missile, she looked like she'd been put together from a child's building bricks – all of them in shades of grey. And then closer still, you could sense that one of those rectangular structures was bigger than an office block.

If the *Celestia* was a whale, the engines were at the end of her tail in two massive, bulbous pods. The command centre was on top, sticking up like a dorsal fin. Along one side were half-a-dozen round landing platforms and the closed bays that held the Warbirds. They would have streamed out of her, or back towards her, like pilot fish. This ship had been a carrier. Originally she would have been home to fifty Warbirds, but her complement had dwindled to about twenty craft at the time that she was destroyed. All of her fighters would have been engaged in the skirmish going on around Saphira, except for a one or two that might have been in the hangar being repaired.

I wondered what those spaceside fighter pilots felt when they saw their mothership – their home – torpedoed and drifting towards the planet. They must have held their breath, waiting to see the *Celestia* fire her engines and pull away from the planet. Instead, they would have seen escape pods and life ships blasting out into space, carrying all those who had been able to abandon ship. All hope would have faded as they watched her pulled closer and closer to Saphira. And their last glimpse would have been the orange-red glow of her hull burning as it entered the atmosphere. What happened to those fighter pilots? Where could they go after their fuel was exhausted?

Celestia, like all the big battleships, had been constructed in a spaceside dockyard. She had never entered a planet's atmosphere and wasn't designed to. Thrusters used to manoeuvre her in space would have been all but useless as she fell. And even if the crew could have controlled her descent, she had no landing gear.

I don't know how long she held together, how much time those trapped inside had to contemplate their fate. Jack Sterling said the battleship broke into at least three pieces while it was falling. From the ground it must have looked like a meteor shower – just pale ribbons of light arcing downwards in the night sky.

Depending on their angle of descent, those pieces could have plunged nose-first or belly-first into the jungle, ploughing through the canopy and flattening the trees. The cherry-red heat of the hull would have ignited leaves and wood sending up clouds of smoke and steam. The sound must have been deafening: a deep rumble that shook the ground like an earthquake, the rending of metal and splintering of trees. The *Celestia* would have torn up the ground like a massive snowplough, sending a tidal wave of soil and other debris forwards and outwards and upwards, the dark scar she left behind her smouldering and smoking.

Weakened by the passage through the atmosphere, the chunks of battleship would have buckled under the initial impact, fractures appearing in the hull. As they scraped across the ground, pieces would have been torn free and hurled left and right.

After the wreckage of the battleship came to rest, there must have been silence. A world in shock. But then the jungle would have started breathing again, doing what all living things do. Healing the wound. Surviving. And, eventually, hiding all trace of the *Celestia's* impact.

According to Old Jack, the three largest pieces of the battleship had travelled in convoy until the unevenness of the ground sent each of them along different courses.

"You wants the middle section," Jack Sterling had said, "that's where all the good stuff will be."

The co-ordinates he had given me were for this middle section. The hunk of wreckage in front of me was supposed to be the treasure chest. Looking at it, it was impossible to judge which part of the ship it was – it was a slightly curved block of grey metal, pitted and scarred by its descent through the atmosphere. Judging from the curve, the section was half-buried – or the lower part of it had been torn away.

All those who were able to, had abandoned ship and the rest had perished. This wreck was their tomb. It seemed almost sacrilege to swazz up the side of her, but there are some things that a man just has to do. I'm not one for prayers, but I would drink to the memory of those who died – once I was safely inside. As I rezipped, I noticed for the first time how quiet it was near the wreckage. There were no insects or birds in the air and nothing scurried through the undergrowth. Perhaps the collective memory of the jungle creatures still recalled the damage caused when the battleship came down – 'This thing turned your great aunt Edith to charcoal' – so they all kept a respectful distance.

Or, more likely, all the little critters had shut up because there was a big critter on the prowl.

I listened, straining my ears. Was that something big I could hear moving through the undergrowth? With images of sabre-toothed lizards in my head, I unsnapped the flap on my holster and practised a couple of quickdraws. Then I set down my pack and opened it. I had a couple of palm-sized drones – I called them Gnat and Mozzie – and I sent them up to survey the area. They fed data back to Trixie.

"What's out there?" I whispered.

"Insufficient data to identify life form. Approximate mass in excess of one thousand pounds."

Definitely something big. "How close is it?"

"Fifty yards and maintaining a path parallel to your current position."

"Passing by?"

"Negative. Pacing backwards and forwards."

"I smell like food and he's wondering whether I'm dangerous. Will a single bullet kill it?"

"Define bullet?"

"Twelve-millimetre explosive cartridge."

"A single direct hit to the thorax offers a fifty-six per cent chance of a kill."

I didn't like those odds, especially when I couldn't even see what I was shooting at. "Perhaps if I fire off a few shots it will scare him away?"

"I am unable to advise."

"Or it might just anger him and make him charge..." I started pacing myself. "To hell with it." I drew my pistol and looked out into the jungle. "Trixie, give me the best sight you can."

The computer projected a target in front of me, giving me something to aim the barrel of the gun at. The target lit up green when I was aiming in the right direction and I squeezed off three shots. The projectiles tore through the jungle and I heard then explode. There was a bellow from the unseen creature, though whether of anger or pain I couldn't tell. And then there was a thrashing in the undergrowth.

"Please tell me it's running away," I said. The pause before Trixie answered was much longer than I was comfortable with.

"The target is withdrawing."

I let out a sigh. "Monitor that area," I said.

Here be dragons. I'd originally thought it was a joke, but Old Jack was deadly serious.

"They're dangerous, Quin. Sneak up on you. I lost one of my men. Gobbled up he was. 'Course, that's one advantage of having a team. If one of them gets took, you get to live for another day."

The trouble with stories like that, even if you don't believe them, is that they sneak into your subconscious and make you uneasy. And if you haven't got a team, odds are that you're the one who will get gobbled up. I wanted to use the drones to find a way into the *Celestia*. They would be able to fly under the jungle canopy and hopefully discover some sort of opening that I could use. But I wasn't going to have them do that until

I was sure the dragon – or whatever it was – was gone for good. The drones had motion and heat detectors that were much more effective than my own in-built survival systems. Gnat and Mozzie drifted off to see what had become of the big bad beastie.

While I waited I twisted open a can of instant coffee and watched it steam as it heated up. I drank it straight from the can because the smell as I poured it into a mug might attract Fangzilla. And flies might squit in it. I'm not a big fan of the instant stuff, but it's a hundred times better than the stuff they served in the prison. I think they reused the water from the cabbage boiler. As I finished up the coffee, a fly buzzed past the end of my nose and I was reassured to hear the jungle coming back to life around me.

"Any sign of the beast?" I asked.

"I am registering nothing of that approximate mass."

"I'll take that as a no. Bring the drones in."

Old Jack Sterling said the crash had torn a hole in what was now the east side of the wreck. I would start my search there. With Gnat and Mozzie hovering just in front of me, I had Trixie project the video into the air in front of me. She could have given me the full immersive experience by firing the images onto my retina, but I wanted my peripheral vision working full-time looking out for anything that might snatch me up for a snack. I gave the drones their instructions and sent them on their way.

While Gnat and Mozzie were doing their thing, I turned my attention to a snack of my own. The packaging of the protein bar claimed it was beef stroganoff, but they all taste like an old man's slippers. As I forced down the last of it, I heard a *ping* as one of the drones discovered something. I squinted at the virtual screen. There wasn't a welcome mat as such, but the opening in the metal looked fairly inviting. I carefully packed the empty coffee can and wrapper away and then had to smile, thinking of the thousands of tons of scrap metal that were littering the jungle. I shouldered my pack and set off for the drone's location. I was about to go into the rabbit-hole and forty years back in time.

Chapter Five

"Tell me about the dragons," I said as we moved along the length of the wreckage.

"Sapphire Dragons," Trixie said, her voice soft in my ear. "Properly called Crichtorax."

"Named after the explorer who first tripped over one," I muttered, "or maybe he was the first person to get eaten. Tell me that they don't really eat people."

"Their diet includes invertebrates, birds and mammals – mainly local deer – and some carrion."

"Not a herbivore, then. Are they poisonous?"

"Two glands in the lower jaw secrete a form of venom which prevents blood clotting, lowers blood pressure, and causes muscle paralysis which is said to be accompanied by severe pain. The victim's body then goes into shock and may suffer hypothermia before loss of consciousness and death."

"Can you tell me anything good about them?" I asked.

"Please wait." There was a brief pause. "They are edible and the flesh is said to taste like chicken."

"How big are they?"

"Adult Crichtorax range in length from twenty to thirty-six feet with approximately fifty per cent of this being tail."

"Show me one," I said. I'd only ever seen the image on a fifty-cent coin. They put dragons on the local currency to try and get tourists to buy some.

Trixie projected the image into the air. The dragon was bipedal, walking on its hind legs like a tyrannosaurus rex. If half its length was tail, then the adults stood between ten and eighteen feet tall. The picture showed a large skull with a narrow snout, long neck and a short thick body. The skin was made of armoured scales and was predominantly olive-green with the female having rusty brown stripes down her back and the male sporting iridescent peacock blue stripes. I scanned through the details under the image, figuring that it is good to know as much as possible about something that is going to try and eat you. The yellow forked tongue provided both taste and sense of smell like a snake's and its teeth were in rows like a shark. They were serrated to saw through flesh and were replaced regularly. These teeth were sought after by tourists as souvenirs.

"A cross between a snake, a shark, and an ostrich – lovely."

The dragons have long arms which they carry close to their bodies. Each has three long clawed fingers with the middle finger being the longest. Their toes are tipped with scythe-like claws used for climbing trees and disembowelling their prey. Their eyes are a milky green with elongated cat-like pupils and they contain predominantly cones, meaning the big beasties have poor night-vision. They can see colours but have difficulty spotting things that aren't moving. The only bit of good news I could see was that they hunt alone rather than in packs or flocks or whatever the collective noun was. A bastard of dragons maybe. With any luck, the bullets had scared my local dragon away for good.

Despite the name, the Sapphire Dragons weren't native to Saphira. Scientists reckon they are an artificially engineered predator and as such, they are banned on all inhabited worlds. One story has it that they were introduced by the Gators as pets or their equivalent of hunting dogs. Another theory is that they were released on Saphira so that wealthy tourists from the orbiting luxury hotel could come down and hunt them for sport, but the owners of the space station strenuously deny this so obviously it can't be true. I'd never felt the urge to go dragon hunting – even when I had my own suite up on the space station.

Old Jack had been right, there was a huge gash in the outer hull of this section of the wreckage. The outer hatch was gone and this left the inner hatch exposed. If I could open that, I would be through the inner hull and inside the ship. It was unlikely that there was any power in the ship to trigger the locking mechanism so I was going to have to open the hatch manually. There is usually a wheel or a crank under a flap beside the door for this. Ten minutes work on a good day.

As I got close I could see that it wasn't going to be a good day. Or even an average one. The impact had distorted the outer hull causing it to collapse like a concertina. And a bent girder now blocked access to the flap beside the hatch, preventing it from opening. I was going to have to cut away a piece of the girder. I briefly considered sending the drones off to look for an alternative way in, but knew this was likely to be my best chance of getting inside before the moons rose.

I was going to have to work in a very narrow space, squeezed between two sections of the mangled hull. That meant having to shrug off my jacket and gun belt – and also that I would be uncomfortably close to the sparks from the metal cutter. Breaking and entering often involves more work than you think. I donned my eye mask and slid into the gap. Wedging myself in place as best I could, I fired up the laser cutter and got to work. Molten flecks of metal flew out like a child's sparkler, burning pinholes in my shirt. I was so intent on the task that a first I didn't register the alarm that the computer was sounding in my ear. I turned off the cutter.

"What is it?"

"A lifeform approaching."

"The dragon?"

"The mass of the lifeform is consistent with the Crichtorax."

"That's not good." The safest place to be was on the other side of the hatch. I looked at the girder – I had another couple of inches to cut through before I could open the access the flap.

"How far away is it?"

"At its present speed, it will be within striking distance in three minutes."

I wasn't sure if the computer meant me striking it or it striking me. My gun belt was hanging on the end of a rope with the rest of my stuff. I could haul it up and sit and wait. Hope it got bored and went away. And if it didn't, hope for a couple of clear shots at its torso. Or I could try and get the job done and get inside.

"Warn me again when it is a minute away," I said. I fired up the cutter again, turning up the heat – this didn't need to be pretty. Metal began running down in thick orange gobbets.

"Sixty seconds," Trixie said, as I got the flap open.

"I've got it." Wary of accidentally touching the hot metal, I reached for the crank. It wouldn't move. After forty years it was no surprise to find that it had seized up. I had a little can of spray lubricant ready for just such a thing.

"Thirty seconds," Trixie warned.

Still the crank wouldn't budge. My hand slipped and my bare arm touched the still hot cut metal.

"Dammit!"

There was an answering roar from the jungle. And then a large phlegm-coloured eye appeared, the dragon's head was too wide to enter the crevice where I was huddled. I froze, hoping the poor light and its weak vision would prevent it from seeing me properly. The head drew back a little and then the yellow tongue appeared, testing the air and flickering towards me. One fork of the tongue brushed my arm lightly and I resisted the urge to bat it away. Licked by a dragon, how many men could say that had happened to them? I hoped I would live to tell the story. The tongue withdrew and the eye reappeared. Did it know I was here? If it reached in with its claws I was toast. I was still clutching the laser cutter and my thumb brushed the starter button. Should I risk an attack of my own? What the hell, I was canned meat as it was. I thumbed the button and thrust the flame towards the dinner-plate-sized eye.

There was a horrible sizzling sound and an even more horrible smell. The dragon's roar almost deafened me. It pulled back and I heard it crashing away through the jungle. I'd had two narrow escapes – I didn't think there would be a third. I needed to get inside before Fangzilla returned.

I reached for the crank, hoping the lubricant had worked its way into the mechanism, but it was still stuck tight. The angle I was working at meant I couldn't get as much leverage on the crank as I needed, but I didn't think I had enough time to cut away more metal to improve this. And there certainly wasn't time to cut through the hatch itself. I had no more than an hour's worth of daylight left and I was sure the dragon would soon be back to give me more than a friendly lick.

I turned on the cutter and adjusted it to its lowest level. I was going to wave it quickly back and forth over the crank mechanism to heat it up. Then I'd spray more lubricant on it to cool it down again – and maybe, just maybe, that would be enough to free it up. I did this twice and the second time I felt some movement in the mechanism. Unless I imagined it.

Trixie spoke softly in my ear, but I didn't need her to tell me that the dragon was on its way. The jungle was silent again – except for the noise of the dragon's approach. It was coming and this time it was angry. And probably blind in one eye. Maybe I could take out its other eye. I hauled on the rope to bring my pistol and the rest of my stuff up. My heart missed a couple of beats when the line snagged, but a sharp tug freed it. And for some reason that made me think of something else. I needed a hammer.

Percussive engineering was what my grandfather used to call it. Anyone who is ever faced with a stubborn piece of machinery always uses it. Either as a first move or a last sign of frustration, you hit it with a hammer. I applied the head of the hammer to the end of the crank. It made a satisfying clanging sound that vibrated along the hull. I hit it again.

"Thirty seconds," Trixie said.

Behind me I felt the hatch move. I hit the crank again and the hatch moved some more. It was open an inch or more now. I leaned back against it, trying to force it inwards and whacking the crank at the same time. Then I felt another *thud!* And it wasn't me hitting anything. The dragon had collided with the outer hull. I could see its shark teeth snapping at the opening and then one of its clawed hands shot in towards me. A talon raked down my boot, scarring the leather as I tried to scramble backwards. I used the hammer to fend off the claws but in the narrow space I didn't have room to swing it like a weapon.

And then I was falling backwards, in through the hatch. I dragged my stuff in after me and I heard the drones zip in behind me. I slammed the door shut.

It was pitch black inside and all I could hear was the dragon's claws scraping on the outside of the door. I turned the wheel on the inside, locking it shut. If the lock got stuck again it didn't matter, I wouldn't be going out that way. I leaned back against the door, gasping for breath. That had been a real squit in the pants moment.

"Let's have some light," I said.

The drones turned on their mini searchlights but they provided only narrow beams of light. The circles of light explored the space we were in. The bare metal room was maybe ten feet square. It was basically an airlock – an airtight room between the outside of the ship and one of its inner chambers. It was strange to think that I was the first person to set foot in here for forty years. Then Mozzie's light passed over something that made me realise I wasn't. I reached into my pack and drew out a flashlight, shining it towards the thing the drone had found.

It was a human skeleton and there were still bits of flesh clinging to it. It wasn't a fresh corpse, but it wasn't forty years old either. One of Old Jack Sterling's team, perhaps? I directed the flashlight beam downwards and saw three good-sized and evenly spaced circular burn marks in the front of its jacket. Bullet hits. He'd either been shot by a rival treasure hunter or... Or he'd triggered the *Celestia's* automatic defences.

These old ships were rigged with all sorts of defence mechanisms and even a self-destruct to prevent them falling into the hands – or claws – of the enemy. We didn't want them to have access to our technology in case they worked out how to defeat us. The *Celestia's* defences would have been activated after the crash – as soon as the ship's Navigator sensed that all of the crew were dead.

I called Gnat and Mozzie back to me. "Don't touch *anything,*" I said.

Chapter Six

The scratching at the outer door had stopped so I assumed the dragon had gone off in search of an eyepatch. Or perhaps it was sitting there wracking its reptilian brain trying to figure out how to operate the crank to open the hatch. I wasn't worried on that score. I'd wedged the mechanism shut with the biggest wrench from my tool roll. No one was getting in that way – not a dragon and not a human bounty hunter. There was a thick glass porthole in the door that led into the battleship, but there was only darkness on the other side.

The air in the bare metal room was stale and there was a whiff of dead flesh that I was trying to ignore. Assuming the seals on both airlock doors were still intact, I had a limited amount of oxygen, but I wasn't too worried about that. I could always use the laser cutter to make a hole in the bulkhead and let air in from outside. Of more immediate concern was my new friend Mr. Skellington. What had killed him? Had he triggered the ship's automatic defence systems? If he had, I very much wanted to avoid doing the same thing. I wasn't sure what my next move should be, but I was going to be very, very cautious. I pulled on my jacket and buckled my gun belt. Mainly because this gave me something to do.

I wanted to set the drones to scanning for weapons, but the ship might interpret their scans as a hostile act and respond accordingly. I told them to power down and save their energy and then I stashed them in my backpack. I'd already warned Trixie not to try connecting to any of the ship's systems. I felt it was safe for her to operate in stand-alone mode, but she had instructions to shut down completely at the first sign of danger. She was currently pulling up the schematics of the battleship that she'd downloaded from an external database. The *Celestia* was old technology and her blueprints and manuals had been declassified more than a decade ago, of interest now only to those who studied historical military technology.

I shone the beam of the flashlight around the room, checking each wall carefully and then the ceiling, trying to see if the weapon that had shot the earlier intruder in the chest was located inside the airlock. I couldn't see anything that might be a hatch. The walls were smooth metal, riveted together and painted with thick layers of pale grey paint.

Turning the flashlight on the dead man again, I tried to figure out what had happened to him. He was slumped against the wall opposite the door that opened into the ship. My best guess was that he had opened the airlock door and been shot in the chest. The force of the three projectiles had thrown him backwards and slammed him against the inside wall. He slid down and into the half-sitting half-lying position he was in now and the door had automatically closed and locked. He'd probably been shot by someone with a gun who had stood outside the airlock or by automatic weapons that were permanently installed there. It would be helpful to know which.

I looked at the schematics Trixie had retrieved. As the images flashed up I swiped them aside, digging deeper and deeper into the battleship's systems, trying to see what surprises she might have in store for me. All I found was a reference to a protocol adopted early in the war to the effect that all combat ships should be retrofitted with defences and self-destruct mechanisms to prevent them from falling into enemy hands. The generals didn't want the aliens taking apart our technology to see how it ticked, in case they figured out how to defeat it. I suppose it was left to the captains of individual ships to decide what internal defences to install.

I closed the technical schematics and pulled up an image that showed the basic layout of the ship. I still had no way of knowing where my airlock was situated. I cast the beam of the flashlight around the room again but could see no helpful markings. The bare metal construction told me nothing apart from the fact that starship decor had come a long way in the half-decade since the *Celestia's* maiden voyage.

"They don't build 'em like this anymore," I muttered. In large part, they didn't build them like this because we were no longer at war. Though we did still have an impressive military fleet on standby. Just in case.

The alien armada had appeared on the edge of known space almost a century ago and broadcast a single message in Earth-tongue:

"We are the Ulthavi Yulori and we declare war on the dry-skins in the name of our glorious creator."

Ulthavi Yulori translates as 'people of the amphibian god' or something like that. Most people just called them Gators because that's what they looked like. They walked upright and wore battle armour, but they looked like alligators. More or less. Official accounts of the conflict state that this was an unprovoked declaration of war. But given mankind's past history, you've gotta suspect that someone somewhere did something to swazz them off. The aliens probably sent an emissary with an olive branch and some redneck turned him into a handbag and a matching pair of high-heel mules for his honey.

A lot of good people – and a fair few disreputable ones – sacrificed their lives to defeat the Gators. The War lasted for fifty years.

No one has seen or heard from the Gators since before I was born. Some folk think they are off somewhere preparing for a second invasion. Others say we wiped them out completely with a haemorrhagic virus cooked up in one of our labs. Official accounts neither confirm nor deny this. But again, referring to mankind's past history, genocide cannot be ruled out.

And now there was a real risk that one of our own battleships was going to wipe me out. That would be a cruel twist of fate given the fact I played no part in the conflict. If I'd been alive back then I would have been a black market profiteer, I'm sure.

I went to the inner hatch and peered out through the glass porthole. There was only darkness out there. I pressed the lens of the flashlight to the glass to try and see what lay on the other side. I wasn't too worried about the light triggering the weapons, the door and the thick glass window in it were designed to endure rapid depressurisation and re-pressurisation and were sturdy enough to withstand a few close-range bullet hits. The round glass in the door was like a lens, distorting what lay on the other side. I could make out a larger chamber but the light didn't penetrate far enough to show me the presence – or absence – of machine-guns on the wall opposite the hatch.

I had to proceed on the assumption that there were wall-mounted weapons outside the airlock, primed and ready to fire at me as soon as I opened the hatch. They were probably triggered by motion-sensors or heat sensors or perhaps both. That's what I would have used. Simple but effective.

I could try opening the door a few inches and stick my arm out, try to shoot the guns off the wall. But not knowing the precise position of the weapons made the chances of success pretty slim. And the risk of having my hand blasted off made this option even more unattractive. A thief, like a pianist, values every one of his fingers.

If I could see the gun mechanism, it would probably be possible to see the limits of its movement and range. There might be a gap that I could sneak through that the bullets couldn't reach – by crawling out on my belly, perhaps. But even then there was the danger of being hit by shrapnel or ricochets.

How do you disable the weapons so you can open the door when you need to open the door to disable the weapons?

I could throw open the door and send out a fake moving target – Mr. Skellington, for example – and stay in hiding until the guns had exhausted their ammunition on him. But how would I know when or if the guns were empty? And again, there might be shrapnel and ricochets.

The drones were another option. I could send one out to draw the fire while I went out and headed the opposite way from the moving drone. But I didn't really want to sacrifice either Gnat or Mozzie. Not this early in the game.

A shield? I could use the laser cutter to remove a piece of hull plate. But that would take ages, even assuming the cutter had enough power to finish the job. And if I was going to cut a hole that big, I may as well cut myself a new doorway to walk through. Though knowing my luck, I'd walk straight into another airlock and face the same problem all over again.

I used the toe of my boot to ease the dead man's holdall away from his bony fingers. A quick glance inside told me that he was even more poorly equipped than me. He had schematics of the ship too – printed on paper. They showed nothing that wasn't on the images I'd already seen.

I sat down and popped open another can of instant coffee and chewed on another protein bar – a roast duck scented slipper this time – and tried to think of some way to avoid being killed. Escaping from tricky situations was supposed to be my speciality. Despite the caffeine boost, I drifted off to sleep. That should have been my first warning that something was wrong.

I was woken minutes later buy an insistent buzzing and chirping from Trixie.

"Warning! Oxygen levels at thirty-eight per cent of normal and falling," she said.

It seemed that the ship had grown tired of waiting for me to trigger the guns. She was bleeding the air out of the airlock and replacing it with carbon dioxide from the fire suppression system. The *Celestia* knew this would either kill me or flush me out. As deaths go, asphyxiation would be a relatively painless one, but my preference was for no death at all. I could cut a small hole in the hull using the laser cutter to let in air from outside. Or I could just stop dithering and get out of the airlock and into the ship.

If the fire suppression system had been squirting water into the airlock, I could have used it to make steam and used it as cover to make my way out, confusing the motion sensors. And if it had been squirting out fairy dust, I could have wished my way out. In the absence of steam, I could use the next best thing. Smoke.

My plan was simple enough. I'd use smoke to hide me from the battleship's visual sensors and hope the fire confused the heat sensors long enough for me to get away from the airlock and out of range of the machine-guns. The difficult part would be making sure I did all the right things in the right order. Smoke first.

Working feverishly, I screwed up the sheets of paper in Mr. Skellington's holdall, pushing some of them back into the bag and a few of them into the front of his shirt.

"I can't offer you a proper burial," I told his grinning face, "but I can probably manage a cremation."

I ignited the laser cutter and directed it at the bag of crumpled paper. It was reluctant to light in the oxygen-poor atmosphere, but the edges began to glow and that's all I needed. I used the laser cutter's flame to set fire to the dead man's clothes. The fabric started turning black and thin whisps of smoke coiled upwards. As soon as I pushed the hatch outwards, air would rush in and the smoke would billow outwards. I hoped.

The rest of it depended on me working quickly. And being very, very lucky. I had to get the airlock door open before all of the oxygen was gone. It wasn't just me who needed it. If the door was welded shut or jammed on the other side, I was in trouble. My only option then was out the way I'd come in. And that meant a good chance of running into my old friend the one-eyed dragon.

I needed to circumvent the locking mechanism of the inner door and prevent the ship from immediately relocking it. A lock this old didn't offer much of a challenge. I could open it with my eyes closed. Which was a good thing, because the airlock was now filling with smoke. And the smell of burning bone. There wasn't time for artistry. I tore the front panel off the lock and plugged in the lock-pick. I needed to send a signal to the lock to say 'open sesame' while at the same time sending a message to the ship that the door was still locked. If the lock said 'I'm locked', the ship would believe it. At least until the sensors outside showed the door opening.

Even as the mechanism clicked open, I was reaching for the smouldering holdall. The smoke was burning my eyes and the inside of my nostrils. I was trying not to breathe it in. Staying low, I pulled the airlock door and it swung inwards on protesting hinges. The air rushing in ignited the flames in the holdall. I swung it around and out through the opening, sending it across the floor of the outside corridor to the left. Almost instantly the machineguns rattled into life.

Not even looking that way, I grabbed my backpack and scrambled out through the hatch and headed to the right. I risked a glance back, but I could see nothing through the haze of smoke. The guns would be swivelling round to target me, I felt sure of it. I headed across the chamber. There was a corner or alcove just ahead on my left. I didn't know what it contained. If there were more guns there, I was going to be the new Mr. Skellington. I skidded around the corner just as the floor behind me was ripped up by exploding bullets. I shielded my eyes. The chattering of guns and the thunder of bullet hits vibrated the hull of the ship and the inside of my skull. The hailstorm seems to go on forever.

When the guns finally fell silent, I glanced around me. I had my pistol in my hand, ready to open fire on any threats I saw, but there was nothing to get excited about. I was huddled against the wall in a small area that had been some sort of administrator's workspace. The desk, chair, and screen of the terminal had been within the sweep of the guns and were completely destroyed by gunfire. They still smoked slightly, adding to the fog in the air. In the wall that had been beyond the range of the guns, there was an ordinary-looking door that opened onto a corridor. Staying close to the floor, I crawled towards it.

I eased the door open quietly and tossed a bit of smouldering seat foam out into the corridor. There was no gunfire. With any luck, this meant that the automatic weapons were only targeted on entrances from the outside of the ship. This didn't mean that I was past all of the ship's defences, but it did seem to indicate that I have passed the first challenge.

I fished the drones out of my pack and sent them ahead to scout the corridor. They sent back an 'all clear' and an image that helped me, finally, figure out where I was on the battleship. The drone was showing me the crew's quarters. That meant that Engineering and the warbird launch decks were above me and that Security was on the deck below. I needed to go down there to reach the vault where the artificial sentience that had been the ship's Navigator was housed. But first I'd explore this deck and see what there was to salvage. This would also give me a chance to blink away the tears that were blurring my vision and blow the soot from my nostrils.

I also wanted to try and get the lighting back online. I had no idea how much charge was left in the flashlight and didn't want to end up wandering the labyrinth in total darkness.

The fact that the machineguns were working meant there was still power in the ship.

I headed towards the crew's quarters, trying to shake off that uncomfortable feeling that always seems to come up in situations like this.

Chapter Seven

At the first T-junction in the corridor, there was a narrow door that opened into a maintenance cubbyhole. There was just enough room for a plumber or an electrician to squeeze inside and fix whatever problem was plaguing this section of the ship. Luckily I was more or less the same size as a plumber and had some of the skills of an electrician.

The power sub-systems on this deck weren't protected by anything more than basic security protocols and the only reason it took me a whole five minutes to bypass them was because I had a sneezing fit. It was going to be days before I got the smell of smoke out of my clothes and hair.

The little orange and black screen showed me that the ship's systems were mostly in hibernation mode. Drawing just enough power from the batteries to keep things ticking over, but ready to respond almost instantly if stirred by external threat. After a couple of tries, I pulled up the correct menu and told the system to kick things up into minimal habitation mode. That would be enough to get the air circulating and the lights on. I hoped. I could hear a humming sound and feel a slight vibration through the soles of my boots. Perhaps these were good signs. Outside in the corridor, the lights flickered on and off a few times and then settled down to a subdued bluish light. That must mean we were in a daylight phase – at least as far as the *Celestia* was concerned. I felt sure it must be night outside the ship now. Who knows what time zone she was mimicking?

The environmental control unit was connected into the ship's main systems and also offered proximity connection, so I let Trixie offer a handshake. Neither of us was surprised when the battleship gave it the cold shoulder. Just because we were inside didn't mean she was going to let us in. That required access to security protocols that we didn't have. We were just going to have to wait until we got into the Navigator's vault where we could force a direct connection.

Behind me there was a loud clicking sound and the lights went out again. After a few seconds the corridor was lit again, but by red emergency lighting only. Some sort of circuit breaker had been tripped – hardly surprising after forty years in the dark. I could try and fix it, but I'd be off this deck soon and heading down to the next one, so decided I could manage with the emergency lighting. While I was exploring this deck, I could keep an eye out for additional flashlights, in case I needed them later.

Back in the corridor, I got a sense that the air was still moving, if only sluggishly, so life support was functioning at some level. As well as smoke there was a whiff of decay in the air, but it was no worse than the jungle outside. My eyes quickly adjusted to the red lighting. Everything around me was painted battleship grey so I wasn't really missing anything colour-wise.

The *Celestia* had nose-dived into the dirt from a great height. We aren't talking about a minor fender-bender. The ground would have shaken like a major earthquake. Anything loose inside the ship must have been tossed around like a bingo caller's balls. It should have looked like a garbage truck exploded in here. But it was tidier than a politician's alibi. Someone or something had been through the ship from stem to stern and cleaned it up. And they had carried on maintaining it for the last forty years. If you ignored the fact that she was broken into three pieces, the *Celestia* looked like she was ready to take flight tomorrow.

This made me uncomfortable, because it meant my feeling of not being alone couldn't be written off as simple paranoia. I was not alone here, I felt sure of that.

Most of the rooms off the corridor were crew quarters. Narrow cubicles containing two bunks, one above the other, or slightly wider rooms with four bunks. This was where the pilots and the engineers that maintained their fighters would have slept. It was functional living space with few creature comforts. Typical military accommodation. There were pictures on the walls of most of the bunks. Curled photographs of family members. Faded pin-ups of actresses, motor vehicles, and porn stars – all of them decades old. There were small toys hanging in some of the bunks, meagre attempts at personalising the space. It was like looking into rooms that had been preserved for a museum exhibit. A hermetically sealed time capsule.

I didn't open any of the lockers or drawers. It would have been disrespectful. 'Treasure hunter' is just a polite euphemism for tomb robber. This was the uneasy feeling I'd had since I came on board. I was intruding in a place that belonged to the dead.

I was seeing little evidence of the impact. There were a few things scattered on the floor or piled in corners, but nothing more. I had expected to see corpses. Though most of the crew from this deck had probably been on duty when the *Celestia* was hit. As I moved inwards towards the centre, there was less evidence of structural damage. Everything seemed normal, nothing crushed or twisted into crazy angles. You could imagine an end of shift klaxon sounding and crew members streaming back down to their quarters to wash up before heading to the mess hall. These imaginings were the closest that I came to seeing ghosts.

The last cubicle in the corridor held only a single bed, belonging to a sergeant or some other lower-ranked officer, presumably. The wall opposite the bed was filled by a mesh-fronted locker that held weapons. Handguns and rifles. I popped the padlock. The weapons all seemed to be loaded. In the bottom of the locker was a row of flashlights. I picked up a couple that showed as being fully charged. The weapons could wait – for now. I asked Trixie to tag the location so we could come back to it later. Depending on what other loot there was to carry away, I would pick up a few guns on the way out.

Around the corner was a small medical bay. There were half-a-dozen of these scattered throughout the ship, as well as the main trauma centre that housed the operating theatres. There was a refrigerated locker filled with blood products and medicines, all long past their use-by dates. And there was a cupboard full of vacuum-packed dressings and other equipment. This was another location to tag for later. I doubted I would be back – there were much richer pickings on the deck below – but you never know. This might turn out to be the first of several visits I made to the *Celestia.*

I figured I'd seen all this deck had to offer. Time to head downwards. By definition, Security was going to be housed in a location that was more secure. And the increased protection meant it was also the ideal place to house the most valuable items of equipment. There would be robots down there and other equally saleable items of hardware. And also the greatest prize of all, the Navigator, shielded in its own (allegedly) impregnable vault. That sounded like my kind of challenge.

How do you travel between decks on a battleship? You take the elevator the same as anywhere else. With only emergency power available, I was thinking that the elevators would be offline. Aren't we always told not to use them in an emergency? The elevator cars usually descend to ground level and sit there until the emergency is over. If you want to escape, you have to use the stairs. I wasn't sure if battleships had stairs. I'd been on space stations and passenger liners where a staircase swept majestically down into the ballroom, but this was set dressing designed for impact rather than practicality. Warships don't have ballrooms. But surely they must have some sort of utilitarian stairway for use in case of fire or flood? What did they do when the elevators broke down? Even on a military vessel you must occasionally see an out-of-order sticker. There had to be some kind of manual back-up.

Looking around me, I couldn't see any emergency exit signs. Presumably the crew were expected to be familiar with the escape routes. They probably got woken in the middle of the night by sadistic sergeants running fire drills and could get to the assembly points with their eyes closed. Or perhaps arrows lit up to direct you to safety when the alarms went off. I considered setting off the fire alarm to test this, but I didn't want to make that much noise – especially when I didn't know how to turn it off. My attention was drawn back to the elevators. Even if they weren't operating, the shaft still went straight down to the next level.

My journey to the wreck of the *Celestia* had been organised at short notice and I had travelled south with only the bare minimum of equipment. My plan, such as it was, was to improvise when I got here. With hindsight, there were a few things I wished I'd brought with me. A bigger flashlight was one. And another was a 'burglar's friend' – a jemmy or crowbar – which would have been ideal for prying open the elevator doors. I was thinking that I'd have to try using the largest screwdriver from my tool roll when I spotted something more promising. At the end of the corridor close to a fire alarm button there was a box on the wall. Behind its glass front, I could see a red-handled fire axe. I used the screwdriver to lever the box open. The axe was heavy in my hands. It wasn't an ideal substitute for a jemmy but it was sturdier than my screwdriver.

I pushed the sharp end of the axe head into the gap between the elevator doors, wedging it in as far as it would go. Then I used a hammer to knock it further in. When most of the head was buried in the gap, I gripped the end of the handle and turned, forcing the doors apart. There was a lot of resistance from the mechanism that was supposed to keep the doors safely closed when there was no elevator car behind them, but gradually the gap widened. I didn't want the doors snapping shut suddenly when I had my fingers between them, so I slid a fire-extinguisher into the gap to stop them closing. I know, I know, you're not supposed to use extinguishers to prop doors open, but I'm not big on obeying regulations.

Setting aside the axe, I used my hands to drag first one door and then the other, and then I got first my shoulders and then my whole body in the gap and used my legs to force the doors fully open. The elevator shaft was dark and the smell of dead vegetation wafting up from the lower floor was stronger. I paused to draw breath. I'd lost track of how long I had been inside the wrecked battleship. This weird red-lit metal labyrinth seemed to have a time zone all of its own.

I lay down on my stomach and edged forward to shine the flashlight down into the shaft. The beam of light showed me the grid-like metal structure with the cables running down the middle – and not much else. The light wasn't strong enough to penetrate as far as the next level. I was about to reach into my pocket for a coin to drop down when I felt a breeze on the back of my neck. It was coming down the shaft.

Adrenaline surged through my body and I pulled myself backwards out of the shaft without even thinking about it. Something big and heavy *whooshed* down the shaft and I felt it brush past the top of my head.

I lay on my back for a moment and waited for the sick feeling in my stomach to fade. I didn't want to think about how close I had just come to being decapitated by the plunging elevator car. It couldn't have been a coincidence. I looked around, trying to see the camera that had to be watching me, but in the red half-light it was hard to see anything clearly. From this point on I would have to assume that I was being observed, that my movements were being tracked.

Knowing that the elevators were operational, I could have jacked into the control system to call a car to take me down to the next level. But I didn't fancy putting myself into a closed metal box that the ship could take control of and send me plunging to my death or leave me trapped between floors until I starved. I had also entirely gone off the idea of climbing down the elevator shaft.

"Trixie, call up blueprints for the ship and show me emergency exit routes for my current position." I was whispering, afraid of being overheard, which was crazy. If the ship wanted to listen, her sensors could probably pick up the gurgle of my stomach digesting protein bars.

The plans showed that there were several staircases connecting the two levels, but none close by. In the event of a fire or other emergency, the crew had to use ladders built into the conduits that ran between floors. These narrow tubes carried the pipes and cables that provided services around the ship – water, electricity, data, sewage, and the like. Engineers called these conduits roach runs because no matter how sophisticated the technology became, those bugs always managed to find their way in. You'd have thought they would have evolved into stainless steel roaches or something by now, but no, their ugly prehistoric form still does the job fine.

I popped the hatch open on the nearest access point and shone my torch inside. It was a much smaller space than the elevator shaft. A ladder was screwed to the wall on one side and the other was filled with pipes and cables of various sizes and colours that disappeared down into the darkness. I didn't see any cockroaches but that didn't mean they weren't there. I also couldn't see any sign of cameras, sensors, or weapons – but again that didn't prove anything. For my own continued well-being, I should assume that defences of some kind had been placed in the conduits. I tried to imagine what a devious military mind might come up with. Lasers criss-crossing the tube ready to chop me up like zucchini? Or could the ship seal off parts of the network and flood them with carbon dioxide?

I took the hatch off its hinges so that the ship couldn't seal it shut behind me. I was about to toss it aside but dropped it down the tube instead. I watched it fall until it disappeared beyond the light from the flashlight and then I listened as it clanged down in the darkness. There were no flashes of laser weapons and no sounds of explosions. Of course, the ship might be watching and could have turned off the defences temporarily. Perhaps it was trying to lure me into a trap? I had to hope that she wasn't that devious.

I fastened the red axe to my backpack and threaded my arms through the straps. I had some of the smaller tools in the pocket of my jeans and the pistol in the holster on my belt – I hoped these would be enough to deal with any challenges I met on the way down. I had a spare flashlight attached to my belt and I could quickly unsling the axe if I needed it. I went back down the corridor and made a quick scouting exhibition to try and find a helmet of some kind, but all I came up with was a moth-eaten baseball cap that I didn't want to put anywhere near my hair. I was just going to have to hope that the ship had nothing it could drop down on me while I was in the roach run.

I stepped into the tube and grabbed hold of the ladder, tugging at it to make sure it was firmly screwed to the wall. The rungs of the ladder felt warmer than I'd expected. They were probably a composite made of recycled plastic waste but the clammy feel of them made me think of bone for some reason –

like I was climbing around inside the ship's skeleton. Trying not to shudder, I started downwards.

Chapter Eight

Initially, I had been confused by the distance between the crew quarters level and the security level below. The deck between them couldn't be seventy feet thick, could it? It wasn't clearly marked on the blueprints, but it turned out that there was a sort of subfloor between the two levels. A basement or attic, depending which of the levels you were standing on. It was basically a warehouse where they stored all of the stuff you needed to run a ship of this size – toilet paper and spare mattresses and all those other things that you never really think about when you imagine a warship. If I had been planning a longer expedition, I would have wanted to have a good look around this warehouse. But given my experiences so far, I had decided that I wanted to be off this wreck as soon as I had enough valuables to take back with me. Preferably in the form of something I could easily carry. Like the core of the Navigator unit. Anything less than that was going to be a major disappointment.

Sweat trickled down my nose and dripped off the end. There was no air conditioning in the roach run. I doubted that the cockroaches cared much, but it must have been unpleasant for the engineers who had to work in these tight spaces. It was dark too and the bobbing of the flashlight was disorientating.

Something grabbed me from behind and tried to pull me up. Or that's what it felt like. My backpack had caught on the little wheel of some sort of valve and was stopping me going downwards. I had to go back up and reach around to unhitch it. I decided to shrug off the shoulder straps so I could lower the backpack down the shaft on the rope – this would avoid further entanglements and would also give me greater freedom of movement. And while I was at it, I took off my jacket and gun belt and tucked them under the flap of the pack. I lowered the backpack down until I ran out of rope and then I let it fall the rest of the way – it didn't fall for long, so I figured I had only another thirty or so feet to go.

As I got closer to the security deck, a glow filtered upwards, getting brighter as I descended. Looking down I could see that the hatch was partially open.

"Level 3: security, weaponry and robot guards, bombs and navigation, space helmets and drones. Going down."

Reaching the hatch I pushed it open and peered out into the corridor. There was no sign of my jacket or backpack. I looked all around in case they'd bounced or rolled and I looked up in case they had snagged on something on the way down. But they were gone. Someone or something had taken them. I was definitely not alone on the *Celestia*. This thought gave me the creeps. But on a positive note, this was a much better class of spaceship corridor. The walls were a clean off-white that the brochure probably called 'desert sand' and sensors turned on the lights just ahead of me as I moved – and they were proper 'evening sun' lights, none of your nasty 'bloodshot red'. It was like being in the office building of an expensive law firm. Any minute now there'd be a corner with a potted palm in it.

With no backpack and no computer, I was feeling vulnerable. Who or what had snatched my things? Out in the corridor, I was more exposed than I wanted to be, so I decided to duck into one of the rooms. I could take a moment to consider my next steps.

"Pick a door, any door."

Again there was a complete absence of helpful signage. Maybe it was a War thing. I remember reading somewhere that planets in the war zone used to remove all of their street names and road signs in an attempt to confuse any enemy invaders. I bet the Gators were furious when they couldn't find the name of the place that they were just about to blow up.

I chose a door at random. It had a standard electronic lock that had probably been state of the art back in the day. I took the lockpick out of my pocket and slid the sensor into the mechanism. It vibrated slightly to let me know that it had tricked the lock into thinking that an 'access denied' signal said 'open sesame.' I snatched my hand away as the lockpick suddenly grew very hot and then exploded in a shower of sparks. I glanced over my shoulder up towards the lens of a security camera.

"Spoilsport."

The door had opened about an inch and then stopped. I grabbed the edge of it and pulled, sliding it open a little further. Eventually there was room for me to squeeze through.

"Mind the gap."

The door slammed shut the moment I was through it. Behind me the lights flickered on. Something, just an odd feeling, warned me that something was wrong. I turned slowly.

The narrow room was filled with security robots. Two rows of them – six to my right and three to my left. I froze, holding my breath. Were they active? I've had some nasty experiences with security robots in the past. The carbon-fibre carapaces of these were painted the usual pale blue and white to mark them as security rather than military hardware and the bare metal of their joints was bright and shiny. I was starting to feel light-headed and had to let go of the breath I was holding.

"Pardon the intrusion, gentlemen, I was looking for the bathroom."

There was no response from the robots. Perhaps they didn't believe me. Looking down, I could see that they were all standing on charging pads and the gently flashing indicators all seemed to be in the red zone – they weren't yet charged. Three of the pads were empty. Did that mean there were more robots out on patrol? Or maybe they were in the repair shop?

I stood directly in front of one of the robots. I dodged left and then right to see if it would follow the movement with its head, but it stood like a mannequin. I raised my hand and slowly reached towards the robot's forehead. I touched the shiny blue plastic. Still nothing. I pushed. The robot tilted slowly on its heels and, reaching the tipping point, fell backwards. It collided with the robot behind it and that fell backwards too. With a loud clattering sound, all six robots in the line went down like dominoes. This made me smile.

The fallen robots made no attempt to right themselves. I glanced towards the three still standing, but there was no response from them – not even a sideways glance or a smirk. Flat batteries, the lot of them. And I didn't want them getting all recharged and coming after me.

I was rapidly running out of equipment, but I still had a screwdriver in my pocket. I used it to take the heads off the six sleeping robots. I took the controller chips from each of the heads, pocketing them, and then set the gleaming domes on the floor next to their bodies. Then I took the heads and chips from the two robots that were still standing. *Two?* Did I miscount?

I half-turned and a straight-armed swipe from a security robot whizzed past the top of my head. He must have been expecting someone taller. I dodged another attempt to decapitate me, feeling the draft caused by the passage of the robot's hand. If any of those karate chops made contact the result would almost certainly be a broken bone. And it would hurt. Backing away from the robot, I almost tripped over one of the heads on the floor. I ducked under another swipe and picked up the robot head, holding it in front of my like a shield. A hand swiped down in a swift and brutal arc, shattering the skull and breaking it in two.

Ducking and weaving, I picked up two more of the heads, hurling them like boulders, and the security robot knocked them aside sending them clattering against the walls. Its arms slicing through the air, the robot forced me deeper into the room. A quick glance behind told me that there was a wall and a door – some sort of inner office – and I would soon be forced up against it with nowhere to go.

The door was locked and my pick was now a puddle of melted metal. Still trying to stay beyond range of the wildly waving arms of the robot, I edged sideways, looking around the room for something I could use as a weapon or as a tool to open the inner door. But there was nothing. This was a bare room that served only as a recharging station for the machines. Robot corpses littered the floor and I had to step carefully to avoid them. I stepped between the two headless bodies that were still standing, trying to put them between me and the kung fu robot. I ducked behind one of them, holding onto its upper arms and turning it, hiding behind it. Chop after chop cracked and splintered the decapitated robot, sending bits of debris flying in all directions. A particularly savage blow to the shoulder cracked the joint and left me holding the arm. I considered using it as a club to fight back, but then I saw markings above the wrist that gave me another idea. This was the robot's identification number and an old-fashioned quick-scan code. I pushed the remains of the dead robot forwards so that my attacker was momentarily entangled with it.

I rushed to the back of the room and pressed the code on the arm up against the scanning pad of the lock. Surely a security robot would have the necessary clearance level to get me through the door? There was a crash behind me as the robot tore itself free from its dance partner and shoved the obstruction aside. As robot Frankenstein goose-stepped towards me there was a long moment when I thought the lock wasn't going to yield. I really didn't want 'Oh, squit!' to be my dying words.

Click. Shush!

The door slid open. I dashed into the inner office and slammed my palm back against the mechanism, hitting the control that would shut and lock the door. I pressed one of the robot fingers to the button that would seal the door shut, not allowing anyone to enter from outside.

Finding that its own code didn't work the door-opening magic, the robot outside began battering the door. I could see small dents appear but I felt fairly confident that the door would hold firm. This was a door on a security deck, you'd have to hope it would be a good one.

Catching my breath, I turned around, half-expecting to see the missing three robots standing behind me with fists raised. But there was only a desk and chair. A supervisor's office. In one corner was another robot charging station, but this one was bigger than those outside. I was pleased to see that it was vacant. On the desk were a jacket and a backpack. *My* jacket and backpack. I wasn't sure if one of the robots had brought them in – they certainly hadn't rolled into there and bounced up onto the desk – but I was definitely pleased to see them. The red axe was lying on the desk too.

Pulling on my jacket, I felt much less vulnerable. The gun belt and pistol helped a bit with that.

The hammering on the door ended and the silence came as a relief. I woke Trixie and got her to scan the area for robots.

She reported no activity. Hopefully, that meant the robot outside had exhausted whatever little charge it had left in its batteries.

There was a uniform jacket hanging from a coat hook in the corner behind the desk. I took it down to look at it. It would have been great to wear to a War-themed fancy dress party. Handling it gave me that weird feeling again. It had belonged to a man who had probably died on this ship. According to the security tag clipped to his breast pocket his name had been Kyle Rose. I hung the jacket back on its peg but I took the tag, thinking it might come in useful later.

"Show me the layout of this floor," I said. Trixie projected the image in front of me. More by luck than skill I was now less than a hundred yards from the vault that held the Navigator. And by 'vault' I mean something comparable to a bank vault. The Navigator was the most valuable thing on the ship and the precautions taken to protect it reflected that. I've seen perhaps half-a-dozen bank vaults in my time – most of them from both the outside and the inside. Manufacturers like to strongly hint that their vaults are impenetrable but they know better than to guarantee the fact. Vault makers are aware that there are people like me around who see the phrase 'impregnable vault' as a challenge – and some of us are very good at what we do. Of course, when rising to such a challenge I would normally make sure I had all the state-of-the-art equipment that stolen money could buy. At this moment I had at my disposal a small tool roll and a fire axe.

The *Celestia's* Navigator was a fully-fledged artificial sentience – which was a good few rungs higher on the evolutionary ladder than an artificial intelligence. Where an AI could control a robot or even a team of robots, an AS could control a whole city. Or a battleship and all of its Warbirds. An artificial sentience is like a human brain – only more so. The earliest ones had been based on a mapping of the human brain. But then AS's started improving themselves. Today only an AS can understand and build another AS. This fact makes a lot of people uncomfortable.

Artificial sentience, like a lot of military hardware, had been outlawed after the War ended. People didn't want their cities – their lives – being controlled by machines. It is no exaggeration to say that people were terrified of them. An artificial intelligence is just a collection of clever algorithms that you could take apart and understand, but a sentient is altogether different. Manufacture of them had ceased almost twenty years ago. When an AS stopped functioning – because of damage or sabotage or whatever – it wasn't repaired or replaced. Those that remain are rare and therefore valuable. More valuable now than when the *Celestia's* Navigator had been placed in its vault. That's why I wanted to break in and retrieve it. But I was going to need more than an axe. Luckily I was on a military warship that was stuffed to the gills with hardware. Everything I needed would be here. Somewhere.

Chapter Nine

The vault that housed the *Celestia's* Navigator was an hermetically sealed room. Almost. It wasn't quite self-contained and had some services piped or wired in from outside. These external connections were vulnerabilities that could be exploited – if you knew how. It's not like you see in the movies – there are no conveniently placed wide metal air shafts that a thief can crawl through. A rat couldn't fit through the widest pipe that passed into the vault. A cockroach might just about manage it, as long as it didn't trigger the intrusion countermeasures when it got inside.

There were three types of sensor in the vault to detect intruders. The floor was one huge pressure mat, sensitive enough to pick up anything heavier than a housefly. Around the walls was a network of heat and motion detectors watching every corner of the vault including the ceiling. And finally there were video cameras linked to the security database. These used facial and gait recognition to check whether a person entering the vault was authorised to be there. If you triggered any of the sensors or your face or movements didn't match an authorised profile, you would be fried by one of six high-power lasers that could target any spot in the room. There was nowhere to hide.

Forty years ago, the defences in the vault would have been state-of-the-art and military-strength – and even today they were pretty effective. The vault's active anti-intrusion measures can only be deactivated for someone who has an appropriate level of authorisation according to the *Celestia's* security database. I didn't have security clearance of any kind.

The Navigator itself was housed in an oblong case like a sarcophagus – though people in my profession tended to refer to these cases as 'treasure chests'. When the artificial sentience was sealed in its case, it was virtually impervious to external attack. The case also contained an explosive device that could be triggered remotely, destroying both the Navigator and whoever had tried to steal it. This in-built bomb cannot be disarmed locally, so it is best not to do anything to trigger it.

All of these details about the vault's security were publicly available and had been when the *Celestia* first came into service. Vault manufacturer's always like to boast about how good their security systems are. It serves to warn off anyone who might think of trying to break into it and it is great publicity for the manufacturer. What you don't find out in the open are details about the internal workings of a new vault mechanism.

With most old technology, you can usually find detailed specifications and video tear-downs that show you how the thing was put together. Bank vaults and safes tend to be an exception. Manufacturers never allow these details out into the wild – because there is always someone somewhere using a twenty-year-old safe. Details only leak out if someone manages to obtain one of the old safes and takes it apart. Manufacturers prevent this by offering good money to buy back old examples. And details are never leaked by disgruntled employees because the manufacturers have ways of dealing with such people. Permanently.

But no matter how good a vault is, it is always placed within a structure of some kind and connected up to that structure's systems. In this case, the vault was housed in a battleship. An *old* battleship. That meant there would, in all probability, be weaknesses I could exploit. In all probability.

When I was a kid, I had a friend, Abbie, who collected old hardware. Her bedroom was full of the stuff. When I first saw it, I couldn't see the appeal. Those old boxes were slow and the software was glitchy and you couldn't play the latest games. And most of them smelled funny – a combination of old plastic and burning dust when you turned them on. Sometimes there were sparks and small fires. But Abbie liked to tinker with them and I learned a few things from watching her. Like the fact that old things often work like simpler versions of new things and helped you to learn how stuff worked. And old boxes didn't have the same safeguards as new ones, so you could often do things that new tech didn't allow you to.

That's an idea I've used a few times in the years since then. But most significantly I learned that some people just enjoyed the challenge of keeping old stuff working. Computers, operating systems, software, watches, handguns, or whatever.

Abbie would have had a field day on the *Celestia* but sadly I'd lost touch with her long ago. Given time I could probably have tracked her down – most people are locatable unless they take active measures not to be. But I didn't need Abbie. There were a lot of people like her out there and I was sure some of them had a thing for forty-year-old military technology.

As far as anyone knew, the *Celestia* had been lost in battle and no one was sure where. But she had a sister ship that had survived the conflict. The *Achilles* had probably ended up as a floating museum or a restaurant. At least the *Celestia* had been spared that indignity. If I could find an enthusiast who had maintained or salvaged the *Achilles*'s hardware and software, I could get an insight into how the *Celestia* was set up. I explained my plan to Trixie. I don't think she was impressed.

"I need you to find me a geek," I said. "I mean an enthusiast."

"I *know* what a geek is."

Was she looking at me when she said that?

Trixie made a connection to one of the satellites orbiting Saphira and in relatively short order had managed to piece together much of the information I needed. She showed me a three-dimensional plan of the *Celestia's* systems, all wrapped around a blank spot that was the lack of details about the vault itself.

There was an impressive refrigeration system that fed ice-cold fluid into the vault. The Navigator obviously needed cooling – and a lot of it when working at full capacity. Though as it was now, with the ship mostly in standby mode, the Navigator could probably get by on passive cooling alone. But an idea was forming in my head that would put the refrigeration system to use.

The Navigator was effectively a self-contained computer system, isolated from the rest of the ship's network. Data was passed into the Navigator by the ship and the Navigator then passed data out again – and that was it. The volumes of data shared were massive, but there was no interaction beyond that. Try to pass anything other than authorised data streams to the Navigator and the firewalls – either the ship's or the Navigator's or probably both – would quarantine the intrusive code and dissect it with lethal force.

The *Celestia's* own computer system was a relatively unsophisticated ancestor of a modern system that I was familiar with. The network that connected the ship's day-to-day systems was more or less isolated from the ship's security network. This wasn't unusual forty years ago and it's still fairly common now. Information technology departments don't trust security departments and vice versa. Each sees the other as a potential source of risk and each wants to be the one with ultimate control of network security – so they have their own systems that barely talk to one another. While this can enhance security, it can also introduce vulnerabilities. People like me delight in discovering and exploiting these vulnerabilities.

The Navigator, the ship's computer network, and the security system all passed data to one another, but lacking the ability to rigorously test this data, they effectively accepted it on trust. If security said something was secure, the other two systems wouldn't – and couldn't – argue, because they had no way of checking for themselves. This was something I was sure I could exploit. Somehow.

Vaults are specifically designed to keep people out. They are created by people whose job it is to think up possible ways of entry and then make sure that these ways won't work. Manufacturers even employ thieves to try and break into their newly designed vaults to test them. I've never been asked to do this. Which is a good thing, because if people know you're a thief and know how to contact you to offer you a job, you're probably in jail.

Prisons are the opposite of vaults. They are specifically designed to stop people from breaking out. Getting out of a prison can be tricky. On the other hand, breaking *into* a prison is relatively easy. I can say this based on experience, having sneaked into penitentiaries on two occasions on different planets. Prison designers don't expect people to try and break in. And this set me thinking...

People who build vaults aren't going to put a lot of effort into preventing someone from breaking *out* of them. Why would they? In fact, many vaults have systems in place to allow people to get out if they are accidentally locked in. Having a bank employee slowly suffocate in your vault is not the sort of publicity you want as a manufacturer. Authorised persons can get out of a vault relatively easily. I wasn't sure where I was going with this idea – I was not an authorised person and I wasn't actually inside the vault, but I felt I was on to something.

I sat down behind the desk in Kyle Rose's little office and put my feet up. When you relax, great ideas sometimes pop into your head.

I was going to need access to the *Celestia's* security system in order to achieve anything. I asked Trixie to bring together all of the data she'd found on the operating system and software that had been used on this class of battleship. She made a tutting noise.

"What?" I asked.

"Nothing."

"No, you obviously have some criticism of my plan – tell me."

Trixie made a sighing sound. I'm not sure where she learned to do things like that. "The problem with lines of reasoning inspired by the exploits of Sherlock Holmes is that people sometimes miss the more obvious solutions," she said. She may have been quoting some long-dead academic killjoy.

"You think there's a simpler solution?" I asked, sceptical.

"No, I'm sure that you spending hours sifting through software manuals and millions of lines of code is much simpler than what I was going to suggest."

Sarcasm, that was another thing she'd picked up somewhere.

"Go on, astound me with your brilliance," I said.

"Why don't you use the security tag you picked up earlier?"

I was silent for a few heartbeats. I'd forgotten about the tag. But even if I'd remembered it, it didn't really solve my problem. "What good is that?" I asked. "It'll open doors but it won't get me into anything else. The security systems all require two levels of authorisation – as well as the card I'd need to pass the bio scan."

"I'll tell you what," Trixie said. "You think about it for a few minutes and if the solution doesn't come to you, you can ask me."

"Just tell me!"

"If I do everything for you, you'll never learn to do it yourself."

That sounded so like my mother it was spooky. I think Trixie had been a school teacher in another life. She had laid down the challenge and my commanding her to give me the answer would have been an admission of defeat. I picked up the security tag.

"Don't smudge it any more than you already have," Trixie warned.

She'd just given me the answer. I held the tag carefully by its edges and tilted it, examining its surface under the light.

"Fingerprints?" I said.

"Or possibly DNA," Trixie said.

"Enough to fool a bio scan?"

"Won't know until we try," she said. It sounded like she was smiling. A virtual smile of virtual smugness.

I held up the tag so that Trixie could scan each side of it. She analysed the images, separating my prints from those left by the tag's original owner.

"Anything?" I asked.

"I don't know what you've touched, but you should wash your hands before you next eat," she said.

"Yes, mother."

"There's no DNA," she said. "Are there any stray hairs on the shoulders of the jacket? Or dandruff?"

I went to look. It seemed that Kyle Rose was one of those military types who used a clothes brush on his jacket every morning – there wasn't a speck on it.

"What about fingerprints?" I asked.

From her scans of the security tag, Trixie managed to recover three fingerprints, but all of them were slightly distorted. She set about teasing the print from an index finger back into shape. It didn't need to be perfect – just good enough to provide enough points of comparison to trigger a positive identification from the security system sensor.

I dug the glove out of my jacket pocket. It looked like a well-worn leather driving glove, but it had some interesting electronics built into it. I hadn't used it for a while and it felt tight and dry when I pulled it on.

"Try it now," Trixie said.

The glove warmed to body temperature and the index finger adopted the pattern of the fingerprint Trixie had recovered. I pressed my finger to the sensor at the side of the security terminal. The little screen above it flashed red and the words 'Please try again' were superimposed on it. I pressed my glover finger down again, rotating it a little as I did so. After a moment's thought, the little screen turned green. The monitor attached to the security terminal lit up. I slid the security tag into the reader built into the keyboard.

Good afternoon, Kyle appeared on the screen. Apparently he had thirteen unread messages, but I didn't want to look at them. I was only interested in his security level. If it turned out he was a 'facilities manager' who only had access to the mop cupboard, I was going to be disappointed and would feel the need to mock Trixie mercilessly. I called up the menu of systems his work required him to use.

"Level four security," Trixie said in my ear. Again with the smug smile.

I wasn't sure how many levels of security there were here on the *Celestia*, nor did I know whether '1' was the highest or lowest, but judging by the menu items, Kyle was relatively high on the food chain.

"Can you make a connection?" I asked.

Trixie chuckled. "You're going to have to plug me in."

"Please tell me you're joking."

"Nope. Wireless communication was regarded as a security risk on these old warships so it is all triple-encoded. You can't access it unless you know the secret handshake."

I pulled open the desk drawer. There was the usual accumulation of old paperclips, decayed rubber bands and blunt pencils. There were also several wires that had that odd sticky feeling and smell that some of the old tech in Abbie's bedroom had had.

"Take your pick," I said, holding up the cables so Trixie could see the connectors on both ends.

"The red one," she said, "plug the larger connector into the terminal."

I did as she asked. Meanwhile, Trixie's nano-bots reshaped the end of her casing, creating a socket to match the other connector. I slid it into place.

Trixie giggled. "That tickles. Give me a minute, I'm going to tap into the communication grid and see if I can trick it into giving me a wireless connection. There we go. I'm not sure what sort of range we'll have and it will only work in parts of the ship where the grid is undamaged."

"But it's better than having a plug up your butt," I said. I disconnected the wire.

"Keep that with you in case we need it again," Trixie said.

I coiled the wire and stuffed it in my jacket pocket. "See if you can get into the security database and look at how the input is structured. Then take my data and format it ready to create a new profile."

"Ready," Trixie said. "I'm inputting basic facial profiling, voice pattern, retinal scan, and gait. Do you want me to set it to auto-erase?"

"Always," I said, "Wipe it after forty-eight hours – we should be long gone by then."

"Who do you want to be?"

Kyle Rose's security clearance would only permit him to create a profile for someone at a lower level than him, which made sense. "Make me an engineer with as much clearance as you can – I need access to utilities and life-support as a minimum. And make me the duty engineer for the current shift."

"I like it," Trixie said. "Do you want to be Mario or Luigi?"

"Just give it my name," I said.

"I'm going to have to reprogram the security tag," Trixie said. "That'll give you access as your new identity, but it will mean you can't use it to get back into the system as Kyle Rose."

"That shouldn't be a problem," I said. "But try and keep this terminal logged on as Kyle if you can – just in case."

Trixie wrote my new identity to the security tag and then set the terminal to playing a game of Hearts to make it look as if Kyle Rose was still hard at 'work'.

"You're all set," she said. "The first blocked toilet that comes along will be yours to fix."

"Now we need to put someone inside the vault," I said. "Find out who was the last person authorised to enter. And retrieve the security video from the vault for that shift."

"Searching," Trixie said. "I don't know who created this database, but I would have serious concerns about his reasoning abilities."

"Or hers," I said.

"What?"

"It might have been designed by a female person," I said.

"Oh, no," Trixie said. "Trust me, this file structure was thrown together by a man. And I would put money on the fact that he wore odd socks."

I decided not to mention the fact that most of my socks were odd.

"I've found you the ideal young woman," Trixie said.

"Remember how well it turned out the last time you said that?"

"Her name's Zola Brandt and she's probably been dead for forty years," Trixie said. "Even you couldn't screw up this relationship."

"When we get away from here, remind me that it's time for your annual check-up," I said.

"I'm not letting anyone in rubber gloves anywhere near me," Trixie said. "I have the video. The quality isn't great."

"Degraded due to age?"

"No, a squitty camera to begin with."

"I need a loop of five or ten minutes – I want to use it to replace the live feed. Give it the current timestamp."

"This is actually not a bad idea," she said.

"Why do you sound surprised?"

"Do you want me to list some of your previous 'great ideas' for comparison?"

"Annual check-up, I'm warning you. And I may ask for a factory reset."

"You need me if you want to get out of here alive."

Trixie had a point.

"I need you to go back into the logs and delete the record of Zola Brandt leaving the vault – we need it to look like she's still in there. Then start the video feed showing her in the vault."

"Just tell me when to hit 'play'."

The next step was for me to go out and sabotage the cooling system that fed into the vault. To do that, I would have to go back out through the robot garage.

"Any chance of you being able to keep the security robots away from me?" I asked.

"Sorry. Control of them requires clearance above Kyle Rose's level. I'll monitor their positions and warn you if they get close."

"What about the one outside the door?"

"Battery currently at less than one per cent but it is back on the charger."

"I'll take his head off on my way out," I said.

Chapter Ten

The plan was simple. I was going to trick the ship so she opened up the vault door and invited me in. To make that happen, we were going to make it seem that someone – Zola Brandt – was trapped in the vault. Then I was going to arrange a fault so that poor Zola was at risk of dying in there, causing the ship to open an emergency hatch so she could get out. As that happened, the ship would send a call to the duty maintenance engineer to come and fix the problem in the vault. I would be playing the part of the engineer. Once I got into the vault, I would improvise. I didn't expect to be in there very long. Grab the Navigator and get out, hopefully before the three remaining security robots were alerted to the theft. Like I said – simple.

"Any sign of those security robots?" I asked. I didn't like not knowing where the robots were. I opened a maintenance hatch that would give me access to the refrigeration system that sent coolness into the vault.

"Negative," Trixie said. "There are large sections of the interior monitoring grid down – dark places that I can't see into."

This wasn't surprising given the damage caused by the crash. It was a miracle that this armoured middle section of the ship had survived as well as it had. It was possible the missing robots had been destroyed when the *Celestia* hit the ground, but I wasn't going to bet my life on a possibility.

"Keep an eye out for them," I said.

"About that factory reset...?"

"It'll never happen," I assured her, "I love you just the way you are."

"You say the sweetest things, Quincy. But you probably ought to find yourself a real girl. Or boy."

"I've sworn off relationships," I said. I was using my new identity to log into the refrigeration system control panel.

"Just because you've had a couple of bad experiences..."

"A *couple*? Would you like me to list my top ten relationship disasters?" I said. "You haven't forgotten how we ended up in this squit hole, have you?"

"She was just one..."

"One of a long line that includes both my first wife and my husband."

"I just think you need to get back into the saddle. It's been six months since you..."

"*Thank you,* I know. But please promise me, no more match-making. How's our friend Zola Brandt doing?"

"She's carrying on as normal, quite oblivious to the disaster that is about to befall her," Trixie said.

"Any sign that the ship is suspicious about us?"

"Nope. It has already added a couple of minor repairs to your job sheet for this shift. Apparently there's a hole in the hull it wants you to have a look at."

"If she thinks that is a minor repair, this battleship has a gift for understatement. Okay, I'm about to flood the vault with refrigerant. Blur the video so that it's not obvious that the lovely Zola isn't panicking about the vapour flooding her work area. And then make it look like she's triggered the panic alarm."

"Aye, aye, skipper."

I now had a toolbox. A proper one, battered metal and lots of compartments, with all the tools a maintenance engineer might need. Plus a few extra bits and pieces that a thief might need. I still had the red fire axe and I'd also picked up a blow-torch from the ship's stores, in case I needed to set fire to another corpse or anything.

"Any communication out from the Navigator?" I asked.

"Nothing. Oh, that's odd."

"Odd? I don't like odd."

"It may be nothing. But there's no data at all coming out from the Navigator. I'm just looking back through the logs. There's been nothing out of there for some time."

There was no way of knowing what this meant. Maybe the Navigator had been damaged during the crash or maybe it had recently suffered a flat battery. I wouldn't know until I got into the vault.

"Incoming message for the on-duty maintenance engineer," Trixie said. "You're wanted in sector 3A."

"Blocked toilet?"

"The next best thing. They need a clean-up in the Navigator aisle."

"On my way."

"You'll be pleased to know that Zola made it out of the vault safely. She's currently catching her breath in a sub-corridor where the cameras aren't working. A medic has been summoned to check her out."

"Unthinking, unquestioning automatic response systems, you've got to love them," I said.

"Technology has sure moved on since then," Trixie said.

"In some ways."

"I'm picking up two – no, three signals. It may be the security robots."

"Where?" I asked.

"There's something wrong with these readings, unless... they may be outside the ship."

"Keep them in sight and update me if they move. I'm approaching the vault."

"I'm sitting on your shoulder, I know exactly where you are," Trixie said.

"I just feel the need to provide some sort of narration. Maybe it's just nerves."

"Maybe you just like the sound of your own voice."

"Humour me."

"I always do. Can you see Zola? I hope she's okay," Trixie asked.

Above me a camera turned, scanning me and comparing my movements against the patterns stored in the security database. If we'd done our work properly, I would show up as the expected duty engineer and given a snappy salute as I walked in through the open hatch into the vault. I wasn't sure if they saluted maintenance men in the military, but anyone who appreciated a hot shower and a flushing toilet owed them respect.

"I'm at the hatch." I slid my security tag into the slot. The little screen hiccoughed and then turned green. The heavy hatch swung slowly open. I tried not to mentally compare it to a prison door.

There was a thick mist inside the vault, lit up by a steady flashing red light. It looked like a low-budget stage set depicting hell.

"You're not going to suffocate in here, are you?" Trixie asked. I like to think there was concern in her voice.

"Not unless some idiot closes the hatch and seals me in," I said.

The hatch clanged shut behind me and I could hear the locking mechanism slide into place.

"You were saying?" Trixie said.

"Nothing to worry about. I won't be breathing this stuff long enough to lose consciousness."

In my inner eye, I could see Trixie call up my heart rate, blood pressure and blood-oxygen levels. "You *do* care," I said.

"My motivation is purely selfish: this is not where I wish to spend the remainder of my existence. Open the coffin, grab the brain, and let's get out of here. You can get us out of here, can't you?"

"Um..." I said. In theory, I could hit the panic button and the ship would let me out. But there was no guarantee it would fall for the same trick twice. I was pinning my hopes on the fact that my newly programmed security tag would open the hatch door and get me out. "Of course," I said. "I planned for just such an eventuality."

"I'm monitoring your vital signs. I can tell when you're lying."

"Stop talking, you're wasting our oxygen."

"I don't breathe."

"Then you'll grow old alone here. Are you picking up anything from the Navigator?"

"Nothing. But I think the three security robots are back on the ship. I picked them up just before they entered another of the dead zones."

Being locked in the vault gave us the advantage of being safe from the robots – for the time being at least.

In my guise of maintenance engineer, I reset the emergency system and turned off the annoying flashing lights. I flipped the switch on the overheads and the vault was revealed in all its silver and white and brown-stained glory. It was like the set of an old science fiction movie. And I wasn't the only actor on stage.

My co-star looked a lot like Mr. Skellington, except that he had much shorter arms. And no hands. He was also a little better preserved – mummified almost. I peered at him more closely. Presumably, he was another of Old Jack Sterling's crew who had made it further than his teammate. But how could he be a thief if he had no hands? Then I realised that the brown stains splashed around the vault were his blood. He'd had hands when he came in here but somehow his arms had been chopped off just below the elbow. Just the thought of it made me shiver. I had to figure out what had happened to him. Because I wanted to be sure it didn't happen to me.

The brown stains were heaviest around the Navigator's coffin. My guess was that Mr. Hands-Free had opened the lid and reached inside – only to have the lid slam shut like a high-tech guillotine. The would-be thief had bled to death in here, unable to do anything to help himself or to summon help. I promised myself that I would be very, very careful about where I put my hands.

I had hoped that shutting down the cooling system would have caused the Navigator to switch over to passive cooling. The top of its casing was designed to rise about half an inch to serve as a vent. With the top raised, it would be much easier to break into. But it was still sealed tightly. I was going to have to warm things up a little more. Unfortunately, that would mean burning up some of the remaining oxygen.

"Is that wise?" Trixie asked as I pulled the blow torch out of my backpack. "Forget I asked that, no part of this plan is wise."

I lit the blowtorch and set it on the ground so that the flame was aimed at the side of the Navigator's casing. In an ideal world, I would have brought a more sophisticated form of heat generation, but I'd been limited to what I could scrounge up on the wreck. I wasn't sure how long it would be before things warmed up enough inside to get it to pop its top.

"Let me know if the Navigator sends any messages to the ship," I said. "If either of them suspects we're doing something naughty, things might get a little... interesting."

"How interesting?"

"They'll fire the lasers at us."

"And if that happens, our plan is to...?"

"Er... hide in the Navigator's coffin?" I said.

"Best get a move on with the opening of said coffin, then, eh?"

When Trixie was right, she was right.

There was a pale orangey spot on the outside of the casing where the blowtorch was pointed at it, but the top of the case was still firmly sealed. The Navigator was probably protected by a layer of insulation – maybe even the sort of stuff they put on the outside on spaceships to stop them burning up when they enter a planet's atmosphere. The blowtorch might not make much impact on that.

I could try firing my pistol at it, but the casing was armoured – thick enough to protect the Navigator if the laser weapons built into the vault were fired. Any projectile I fired at it would probably bounce off and take my eye out.

I looked around the room at the points where the lasers were fixed to the walls. They seemed innocent enough – more like cameras than guns. They would be fitted with tamper-prevention devices. If I tried to disable them, the one I was working on would probably blow up in my face and the others would fry my body as it fell, just to be sure.

As I looked around the vault, I saw one of the video cameras following my movements.

"Something's happening," Trixie said.

"The cameras are back online – they're watching us, not the pre-recorded video loop."

"What will happen now?"

That was a good question. If the ship had been fully-manned, a security guard in a monitoring station somewhere would have seen us on his screen and manually triggered the lasers. But at this moment I didn't know who or what was watching the video feed. If the ship was seeing us now, there was no way of telling how she had been programmed to respond. What I did know was that between the falling oxygen levels and the waking of the ship's security systems, we were rapidly running out of time. I ought to concentrate my efforts on getting the escape hatch open.

I looked back towards the Navigator's coffin. Having gotten this close, I really didn't want to give up on my quest. Not until it became a choice between success or death. But how would I know when I reached that point?

Chapter Eleven

What I was facing here was, more or less, a locked metal safe inside a locked bank vault. I'd managed to get inside the vault. Now all I had to do was crack open the safe. But there was an additional complication here. I wasn't simply trying to get something valuable out of a locked box. This was more like trying to get at somebody who had locked themselves inside a box. To get them out, I had to pick the lock that was inside the box. There was no external keyhole.

The most elegant way of tackling this would be to trick the person in the box into opening it, which you could do even with a super-smart artificial sentience given the right circumstances. You just had to convince it that you were someone it wanted to interact with face-to-face. Failing that, you had to pick the lock. From the inside. This was going to require a combination of brute force and finesse.

My original idea was to heat up the metal casing with a blowtorch so that the 'person' locked in the box opened the lid a crack to let the heat out. But I hadn't managed to generate enough heat to do that. Once I had the lid open a little, I could force it a bit more and then wedge it so it couldn't seal closed again. Then I could poke my tools in through the crack and first deal with the hidden bolts and then tackle the main locking mechanism and get the lid to fully open.

The skeleton in the vault appeared to have achieved partial success. Judging by his lack of hands and forearms, he'd gotten the lid open wide enough to reach inside – but he'd failed to prevent it slamming shut on him. A methodology that results in loss of limbs in this way has to be regarded as less than optimal. Leaving your fingerprints at the scene of a crime marks you as an amateur whose criminal career is likely to be short-lived. Leaving your actual hands behind will have even more drastic consequences. Bleeding to death being the most significant, I would say. I looked over at the skeleton and determined that I would take care not to suffer his fate.

Opening the lock on a safe, any safe, is only half the job. You have to prevent the safe from engaging additional bolts when it senses that someone is mounting an attack. Heat from a cutting torch or vibrations from an explosion cause a safe to activate hidden mechanisms that are independent of the main lock. If you don't know what you're doing, your joy at having cracked a safe's lock will quickly turn to despair when you discover the door is still bolted shut. The purpose of these 're-lockers' is to massively increase the time needed to open the safe once they've been triggered, in the hope that the thief will give up or take so long working on them that it gives the police time to turn up and catch him in the act.

The trick is to deal with these hidden bolts first, by either disabling the mechanism that triggers them or by blocking the bolts so they can't lock into place. To do this you need to know how the mechanisms are constructed and where they are placed. There are a limited number of options and an experienced thief soon learns to recognise what he's up against. As with most professions, we have to stay current, reading up on the latest technology. But my knowledge of the current state of the art was doing me no good on the *Celestia*. I needed to be an expert in vintage technology. Fortunately, modern mechanisms are often only more sophisticated versions of vintage ones.

When opening a safe, explosives are always a possibility. The noise involved is a disadvantage that has to be considered. But more significant is the risk of damaging the valuable items that you are seeking to extract from the safe. An artificial sentience is just about the most delicate bit of equipment you will ever come across. Even if you don't blow it to smithereens, there is still a risk that the concussion caused by setting off a small bomb inside its storage box will damage it severely. I wouldn't set off a bomb under my own hat, and similar consideration was needed here. I had to open the lock manually.

My first task was to get the top of the casing to pop open. For that, I needed to trigger the passive cooling system built into the box. And to achieve that, I need to generate heat. Much more heat than a blowtorch could manage. Something like the temperature of a small sun. Except, I realised, I didn't. If Mr. Skellington's twin brother had done this, there would be obvious scorch marks on the casing. But it had been pristine when I entered. Apart from the bloodstains. That meant there was an easier and less energetic way of triggering the lid.

The answer, like many such problems, was easy once I figured it out. Computers deal with data about situations rather than experiencing the situations themselves. If a machine receives data from a trusted source that tells it something is occurring, it accepts this as true. Unless programmed to do so, it won't conduct independent analysis of the incoming data. If I could convince the computer that the temperature inside the box had risen to a critical level that threatened the continued existence of the Navigator inside, the ship's computer would respond accordingly. That is, it would pop open the lid to provide physical ventilation.

"Trixie, is there any evidence of the Navigator communicating with the ship?"

"Still nothing."

I wasn't sure why the Navigator and the ship's computer weren't on speaking terms, but it made my task easier. If I told the ship that the Navigator was getting fried, she would ping a message to the Navigator asking for confirmation of the danger. If the Navigator said 'No, I'm cool,' my plan was doomed. If the Navigator failed to respond, the ship would trigger an emergency cooling protocol, fearing that non-response was due to the Navigator over-heating.

I tapped into the data link from the Navigator to the ship. I would send an 'overheating' signal to the ship, making it look like it had come from sensors in the Navigator's box. I could then intercept the query from the ship to the Navigator and make sure it was never received or answered.

"Trixie, what's the optimal temperature range for Navigator operation?"

"Minus forty to plus one-hundred-and-twenty degrees centigrade."

I decided to increase the reported temperature slowly until it got to a hundred and then more rapidly after that. This would hopefully mimic a rapidly failing cooling system.

The result was disappointingly undramatic. There was a soft sigh and a gentle breath of air as the lid of the Navigator's casing rose about a half inch. It was held up by a round silver bar at each corner, like a table leg. Stage 1 complete.

I used a small rotary tool with a blade attachment to cut some strips of metal from the bottom of a control console. These strips were flexible but relatively sturdy. Working carefully so as to avoid any sudden vibration, I slid four of the strips into the Navigator casing so that they blocked the holes that the secondary bolts would lock into. With a bit of luck, the metal would be strong enough to prevent the hidden bolts locking if the lid was lowered again. That was Stage 2. Enough with the finesse, now it was time for a bit of brute force.

The fire axe was hanging from a loop on my backpack. I was beginning to think I should make the axe part of my standard equipment. The robot arm I was less sure about. It was threaded under the flap of my pack and I'd brought it along in case I needed the code on its wrist to open another lock.

I wasn't sure how much force the lid could muster in order to try and close itself, but given that amputation was a real risk, I decided to err on the side of caution. I wanted to wedge the gap open with the most substantial bits of material I could find. I used a military-grade laser cutter to chop four lengths of steel H-beam from the criss-crossed girders that supported the ceiling.

I slid the head of the axe into the gap and levered the lid of the Navigator's box open wider. There was a loud whining sound as the internal hydraulics tried to close the lid, but I slid a section of the H-beam into the widened gap, positioning it across the corner. I did the same thing for the other three corners. There was some creaking and groaning as the lid strained against the bits of girder, but it didn't look like the gap was going to be closing again any time soon. It was now safe to put my hands inside the box. Probably.

I shone a flashlight into the box. There was a metal mesh inside and under it a glimpse of something that might be the navigator. I didn't look more closely because I was distracted by what was lying on top of the mesh. Two mummified forearms complete with hands. I didn't want to touch them so I used a pair of long-handled pliers to lift them out. I put the arms in the skeleton's lap – I couldn't tell from his expression whether he was grateful. I looked back at the box. Even with the bits of girder propping open the lid, I really didn't want to put my hands in there. Then my eyes wandered over to the robot arm. I picked it up.

"Trixie, can you operate this?"

"I'll need two if you want me to play *Chopsticks*."

Piano playing wasn't on the agenda, but what I had in mind was going to require two hands and at least one eye inside the Navigator's box. If we used the robot arm, I would have to risk only one of mine.

I had to plug a tiny receiver into the end of the arm so that Trixie could send control signals to it. She demonstrated that it was working by closing the hand into a fist and extending the middle finger upwards. I ignored her and reached into the backpack to pull out one of the drones and the little medical kit. Just in case. I took off my belt, ready to use as a tourniquet if the worst were to happen.

"Not brimming with confidence, are we?" Trixie asked.

"Tell me where the security robots are," I said. "How much time have I got?"

"They are currently in the charging area we passed through earlier."

"Trying to revive their fallen comrades, probably," I said. I hoped they didn't have access to the spare parts necessary to reactivate the decapitated robots. "Let me know if they head this way. And monitor the lasers in here, I want to know if they come online."

The smart thing would have been to get out of there while the security robots were distracted. But that would be to admit defeat. I wasn't defeated. Not yet.

Chapter Twelve

You can increase the thickness of the walls and door of a safe, but ultimately security depends on how good the locking mechanism is. A safe is simply a strong box with a door and a lock. The lock and the door hinges are typically the weakest points. The Navigator's casing did away with hinges altogether – the lid opened on four rods which slid out of the casing. They had notches in them like the end of a padlock clasp and also functioned like bolts. The rods were about three feet long when fully extended. So far I'd gotten them to extend only a couple of inches.

The lock on the casing was inside and there was no external keyhole or keypad or dial. To open the casing you needed to get inside the casing to manipulate the lock. It was an ingenious bit of design.

I decided to send a drone into the coffin to have a look around and Gnat got picked for the job. He floated in through the gap and turned on his mini spotlight. He sank slowly downwards, sending pictures to Trixie who projected them on the side of the coffin for me to see. I needed to get a look at the mechanism to see what I was up against. I knew it would be a mechanical lock, they always were. It made the Navigator invulnerable to cyberattack. A mechanical lock cannot be tricked or countermanded. It had to be opened by the Navigator. Or picked from the inside by an expert thief – but what were the odds of that ever happening?

The Navigator didn't carry a key to open the lock. It *was* the key. It would extend a quicksilver-like pseudopod towards the lock. The nano-bots in it would turn the silver sliver into the shape of the key. This perfectly matched shape would slide into the lock and at the same time release a code that was known only to the Navigator, triggering more nanos to realign themselves, creating a gap that had not existed moments before. The lock would then turn and there would be a gentle click as it opened.

Mimicking the key shape was easy enough – Trixie's scanners were more sophisticated than anything available when the lock was created. She could map the inside of the keyhole and create the shape almost instantly. Generating the right code to tickle the lock's nanos into doing their thing was a different matter. Human beings were notoriously bad at thinking up passwords or numbers, relying on easily-remembered dates, pet or family names, or other mnemonic devices that thieves could easily work out themselves or obtain with a bit of simple social engineering. In days of old, even numbers or codes 'randomly' generated by computer turned out to be a lot less random than anticipated, though again this was the fault of human fallibility in determining the definition of 'random.'

A machine like a Navigator could generate a key code that was impossible to guess. The strings they came up with were of variable length and drew from various sets of symbols, numbers, and letters. Only a Navigator could estimate how many billions of combinations were possible. And a Navigator never wrote the key on a bit of paper and stuck it on the bottom of a drawer in case they forgot it.

If the Navigator had been active, I could probably have nudged it and got it to try and relock the mechanism, during which action we could have picked up the key code like the signal from a cheap vehicle's keyless lock. But the artificial sentience was still asleep, evidently oblivious to what we were doing. Unless it was lying in wait, ready to spring to its own defence when I least expected it.

I took Trixie from her loop on the shoulder of my jacket and placed the slim metal tube into the hand of the robot. The Trixie closed the fingers around herself.

"I bet this reminds you of something you do regularly," she said.

"What?"

"Holding yourself in your hand? Never mind."

"You just compared yourself to a penis."

"Yeah. Usually it's you I'm comparing to one."

I picked up the robot arm and used the pliers to place it into the case where the two mummified arms had lain.

"Keep your hand out unless you really need it down there," Trixie said.

"Are we still talking about...?"

"I'm talking about the lock. I'm scanning the inside of the hole and getting ready to insert myself. Oh, for heaven's sake, stop sniggering and grow up!"

"Sorry."

"Okay, I'm in. I'm examining the lock mechanism."

There was a loud 'snap' and I threw myself backwards away from the casing.

"Sorry," Trixie said in my ear, "I accidentally triggered the secondary locks."

So far the metal strips and sections of girder I'd put in place were holding.

"How do the nanos feel?" I asked.

"Primitive," Trixie said. "I think they were man-made."

Man-made nanos were a joke machine intelligences like to make – as if a human could ever make anything as small as a modern nanobot. They seem to forget that we made the machines that made the nanos.

"Can you control them?" I asked.

"It's going to be like herding cats," she said.

"But they're binary cats," I said, "they sit in one of two locations, you just need to get them off the mat and point them in the direction of the patch of sunlight."

"You know how to bludgeon a metaphor to death, don't you? I'm checking to see if the material structure of the lock was fully reset."

If you make a model out of clay and then screw it up into a ball, it may be possible to 'unwrap' the ball of clay and see what the model you made looked like. Unless you completely kneaded the clay over and over until there was nothing left. If you imagine the lock as a piece of clay, Trixie was trying to see how much of the model was still discernible. If she could see the residue of the shape, she could try and urge the nanos back into it. The shape, in this case, being a lock that can be opened as opposed to something that looks like a solid block of metal with a key-shaped hole in. If she could reshape the nanos, we wouldn't need the navigator's secret code.

"They're moving," Trixie said.

I imagined video of a melted object being played backwards from a pool of goo back to its original shape. Trixie would have scoffed at the simplicity of this analogy. On the video image transmitted by the drone, I could see the surface of the lock mechanism start to shift. A hair-width gap appeared, extending around until it formed a complete circle around Trixie's skeleton key.

"Do you want to reach in and work your magic on it?" Trixie asked.

"No, let's open the lock first. You've earned the honour."

There was a metallic click and a hiss of compressed air. The lid of the Navigator's casing rose upwards on its metal rods, like a table whose legs were getting longer.

I leaned closer, peering into the casing. I didn't want to stick my head inside in case the lid descended again suddenly.

"Something isn't right," I said.

I used the pliers to lift the robot arm out of the case. The drone floated out after it. Then I used the pliers to grip the mesh that the arm had sat upon. It came away easily – the four screws that normally held it in place were missing. The drone hovered over my shoulder as I peered into the bottom of the case.

"I've never seen one up close," Trixie said, "but that doesn't look like a Navigator."

No, it didn't. It looked very much like a Bertie the Bear soft toy. In all probability because it *was* a Bertie the Bear soft toy.

"Someone got here before us," Trixie said.

I reached into the case with the pliers, intending to pluck the bear out and tear its head off. This proved to be a bad move. As I lifted the toy, something shifted under it and there was a *click*. An alarm sounded somewhere outside the vault.

The cameras on the walls all turned towards me. And then the lasers all turned as well. In a fraction of a second, I would be toast. I did the only thing I could. I jumped into the Navigator's casing, pulling the lid shut as I did. I knocked the pieces of girder out as the lid descended. The last thing I saw before being swallowed by darkness was a bright red flash as the first of the lasers fired.

Inside the box there was complete silence and I could feel only the slightest vibrations. Outside, I could only imagine that the vault was criss-crossed with bolts of energy. I held Bertie the Bear close and waited for the nightmare to end.

I was lying on top of the robot arm and I felt it begin to move.

"Stop doing that," I said.

"Why, have you got something better to do?" Trixie whispered in my ear.

"I need to conserve oxygen," I said. "I'm not really into that asphyxiation thing."

"Kill the moment, why don't you," Trixie said.

"It's stopped," I said.

"You told me to."

"No, outside The lasers have stopped."

Trixie's sensors confirmed this so I decided to open the lid of the box enough to peek out. All I could see was swirling smoke. The drone floated out and scanned the area and it drew no fire from the lasers.

"All clear?" I asked, ready to push the lid open and climb out.

"Not quite," Trixie said. "The security robots are just outside the hatch. Hatch is opening." She called the drone back into hiding and I pulled the lid back down, leaving a tiny gap to allow the drone to watch what was happening. It fed video that Trixie projected for me to watch.

Three robots identical to those I had encountered earlier entered the vault. Identical except for the fact that these carried weapons – stubby rifles with long, curved ammunition clips. They scanned the inside of the vault. Apparently satisfied, two of them slung their weapons over their shoulders and reached down to something on the floor. They lifted the smoking remains of the skeleton and dragged it out. Hopefully, they would decide that Mr. Skellington had triggered the alarm in the vault. The third robot scanned the vault a final time and then followed the others out. As it left, I pushed up the lid of the box and jumped out. I wanted to get to the door before it closed. I slid one of the cut sections of girder into the gap to stop the door closing fully.

"We need to get out of here," I said. I slid Trixie back into her loop on the left shoulder of my jacket. I put the fire axe and the robot arm back into their slots and put my arms through the straps of the backpack. The pliers had been blasted into a molten mess by the lasers. I left Bertie sitting on top of the Navigator's coffin. Keeping a wary eye on the lasers, I moved to the door. A quick glance showed the corridor outside was clear. I slipped out, allowing the door to the vault to swing shut behind me.

"What now?" Trixie asked.

"We leave," I said. "But not the way we came in." I was worried that the dragon might still be lying in wait outside the hatch.

"If we head north," Trixie said, "there are fewer cameras and sensors active."

"Which way's north?"

Trixie projected the outline of a compass onto my retina. As long as the arrow was green, I was heading in the right direction.

"Where are the robots?" I asked.

"Last known position is a hundred and two metres northwest of this position," Trixie said. "They're not showing up at the moment, so presumably they're in an area where the sensors aren't working."

If we headed north, there was a chance we would run into the security robots. The *armed* security robots, I reminded myself. And as well as the three robots, there was evidence to suggest that there was someone else on the ship. Another person. Someone had been responsible for the primitive booby traps in the vault and for the Bertie the Bear booby prize in the Navigator's box. Robots didn't really do boobies of any kind.

"Are you picking up any other life signs?" I asked.

"Negative. But again, I am restricted to data from a limited number of working sensors on the ship. Do you think there is someone else on board?"

"Somebody has definitely been here. We should keep an eye out."

"I would suggest having a drone ten metres ahead of us and one ten metres behind."

"Do it." I drew my pistol and we started forward, heading north.

As we made our way through the deserted corridors, I started to get a sense of how big this ship must have been. And the chunk we were in was only the middle third.

At the coming together of three corridors, we found a metal spiral staircase.

"Let's go up," I said. "Maybe the robots will stay down here on the security deck."

The hatch at the top of the stairs was locked, but Trixie and I knew our way around the systems now and soon had it open. I felt more comfortable back on the dingy grey metal deck. It was a couple of minutes before I realised that the lights were on. The deck was no longer bathed in red emergency light. Perhaps because we were in a different section. Or perhaps for more sinister reasons.

If there *was* someone else on the ship, who might it be? Could it be a survivor of the crash – one of Old Jack Sterling's crewmates? I started to imagine a wild-eyed lunatic with a massive grey beard and long hair – a cross between Robinson Crusoe and Ben Gunn. Perhaps this shipwrecked soul would be unaware that the War was over. He would cry tears of joy when he learned the good news. We'd won. More or less. This was all contingent on the fact that he didn't blow my head off as soon as he saw me. I hoped he wouldn't mistake me for a Gator spy.

"Past this point most of the sensors and cameras are offline," Trixie said.

This meant there was less chance of us being tracked but it also meant we couldn't scan ahead and wouldn't know what we were walking into. I would have to depend on the drones to warn me of approaching danger.

Chapter Thirteen

The overhead lights dimmed slightly and there was a humming sound somewhere ahead of us.

"What was that?" I asked.

"Something drawing power," Trixie said. "Possibly an elevator at the end of this corridor, but I can't be certain."

"The security robots?"

"I don't think it's the janitor," Trixie said.

I stopped to consider my options. We were in a long straight corridor with no sub-corridors running off it. There were three doors in front of us, one in the wall on the left and two on the right. At the far end were two sets of elevator doors. If the robots appeared there, I was going to be a sitting target. And despite what you see in the movies, robot security guards are excellent shots. Once they acquire a target, they just keep firing at it.

"Let's go back," I said, starting to turn as I said it.

"Mozzie is picking up motion in the corridor we came down," Trixie said.

"Then we take the other fork," I said.

We were close to a junction where three corridors met in a sort of Y-shape. If we had robots in two of the corridors, there was only one way left open to us.

"Send Gnat to check it out," I said. I didn't move. I already knew what the second drone was going to report.

"Movement there also," Trixie said.

The ship's computer had chosen an excellent place to ambush us. But how had it managed to locate us if the sensors were out in this section?

"Show me the plan for this corridor," I said. "And try and work out how they found us."

I didn't want to be caught out in the open, but I wanted to know where each of the three doors led before I went through one of them. There were two robots coming up behind me and one in front, so going forward seemed to offer the best odds. I told the drones to keep watch for the robots coming from the rear.

The explosive rounds in my pistol could stop a security robot. But only if I fired all six at the right spots in its head and chest. Easy to do if you're shooting at a stationary target on a range – less easy at a moving target that is also firing at you. I didn't want to face any of the robots head-on if I could avoid it.

"Ah," Trixie said. "This is my fault."

"It is?"

"The ship's computer has been following me. It isn't supposed to be smart enough to do that."

"Maybe it got an upgrade," I said.

"I'm disconnecting."

I was only half-listening. The floorplans showed that the two doors to my right were for a latrine and a small gymnasium. I didn't want to mount my last stand in a toilet and I didn't think I could defeat three armed robots with a couple of dumbbells and a medicine ball. The door on the left was more promising. It was a mess hall – what normal people call a cafeteria. 'Gunfight at the OK Canteen' had the right sort of ring to it. And maybe there was a goods lift or a dumbwaiter I could use to make my escape. Failing that, there were probably various bits of kitchen equipment that I could put to good use.

I heard the *ping* of the elevator door opening as we ducked into the canteen. When both of the drones were safely inside, I slapped a small explosive against the lock and set it off. With the lock fused, the robots wouldn't be able to get the door open – they would have to batter it down. It wouldn't keep them out for long, but it bought me a little time to prepare for their entrance. I left one of the drones watching through the round glass window in the door and went to check out the kitchen area.

When I'd gone rooting through the *Celestia's* stores looking for equipment, I had been preparing for a robbery not a war. I'd taken flashlights and a few small explosive devices for use on locks. There had been some plastic explosive, but it hadn't aged well so I didn't touch it. And I took no weapons at all. At this moment I was left with two small palm-sized explosive devices that were marginally more powerful than a sneeze and a beltful of explosive bullets plus the six that were loaded in my gun. In comparison, the rifles the robots were carrying were small cannons that could blow a hole in the side of a tank.

Ordinarily, if I know I'm going up against robot security guards, I carry the appropriate equipment. They use a combination of vision, motion sensors, heat detection, and sound pick-ups. With the right gear, you can confuse these for long enough to make your escape. You send out a handful of 'flickers' to flap around like birds' wings and distract the robots' motion sensors. A scattering of mini transmitters to all corners of a space can broadcast sounds that make the robots think you're in places that you're not. And I would normally wear a hooded suit that masked body heat, keeping it contained until I could get out – or until I passed out from heat exhaustion. The kitchen offered me none of these things, so I was going to have to improvise. I had the two drones, but I didn't want to risk losing Mozzie or Gnat unless it was a genuine life or death moment.

The kitchen was pretty basic, the sort of thing you'd find in a fast food place on dozens of inhabited worlds. It was designed for preparing the usual fried high-carbohydrate goodness plus whatever tasteless proteins a food synthesiser could concoct. The grease in the bottom of the fryer looked like varnish, but I turned on the heat anyway. I also fired up the toaster and the rings on the stove. The robots' heat detectors would see these as bright spots and in comparison, I'd look cooler. In these situations, it's always important to look cool. There was an old fan beside the stove – maybe the cook couldn't stand the heat. I tore off the protective mesh and switched it on. The blades weren't quite a flicker, but they were motion that the robots would have to check out and discard. For the same reason, I opened a refrigerator and a cupboard door and placed cans of beans to stop them closing properly. The doors tried to swing shut and when they encountered the cans, they swung open again. Then they tried to close and started the process all over again. I also set the whisks on a food-mixer whirling.

I was checking another locker, hoping to find a can of cooking oil that I could spread across the floor in the canteen's seating area. A greasy floor might slow the robots down and even if it didn't, I could set light to the oil and make things difficult for them. But I didn't get a chance to put this slick plan into operation. Gnat was looking out through the glass panel in the door and he flashed a silent warning. Our guests had arrived.

I set more canned goods on the ground, ready to set them rolling as visual and audio distractions – and then I opened the door on the food synthesizer so I could cook up a little something else.

Gnat's video feed showed me the three robots coming together in the corridor outside. They stood motionless for a moment, engaged in silent communication with the ship's computer, and then separated. One headed towards the gymnasium. The other stomped towards the latrine – probably muttering to himself that he always got the crappy jobs. The third robot headed towards the canteen door. Finding the door mechanism jammed, I expected that the robot would apply brute force and smash his way in. But it stepped back and raised its rifle.

Gnat sensed the danger and with a high-pitched *whee!* sped backwards out of the line of fire. The door exploded inwards, shrapnel and shards of glass filling the air and smoke billowing behind them. The robot stepped in through the smoke, scanning the room. I had ducked behind the stainless steel serving counter before the robot fired the rifle. Gnat was hiding in the shadows, still transmitting video.

The explosion had drawn the attention of the other two robots and they entered and took up positions behind the first, rifles held ready to fire. They stood in their eerie motionless way and then their heads began to sweep left and right as they scanned the room. I rolled a can of prunes across the floor. The nearest robot swung its rifle and the explosion splattered preserved fruit and bits of metal against the far wall. The smell made me think of Christmas.

Moving as silently as I could, I crawled to the opposite end of the counter and lobbed a can of carrots over-arm into the air. The explosion splattered orange pulp across the suspended ceiling and took out a couple of the tiles.

Again I shuffled to a new spot, knowing the robots would try and track back to the spot where the canned goods were being launched.

There was a loud *click* and then an amplified robot voice echoed around the canteen. "ATTENTION UNIDENTIFIED INTRUDER. THEFT OF THE SHIP'S NAVIGATOR IS A CAPITAL OFFENCE. USE OF LETHAL FORCE IS AUTHORISED. SURRENDER OR FACE THE CONSEQUENCES. YOU HAVE TEN SECONDS TO COMPLY."

The ship thought I had managed to steal the Navigator? That was flattering. And also massively inconvenient, since it meant the robots wouldn't give up their pursuit and would do anything and everything to recover the missing Navigator. The military didn't go a bunch on all that 'a robot must not harm a human being' stuff. Not for the first time, I wondered who had taken the Navigator. Whoever had done it had been smart enough to hide the fact that it was gone – until I had gone blundering into the vault.

My ten seconds was almost up and the robot was waiting for my response. "Trixie," I whispered, "help me target the middle robot's rifle."

I raised my pistol above the edge of the counter without looking. It would have been more or less invisible to the robots, I hoped, due to the thick black smoke that was billowing up from the fryer. Crosshairs appeared on my retina and turned green when I had the gun pointed at the target. I squeezed off a round. I thought that a direct hit might trigger the rifle's own explosive cartridges – perhaps even generating enough force to disable one robot and knock the other two off their feet. I've always been an optimist.

The explosion was deafening and the blast was so bright it temporarily whited out the drone's video. As the image re-stabilised, I could see that my optimism had been misplaced. The two outer robots stood unmoved – they were obviously heavier than they looked. The one in the centre had been pushed backwards by the blast but was now recovering and stepping forward again. There were scorch marks on its breastplate and its gun and right hand were gone, but otherwise it looked unharmed. The three robots took one step towards me in unison – it was quite menacing. I was going to need a bigger explosion.

The two-armed robots opened fire, their explosive rounds completely demolishing the metal serving counter and much of the wall behind it. Luckily they were aiming at a spot that I was no longer occupying. I was in a corner behind a refrigerator.

I've never been a big fan of direct brain-computer connection, but this was one of those situations where I wished I had specified that option. Even with the food mixer and everything else making noise, I was afraid that the robots would pick up my whispered conversation with Trixie. I used the virtual keyboard to type, telling Trixie what I was planning. She flashed back a simple 'OK' in response. The fact that she didn't type 'Are you crazy?!' gave me a bit of a confidence boost. It *was* a crazy plan. And it meant putting one of the drones in the firing line – but I think this qualified as a life-or-death moment. My preference was for the 'life' outcome.

The little drone drifted through the smoke that was rolling across the ceiling. I could see that this was Mozzie going into battle for the good guys. I wished him well. He attached himself to the front of the food synthesiser and began broadcasting. I'd asked Trixie to create the sort of signal that a Navigator would broadcast. Mozzie was now pretending to be the stolen artificial sentience and was sending out an 'I've been stolen, rescue me' message on auto-repeat. I knew this would get the robots' attention. Hopefully, they would think I'd stashed the Navigator in the food synthesizer.

The robot with the missing hand moved towards Mozzie. The other robots followed a little behind and on either side. They continued to look left and right as they approached their target.

There are some things that you are not supposed to cook in a microwave oven – but I'm not sure that exploding eggs can be weaponised. The ingredients I'd wrapped in an old tea towel promised to be much more exciting. A couple of flashlights with good-sized energy cells, my last two mini-bombs, and three of the explosive cartridges from my gun belt. I wasn't sure of the optimum cooking time or temperature, so I'd whacked all the dials up to maximum. If it turned out all right, I was going to call it kaboom cake.

5–4–3–2–1. Beep! BOOM!

There was a rule in our house when I was growing up – whoever cooks doesn't do the washing up. I was happy not to be on the clean-up crew in the canteen. The explosion was *massive.* It blew the door off the food synthesiser and that hit the robot in the chest, knocking it backwards. At the same time, the other two robots were knocked back by the expanding heat and gas. The force of the blast also carried the whole cooker backwards and through the wall – but this wasn't immediately obvious because of the smoke. My plan had been to take out one of the robots – the hole in the wall was a bonus.

I had to move quickly. I had no idea how badly the robots might be damaged or how long it might be before they recovered. I scrabbled across the floor, slipping on the debris. The smoke thinned for a moment and I saw a pair of robot legs that weren't attached to a body and this gladdened my heart. I'd taken out at least one of them. Ironically, I'd learned the trick with the microwave from a robot rights activist. Not far from the legs I could see one of the rifles and I crawled towards it. It was heavier than I expected, but I was happy to bear this extra burden. I'm not usually a fan of heavy artillery – but in the right circumstances, I will make an exception. Trying to avoid anything that seemed to be smouldering or glowing, I crawled over the rubble heaped under the hole in the wall.

Something gripped my ankle, clamping onto it like a vice. I rolled and looked back. One of the robots had hold of me, its hand wrapped around my leg. It was dragging itself towards me with its other arm – and there was no hand on the end of that arm. As it shifted position I could see that the robot's legs were missing.

"Don't you ever scracking die?" I yelled at it. I swung the rifle round and aimed at its head. I like to think that its eyes widened in fear just before I pulled the trigger. The recoil threw me backwards. The robot released its grip on me when its head exploded like a pumpkin hit by a cannonball.

I could hear movement back in the canteen – the other robots, presumably. I didn't wait around to find out.

The room I was in was filled with smoke and dust. There was a lectern at the front and rows of seats had faced this before being swept aside by the remains of an exploding food synthesiser. Maybe this was where the pilots got their briefings. I crossed the space as quickly as the rubble-strewn floor would allow and got out of the door into a corridor I hadn't seen before. I didn't have anything to blow the lock with so I just shut the door behind me and ran.

The lights were out in the corridor – not even the red emergency glow to light my way. The drones flew ahead of me, projecting as much light as they could from their little spotlights.

Trixie projected the compass for me and kept me heading north again. Behind me I heard a blast from a rifle. I'm guessing the robot didn't even test whether or not I'd locked the door. They were in pursuit and they weren't far behind me.

Dead end. Or so it appeared at first. The way was blocked by a steel wall that, on closer inspection, turned out to be a pair of heavy doors. They must have been sealed shut when the ship was damaged. Doors like this usually operated when there was a hull breach. I looked down at the gun – it was heavy-duty, but not quite up to the job of blasting through metal like this.

"Robots!" Trixie warned. I turned and fired back down the corridor.

"Mozzie, try and get that door open!" I threw myself to the ground as a projectile flew through the air and hit the door behind me, showering me with sparks. The impact left a nasty black mark but didn't even dent the door. I fired off another shot, hoping to encourage the robots to keep their distance. Looking down at the indicator on the rifle, I saw that I had eight shots left – I would have to make them count.

"How are we doing?" I asked.

"There's a manual override," Trixie said, "in the hatch to your right."

"Gnat, try and distract them."

I crawled towards the hatch. I didn't like the fact that the robots could see me in the dark and I couldn't see them. Gnat began a bizarre aerobatics display, corkscrewing through the air and make sounds like a demented buzz saw. I swear the drone laughed like a loon when a blast from the other end of the corridor skimmed the surface of its casing. I flipped open the hatch. There was a huge lever that looked like something out of Frankenstein's lab. I grabbed the top of it with both hands and pulled down with all of my body weight. My arms shook with the strain and I didn't think it was going to budge. When it did finally move, it went suddenly and I went with it, almost planting my face into the floor. There was a pause and then a heavy clanging sound as the bolts securing the doors disengaged. The doors slid open with almost painful slowness. As soon as the gap appeared, the robots down the corridor opened fire, knowing I would try and fit through the gap.

With sparks and bits of molten metal raining down around me and smoke filling my lungs, I lunged and rolled towards the widening gap. Knowing I was exposed, Gnat tried to draw the robots' fire. I heard an electronic shriek from the little drone as he was hit. He shot out through the gap, trailing smoke like a damaged fighter-plane, hit the floor, rolled and then slid to a stop. I scooped him up as I went through the gap.

On the other side of the doors, I dodged right and got to my feet. And then stood rooted to the spot.

I was standing on the edge of a cliff with the jungle spread out beneath me. Behind, the doors opened wider and wider and I could hear the rapid footsteps of the approaching robots.

Chapter Fourteen

The floor that should have stretched out in front of me was gone, torn away when the *Celestia* crashed. I was looking down at the tops of trees that had grown during the last forty years, filling the scar that the ship and gouged in the earth. Under less fraught circumstances I would have stood and admired the view.

The treeline began less than six yards from where I was standing and perhaps three yards lower. I briefly considered trying to jump across to the nearest tree. But if I made the jump successfully, there was a risk of crushed ribs and impalement on a tree branch. And if I was unsuccessful, it was a long way down to the ground below. The huge doors were still grinding open behind me. In a few seconds there would be nothing between me and the three security robots. I pulled on my gloves and headed for the edge.

The sky overhead was a sort of purplish slate colour. It was mid-afternoon and it looked like clouds had been building for a while. There was a storm coming. I didn't want to be climbing down the side of the ship when the rain hit. If I could make it halfway down, I might have the option of sheltering on the subfloor that held the ship's warehouse – or do they call it the quartermaster's stores? I wasn't familiar with the lingo. I've made use of military uniforms on occasion, but I've never officially been a soldier. I don't think I have the personality for it.

The tear in the ship's hull was jagged and warped, but offered plenty of hand- and foot-holds. It was perhaps a hundred feet down to ground level, but heights didn't bother me. I'd climb up and down buildings much higher than this. What did bother me was being shot at by robots with big guns. The unevenness of the metal would make it more difficult for them to target me, but they were still going to hit me if they could see me. As far as possible, I would climb between the two skins of the hull so I couldn't be seen from the ledge above. But in places, the hull had been crushed and mangled so there was no gap between the layers of plating.

Climbing would have been easier if I'd slung the rifle across my back, but I wanted to keep hold of it. One or more of the robots would start down after me very soon, and I would have to shoot it before it shot me. I kept glancing upwards, waiting for it to appear.

"Trixie, send Mozzie out and see if you can show me the robots positions."

"Aye, aye."

The video feed showed two of the robots standing on the edge of the ledge scanning left and right. The third moved to the side of the platform where I'd climbed down. I needed to be ready. I saw a space a few feet below me where I could wedge myself in and take aim at the robot as it came down after me.

There was a sound above and I looked up. The muzzle of a rifle pointed towards me. Gripping tightly with one hand, I swung out and round to get the metal of the ship between me and the robot. I almost made it. The projectile sizzled past my right ear and I felt the heat on my cheek and neck. I felt a slight tug at my jacket shoulder and I could smell burning. The bullet must have grazed the fabric. I heard the explosion in the trees behind and below me when the projectile struck. At the same time, the projections in my retina blanked and there was just static in my ear.

"Trixie?"

No response. The passage of the bullet must have knocked out her systems. I'd have to wait while she rebooted in self-repair mode. Her nanos would then scurry around like sub-microscopic ants, repairing whatever damage had been done. Without Trixie to control him, Mozzie floated back towards me, his system in limp-home mode. I could control the drone manually, but right now I had other things to worry about – like being shot by a robot and falling seventy-odd feet to the ground below. I flipped Mozzie's 'off' button and put him in my jacket pocket. Trixie could wake him when she was back online.

I peered around the edge of the bulkhead. The robot was climbing down and it was moving fast. It looked like video that had been speeded up. The thing had no fear of falling – it would almost certainly survive the drop. Wedging myself in as tightly as I could, I aimed the rifle upwards. The recoil almost dislodged me. I can't be sure, but I think I shot it in the ass. There was a bright orange flash and its legs separated from its body and flew outwards. And I think the thing that went upwards was its head. It must be a little-known weakness. If you're ever up against a security robot, shoot it in the asshole. Who knew?

I dodged the smouldering bits of robot anatomy as they fell past. Above, a second robot climbed over the edge and started down. Its rifle was slung across its back, so I assumed it had decided to climb down to me, rather than try to target me from above. Perhaps it had learned from its comrade's mistake. I wondered if it had learned enough to cover its ass? I didn't wait around to find out, I wanted to try and get down to the warehouse level before the robot reached me.

From the corner of my eye, I saw something dropping and flinched. At first, I thought the robot above me had fallen and I felt a moment of joy. But glancing up, I could see that he was still double-timing it down. The third robot must have leaped down from the platform. It would be waiting for me on the ground below, aiming upwards as I descended. This made my decision for me – if there was a ledge at the warehouse level, I'd stop there. With any luck, I'd be able to target the robot that was climbing down. And if Trixie was back online by then, we could maybe open the airlock and get back inside the ship. It was the closest thing I'd had to a plan in some time.

The warehouse floor had twin steel doors similar to the ones I'd come through on the floor above. They had been more heavily scarred by the crash, but they didn't appear to be buckled. With a little encouragement, they would probably open – at least wide enough for me to slip through. The platform in front of the doors was much narrower, just wide enough for me to be able to squat in a corner with the rifle ready to fire at the robot as soon as it appeared. I didn't have long to get in position, the robot was only a few seconds behind me.

"Trixie, you there?" I was still hearing static in my ear. I flicked my eyes to the right and my heart sank as I saw why

Trixie wasn't responding. There was not enough of my box of tricks left for the nanos to rebuild. There was a splat of melted silver on my shoulder that looked like stainless steel parrot squit. I suddenly felt very, very alone. But there was no time to feel sorry for myself. I had a robot to deal with. I aimed the snout of the rifle at the spot above me where I thought the robot would appear. It must have slowed down to assess the situation.

I heard the sound of a soft impact and thought a bird had landed in the tree opposite where I was huddled. There was a dark shadow, a crash, and the top of the tree waved wildly under the impact. It was the robot. Of course, it didn't share my fear of broken bones or impalement. It was gripping the top of the tree with one arm and raising the rifle with the other. I swung my gun around and squeezed the trigger twice. A hole appeared in the robot's chest that I could see daylight through. Apparently unaware of its new body piercing, the robot continued to try and compensate for the wild swaying of the tree and get me in its sights. I aimed for its head – but then its limbs stiffened, jerking backwards, and the hollowed-out robot swallow-dived into the ground. Two down, one to go.

I lay on my stomach and slid towards the edge. Looking down, I could see the fallen robot. Its comrade stepped out from the cover of the trees and examined the robot carcass, then it looked upwards. I ducked back as a blast struck the metal above me and showered me in sparks and bits of hot shrapnel. Down below, I could hear the robot begin to climb, probably using the route I had planned to use for my descent. I didn't want to risk poking my head over the edge again – there was every chance that the robot was climbing with one hand and pointing the rifle at my last position.

The metal door was cool against my back. I looked over at the locking mechanism but knew I didn't have the time or the equipment to get it open before the security robot crawled over the edge. If I'd had Trixie's assistance, I might have risked it, but on my own... A more desperate plan was called for. But I wasn't sure if I was desperate enough to do what I was thinking.

They tell you that Fortune favours the brave. What they don't say is that Death also welcomes them with open arms. The difference between heroic success and death by misadventure is only one small miscalculation. I looked sideways at the tree opposite. On the plus side, it had supported the robot's weight, so it would certainly support mine. And the gap from the edge of the ship to the tree was only twenty feet or so. On the negative side, the ledge I was on was so narrow that I wouldn't be able to take a running jump. Unless... It was at times like this that I wished I had one of those little crossbow things that thieves in movies used to fire a rope across to the other side. The crossbow arrow – or is a bolt? – always embeds itself deeply enough to support the thief's weight as he uses the rope to make his escape. I've talked to technicians on a dozen worlds and none of them could make one for me.

The sound of the robot's approach spurred me on. I didn't want to be a sitting duck – I wanted to be a flying one. Or something. I ran along the ledge from one side to the other, swerving at the last moment and planting the sole of my boot against the edge of the deck to push myself out into the void. Normally I would have screamed something loud and obscene, but I didn't want to draw the attention of the robot.

For a horrible moment, I thought I was going to fall short. My legs cycled through the air, like a cartoon character trying to run closer to the tree. And then my face was buried in its foliage and I wrapped my arms around it like a favourite nephew greeting a wealthy aunt. The top of the tree bent under the impact and that may have saved my life. A projectile from the robot's rifle whizzed by and exploded some distance away, starting a small fire. The tree then sprang back, threatening to catapult me back to where I had just leapt from. I clung on tightly as another bullet burned through the air and arced towards the ground. Holding tight with one arm, I brought the rifle round and aimed at the robot. I had three shots left. I didn't want to waste any of them.

The blast struck the robot in a spot that would have been between its shoulder blades if it had had any. The robot fell backwards, firing its rifle into the sky. It hit the ground and lay twitching like an overturned turtle. Was it dead? I wasn't going to bet my life on it.

Leaping from ship to tree had gone remarkably well. Attempting another leap – from treetop to treetop – would be tempting fate. Only a fool would try it. But I wasn't thinking straight. Fuelled by adrenaline, I was feeling invincible. Of course, this wasn't going to end well. But the risk of injury from travelling tree to tree seemed less than the risk of being shot by a damaged robot if I headed down to the ground. So I jumped.

Chapter Fifteen

The target tree wasn't nearly as soft and springy as the first one. It was like throwing myself from a feather duvet towards a concrete post. Continuing my cartoon exploits, I smacked face-first into the trunk and began to slide down. I tried to grab a branch to stop the fall and felt a tearing pain in my hand – it felt like I had lost at least two fingers. My feet hit another branch hard enough to rattle my teeth and the branch bent as if preparing to springboard me on toward even greater agonies. I wasn't going to let that happen. I bent my knees and grabbed the branch with my undamaged hand, clinging on as the branch snapped back up. Leaves rained down from the tree, but I managed to keep my perch.

Despite the burning pain in my hand and the fact that vision in my left eye was blurred and the flesh around it swelling, I wanted to keep moving, to get as far away from the fallen security robot as I could. I made myself look down at my hand. The fingers were still there but they didn't look like they were where they should be. They were either dislocated or broken. I didn't bother trying to get the glove off.

I was about ten feet below the tops of the trees now. At this height, the branches of neighbouring trees were quite close together. With care, I was able to step from one stout branch to another, increasing my distance from the ship. I didn't encounter birds or any of the monkey-like creatures – I assumed the noise of my falling had frightened them away. Apart from the stirring of leaves as I passed from tree to tree, the forest was eerily quiet. This was a good thing, as it meant I stood a better chance of hearing the robot approach – assuming that it hadn't been paralysed by the fall.

After half-an-hour I decided I could pause and catch my breath. I climbed down to the ground and sat between the roots of a huge ancient tree. My hand was throbbing and sending flashes of red-hot pain up my arm. Contorting my body so I could get my backpack off without touching the injured fingers took a little time. I fished out the little medical kit. There were antibiotics, which I didn't think I needed, and a hypospray of anaesthetic which I was sure that I did. I pressed it against the inside of my wrist and injected it. My hand and the lower part of my arm grew numb and cold. It was a nice feeling.

I carefully peeled off the glove and exposed my poor twisted fingers. The pinkie finger and the one next to it – the one I had twice worn a wedding ring on – had been pulled out of their sockets. Thankfully, the skin was unbroken. I needed to get the fingers back into place before the pain-killer wore off. I knew it was still going to hurt and I knew I had to avoid screaming because that would just alert the robot to my position. One at a time or both together? I gripped the ends of both fingers tightly and pulled as hard as I dared.

I passed out for the best part of ten minutes. Whether or not I screamed, I don't know. There was a good chance I did. My injured fingers looked like they were back where they were supposed to be. But they looked a lot fatter than they used to. I used a piece of clean white bandage to bind them together with my middle finger and then wrapped the rest of the bandage around my hand. That was as much protection as I could give them. The anaesthetic was wearing off, but the pain that was resurfacing was just a dull throbbing. I used an antiseptic wipe on my face – there wasn't much blood on it when I looked down at it. My left eye was almost completely swollen shut now. During all of this I had been listening carefully, but the jungle around me was silent except for the gentle swooshing of the trees. And the distant rumble of thunder.

I looked into my backpack, doing a quick inventory. I had just under a litre of drinking water left and a protein bar that claimed to be chili con carne flavoured. And I was all out of clean underwear and socks. As near as I could judge, the Trekker was parked about ten miles north-east of my current position. It was now late afternoon and there was no way I could reach the vehicle before nightfall. That and the threat of a rainstorm set me to thinking that I would need to find somewhere to shelter. Preferable somewhere I could defend if the security robot made an appearance. I had two shots left in the rifle. My pistol was fully-loaded, but unless I was at point-blank range, it wouldn't do me much good. And I didn't want to get that close to the robot.

A nice dry cave would have been an ideal spot to hole-up for the night, but I had no idea whether the jungle offered anything like that. Without Trixie, I had no way of finding out. Lacking any other data, I had to consider the fact that the best source of shelter within easy reach was the wreck of the *Celestia*. But did I really want to go back there? And if I did, how was I going to get in? I couldn't use the hatch I'd originally opened because some fool had jammed it shut from the inside. And was that last security robot still at the crash site, waiting for me? I soon had the answer to this last question.

I was just about to get to my feet and choose a direction when I saw something that kept me frozen in place. Through the leaves of nearby undergrowth I could see the security robot. It stood motionless, rifle held ready, scanning the area. If I moved from my hiding place among the tree roots, my body heat would provide the robot's vision with a bright orange-red target to fire at. I slowly raised my rifle, resting it on the tree root and taking careful aim. I couldn't afford to waste my last two shots. The chest provided the best target and I breathed out slowly and then squeezed the trigger.

A hit! But only in the shoulder. The robot staggered backwards, firing its own gun up into the trees. I didn't wait to see what happened then – I scramble to my feet and ran.

I could hear the robot crashing through the undergrowth in pursuit. But worse than that was a sound somewhere off to my right. It was the roar of a dragon. The gunfire had attracted its attention. I veered left, away from the sound.

Another rifle blast and a tree just in front of me exploded, a hole blasted through the trunk. The tree shook, shedding leaves, and then started to fall. I tried to curve around it, but I couldn't get away far enough and the branches of the falling tree knocked me to the ground. I tried to get out from under it, but a branch was pinning my leg to the ground. Hearing the robot approach, I lay as still as I could and looked out through the leaves.

The robot appeared from the shadows and stopped in the little clearing, scanning the ground and the trees around it.

The still smouldering fallen tree might be shielding me from the robot's infrared sensors, but as it got closer it was sure to see me. The rifle had been knocked from my hand when the tree fell. I drew my pistol, knowing it would be useless unless the robot was right on top of me.

The robot took a step towards me. Then another. Its head swept from left to right as it scanned. Another step. The head stopped and its eyes were pointing directly at me. It had picked up my heat signature. It raised the rifle. Foliage to the right of the robot seemed to explode suddenly as something big leapt into the clearing. The robot half-turned, swinging the rifle round as it did so.

The dragon darted forwards, jaws open wide. Tilting its head it closed its teeth around the robot's midsection and lifted it from the ground. It shook the robot so that its shark-like teeth could saw through it. The robot tried to get the rifle in a position where a shot would do some good. A bullet blasted a chunk of flesh out of the dragon's side, but this only served to anger it. The robot was shaken like a doll and the dragon's teeth finally did their thing, cutting the robot in half. The two parts fell to the ground. The robot's upper body adjusted its position, turned the rifle on the dragon. A shot grazed its neck and as the dragon leaned forward to roar at its attacker, I saw the damaged eye. This was the same dragon I had encountered before.

While robot and dragon fought, I had to take my chance and try to get away. I used my good hand to scrape dirt away from under my trapped leg and managed to free it. Then I grabbed up the rifle and ran – or rather hobbled – as fast as my legs would carry me.

I ran blindly through the undergrowth. Behind me, I could hear the fight continuing. A shot and then a roar from the dragon. A hit but not a fatal one. And then there was another sound, off to my left – something big crashing through the jungle. A second dragon? It too must have been drawn by the sound of gunfire. I headed away from the sound. Multiple rifle blasts – and then a triumphant bellow from the dragon. I guessed that he had won. At least I didn't have to worry about the robot anymore.

In the quiet that followed, I kept running, not worrying how much sound I was making. And as I went, I wondered whether it had really been the sound of gunfire that had attracted my one-eyed dragon friend. The data Trixie had pulled up about the sapphire dragons had said that their tongues could pick up the scent of its prey from six miles away. It knew my scent. And it had an old score to settle. The robot had probably just been in the wrong place at the wrong time. I hoped the wounds inflicted by the robot would slow the dragon down. I had one shot left in the rifle and I didn't think it was going to be enough to stop a charging dragon. And my pistol would be about as much use as a rubber band gun.

I thought about the movement I had heard before. Were there now *two* dragons out there? And if so, would they fight each other or would they team up to track me? I wished Trixie was there to whisper in my ear and advise me on the behaviour patterns of sapphire dragons.

Without really being aware of it, I had been running in a wide arc back towards the wreck of the *Celestia*. Perhaps I was drawing on some primitive survival instinct. I wasn't navigating by the position of the sun – because I couldn't see it. I wasn't sure how long it would be until nightfall, but it did seem to be growing darker. But that could have been the storm clouds piling up overhead rather than the fact that the sun was going down. I wanted to get back to the wreck before it got too dark to see. Could dragons see in the dark? Another question that Trixie could have answered.

Even when I reached the *Celestia* I was going to have to deal with the problem of getting inside. Climbing with two damaged fingers and a bruised knee was going to make for slow, painful progress. But I'd worry about that when I got there. I believed that my very strong desire not to be eaten would allow me access to previously untapped reserves of energy and luck.

I was aware of sounds of pursuit without really listening for them – another instance of that survival instinct, I presumed. There were two pursuers, I was sure, one behind and to the left and the other on the right that was much closer. If I had had the energy, I would have cursed loudly, blaming Old Jack

Sterling for getting me into this mess. But I couldn't spare the effort – and if anyone was to blame for all this, it was me. I decided that if I got out of this alive, I would forgive myself and buy myself a drink. And if I didn't, well, I wouldn't be around to blame anyone.

The trees thinned out ahead of me and I caught sight of the stained metal hull of the ship. I was afraid it might be a mirage caused by lack of oxygen – like an oasis glimpsed in the desert. But as I approached, it didn't shimmer and vanish. A safe haven was within sight. I didn't need to get inside, I just had to climb high enough that the dragon couldn't reach me. His claws might allow him to climb trees but I doubted they'd get much purchase on smooth metal. My limping jog became a near sprint. I almost made it.

The dragon broke through the undergrowth and stood between me and the ship. I skidded to a stop on the wet leaves. As if this moment wasn't dramatic enough, thunder rumbled overhead and lightning lit up the scene. The dragon leaned towards me and roared. It turned its head slightly, showing me the socket where I had ruined its eye, and then it roared at me again. I think it was saying 'It's payback time!' It raked its claws through the soil, gouging out deep cuts. 'I'm going to do this to your flesh!' The crowd in the arena would be roaring at this point – waiting for the thumb to jab downwards, signalling that the dragon should attack. More thunder and heavy raindrops began to spatter on the leaves like drumbeats. 'Kill him! Kill him! Kill him!'

My options were limited. I could raise the rifle and try to take out its other eye – and hope that it would flee rather than attack blindly, relying on its sense of smell. Or I could make a dash off to one side and try and climb one of the taller trees. Up there I might be able to make my way to the ship and jump back onto it. But even if the dragon didn't manage to claw its way up and drag me down, my chances of reaching the ship safely in my present damaged state were slim to none. Any sudden move would almost certainly trigger an attack, but standing still wasn't going to achieve anything. I glanced left and right, trying to spot a tree that might offer a chance for escape. It had to be sturdy enough that the dragon couldn't throw its weight against it and topple it. And high enough that I stood a chance of getting up beyond its reach. There was a gnarled old tree about ten feet to my right. It was covered in moss and vines that stood out like veins. There should be enough purchase there for me to be able to climb rapidly. I couldn't see the top of it, which I took to be a good sign.

Three-two-one-GO!

I ran. The dragon roared. Thunder exploded overhead. And I screamed like a wild thing. I heard crashing behind me but didn't look back. I reached the tree and scrambled up, hoping it wasn't so wet that I would slide straight down into the waiting jaws of the beast. Keep climbing. Don't look down.

The tree shook as the dragon slammed into it. I clung on as if my life depended on it. Oh, wait, it actually did. I climbed higher as I heard a scratching and scraping sound below – the dragon using its claws to try and climb up after me. I risked a glance down. And saw the vines breaking, unable to support the dragon's weight. It tried again, digging its massive toe claws into the bark of the tree. It managed to draw itself up a few yards, but again its weight made the claws rip through the bark and slide downwards.

I reached a higher branch and sat there for a moment to draw breath. The rain was heavier now and it gradually worked its way through the canopy of the trees and dripped down in large drops. The wet would make it harder for me to climb – but hopefully the same was true of the dragon.

The dragon was on the ground, glaring up at me and roaring occasionally. It leaned back on its haunches and launched itself upwards. Its leap brought snapping jaws close to me and I pulled up my feet – but the jump had been eight feet short. Shaking its head, the beast coiled itself again, ready to spring. Its teeth were a little closer, but still some way short.

If I fired the rifle into its gaping mouth, would that be enough to kill it? At the very least, it would do it some serious harm – and it might be enough to discourage it and send it on its way. As the dragon prepared to make another jump, I raised the rifle and took aim. Leaning forward, it seemed as if its teeth would reach me this time. My finger tightened on the trigger.

The ground underneath the dragon exploded, showering me with compost. The force of the blast almost knocked me off my perch. I hadn't fired the shot. I spat out bits of rotted leaf and peered down, trying to see the dragon. It lay on its side twitching, stunned by the blast. It shook itself and got to its feet. For the moment I was forgotten and it turned its attention on the source of the explosion. It roared at the shadowy shape and then turned and fled.

I blinked, squinting with my one good eye to see through the rain, trying to catch sight of my saviour. And I saw that the second 'beast' that had pursued me wasn't another dragon.

Chapter Sixteen

It was a big military robot – perhaps eight feet tall and almost as wide at the shoulders. Its battered and scratched paintwork had once been bright red, so maybe it had originally been a firefighter on the *Celestia's* launch deck before someone remade it into a walking tank. The armour protecting its shoulders looked like it had been made from salvaged steel plate and its mid-section featured the same badly-welded patchwork of scrap. Its head sat low between its shoulders and looked like it didn't belong there – it was bright yellow and would have been better suited to one of those waiters that say things like 'Glad to be of service.' Large feet and hand made it look like a giant metal ape. I say 'hand,' singular, because in place of a left arm it had some sort of cannon that was still smoking.

I was just about to wave and shout 'Thanks' – but the robot turned and pointed the cannon towards me. This wasn't a rescue, it had just targeted the dragon first. I was next.

I scrambled to my feet and launched myself from the branch towards the tree behind. I felt the heat as the tree I had been in blossomed into flame and the force of the blast gave me an extra push. My chest slammed into a thick branch and I grabbed hold of it, gasping for breath. I pulled myself up, wanting to keep moving before the robot targeted me again.

The rain was coming down heavier now, making the branches slippery and reducing visibility. Drifting smoke from the burning tree only made things worse. But I had to keep going. Some of the trees were so close together I could run along the branch of one and step onto a branch of its neighbour. In other places, I had to launch myself across the gap and hope the branch I was aiming for would support my weight when I hit it.

There was no time to think of anything except getting to the next tree. I had no idea how much time had passed since the red robot had opened fire on the dragon.

My foot slipped on a wet branch and I had to wrap my arms around the trunk of the tree to save myself. As I waited for the jackhammer in my chest to slow down again, I listened to see if I was being tracked by the robot. But all I could hear was the drumming of raindrops on leaves. I hoped the robot was satisfied that it had scared me away from its territory and had returned to the *Celestia*. There was little chance of this if it thought I had run off with the Navigator under my arm.

I was amazed that something that big could move so quietly. If I hadn't been staring down through the leaves, I would not have been aware that it was there. I clung to the tree, holding my breath as the big metal monster approached. It stood directly under the tree I was in, head moving from side to side as it scanned the jungle all around. It was close enough that I could see the water beading on its bodywork and trickling down. I could have dropped down right on top of it, but I couldn't think of a good reason to do that. I had no explosives to thrust inside its casing, so a direct attack would be like an ant picking a fight with an elephant. I'd just get squished.

The robot moved quietly away, still scanning ahead as it went. I relaxed my grip on the tree trunk and shifted my weight. There was a loud *Crack!* as the branch under me broke. Before I was even aware of what was happening, I was falling towards the ground. I remembered to bend my knees as I hit and rolled with the fall. I could hear the robot swiping aside the bushes as it headed back, alerted by the sound of the snapping branch. I got to my feet and ran.

I'm not sure what's worse, being pursued by a bad-tempered one-eyed dragon, or being chased by an emotionless robot tank. I didn't have time to weigh the pros and cons of each. At that moment, Death was a red bulldozer crashing through the jungle after me. If I stumbled over a hidden tree root or slipped on wet leaves, I would probably be splattered across the foliage. I kept my head down and my legs pumping. My world consisted of the few yards of undergrowth I could see in front of me.

The ground slipped away under me. A layer of wet leaves slid over the dirt, carrying me with it. I pinwheeled my arms, trying to remain upright, but smashed down onto my back. And kept sliding – forwards and downwards. The rifle flew from my hand when I hit the ground and I had no chance of retrieving it. There had been no warning that the ground sloped so steeply. I was skidding down a path of some kind that was now channelling rainwater like a mini river. I dug in my heels, trying to slow my descent, but it had little effect. Unable to do anything else, I crossed my arms across my chest and tucked my chin down. I was going to have to ride with it and hope I didn't crash into anything substantial on the way down.

Trees and bushes and rocks flashed by on either side of me. Pebbles and sticks bruised my back and my butt, and mud and debris were piling up in the back of my jacket and under my shirt. My backpack was torn away and thrown aside and I slid onwards, losing sight of it.

And then there was no more ground. I had been pitched over the edge of a precipice and was falling through the air. I looked down, hoping to see a wide expanse of deep water that would cushion my fall, but all I could see was the tops of trees. There was nothing I could do. A curious calm came over me and I relaxed.

I crashed through the canopy of leaves and for a moment it did feel like I had fallen into a lake. But then the small snapping branches gave way to larger ones and they buffeted me around like the flippers in a pinball game. I was bounced from one stout branch to another as I fell, first my chest and stomach then my back being pummelled. I tried to grab at branches with my good hand, hoping to at least slow myself down before I slammed with deadly force into a thick branch or the jungle floor. I caught a branch but my fingers slipped over the wet bark. My right leg scraped painfully against a broken branch and I felt something tear. And then I collided with a branch that tipped me, turning me so that I was falling head-first. I raised my left arm to protect my face and tried to grab something – anything – with my right arm.

My stomach struck a branch hard, driving the air out of my lungs. I slid off the branch and fell the last ten or fifteen feet, crashing through a dense patch of ferns and landing with a thud on the soft wet earth. I lay on my back trying to drag air into my chest. I could feel consciousness slipping away and had to fight to stop the red cloud overwhelming me.

Every part of me felt battered and bruised. I had cracked some ribs I was sure, but aside from that, my bones seemed to be intact. Beyond the general level of pain, there was something seriously wrong with my right thigh. I didn't want to look at it but knew I had to. I struggled to a sitting position. There was a long tear in my jeans where they had been ripped by a broken branch and they were soaked with blood. The gash in my thigh was maybe five inches long and was oozing blood. I'm generally okay with the sight of blood – except when there's a lot of it and it's my own. I waited for the sick feeling in my stomach to subside.

My backpack was gone – and the medi-kit with it. I had no bandages and no antibiotics. I needed to bind the wound and stop it bleeding so I was going to have to improvise. I shrugged off my jacket. My shirt was wet and filthy, but it was all I had. I pulled it off and turned it inside-out, pressing the cleanest surface to the wound, wrapping the shirt around my leg and tying it tightly in place.

I had no idea how far I had fallen – either horizontally or vertically. My joyride had carried me away from the robot, which was a good thing. But I didn't know where I was in relation to the *Celestia* or my Trekker. I needed medical supplies and the ship or my vehicle were the only places I was going to find them.

Using my arms and sliding on my bruised butt, I dragged myself further into the undergrowth. Using my knife I cut a strong sapling and tripped the twigs and leaves from it. I used the stick to help me get to my feet, keeping my weight on my left leg. I hobbled around in a circle, looking for – There! A tree with the round leathery yellow gourds. I cut one down and jammed it on top of my stick. Tucking the gourd into my armpit, I could lean on the stick like a crutch. I just hoped the gourd wasn't the local equivalent of poison ivy.

Without my shirt I was feeling chilly. This was possibly my body going into shock. But I still thought it was a good sign. When I started feeling hot – burning up inside – it would mean that my wound was infected. I pulled on the leather jacket. It had survived the battering remarkably well. Zipping it up, I could feel the bulges of the drones in the inside pockets. Gnat was out for the count, but Mozzie was still functional. I powered him up and sent him skywards to get an idea of my location.

I thought about trying to use the drone as a communicator. I could call for help. Hell, maybe I'd call the bounty hunters and tell them where to find me. Being back in Margotsville jail would be a massive improvement on my current situation. But, of course, there was no signal down here in the jungle. If I waited until there was a satellite overhead, I might be able to make contact. But I had no way of tracking satellites. Given enough time – and a college degree in electronics and astrophysics – I might have been able to come up with a solution. But my life-blood was leaking away and I needed to act quickly.

The thing about jungle is that it all looks the same. The images Mozzie came back with told me nothing useful. Operating the drone manually, without Trixie's input, meant I could achieve very little. I pinged the location of my Trekker – it was fifteen miles away, due east of my position. Running from the robot and the subsequent fall had taken me further from it. There was no tracking device in the *Celestia* that I could use to pinpoint its location, but I could scan for non-natural energy sources. The ship was a little over five miles away – as the crow flies. The Trekker was a safer option, but I doubted I could reach it in my present state. The battleship was closer. But both of them were above me. I was going to have to get back up to the top of the cliff that I had fallen from. And I couldn't fly up like a crow.

I drank some water that had collected in the centre of a large leaf. I would have been glad of a protein bar at that moment – the thought of that rubbery old slipper texture and indeterminate flavour made my mouth water. I would probably find some back at the ship, I told myself. All I had to do was get there. Before I bled to death.

I sent Mozzie back up again, scanning the layout of the land to find a less vertical slope that I could trek up. The one he found would add a couple of miles or so to my journey, but it was a much better prospect than trying to climb a vertical cliff face with only one good hand and one good leg. A journey of eight miles begins with one unsteady step. A little voice in my head was telling me to find a sheltered spot and go to sleep – start my journey in the morning. If I listened to that little voice, I wouldn't wake up in the morning.

Chapter Seventeen

The rainclouds drifted away westwards and the sky faded from dark blue through a rich purple to black. Saphira has two moons, Smaug and Fafnir. The first of them came out; I didn't know which it was, but the bright yellow disc lit up the jungle and made it look unreal – like a theatre set. The second moon would rise about an hour after the first. The two would give enough overhead light to travel by and I had the drone shining its little spotlight on the ground so I could avoid any immediate obstacles.

On top of the fear of bleeding to death, I had some concerns about the things that came out after dark. I could hear small things scurrying through the undergrowth – but I wasn't worried about them. I was worried about the big things that ate the small scurrying things.

Something large like a white sheet flapped towards me, as big as a man. A gauzy ghost-moth, attracted by the drone's light. It was an eerie yet beautiful creature. Later in the evening I stood and watched a host of them dipping and gliding through the trees, dancing to music I couldn't hear.

I had the drone's audio sensors tuned to pick up sounds I couldn't hear. If the *Celestia's* guardian robot came stalking through the trees, I wanted to know earlier rather than later. And there were other denizens of the jungle that I wasn't keen on encountering. As well as dragons, I had heard tales of giant vampire bats. Not as big as the ghost-moths, but still large enough to bring down a man. These might be a local myth – but if Mozzie picked up their ultrasonic cries, I wanted to be ready with my sharpened stakes. Or my pistol.

I plodded through the night, one step after another, resting often. When I stopped, I would lean against a tree, knowing that if I sat down I wasn't going to get up again. More than once I managed to fall asleep on my feet. Progress up the slope was slow. When I reached the halfway point, both moons were almost directly overhead. It would be daybreak when I reached the wreck. *If* I reached the wreck. *When* I reached the wreck.

In an effort to find a silver lining, I told myself that an advantage of my chosen route was that it would bring me back to the *Celestia* from a different direction. And I would probably be able to find a new way in. Probably.

I retied the shirt around my leg, trying to ignore the fact that it was soaked with my blood. How much had I lost? How much can you lose before your situation becomes critical? Perhaps it was better that I didn't know the answer to these questions.

Mozzie buzzed an urgent alert. I had dozed off again, standing against a scrawny old tree that stood close to the top of the slope. His alarm wasn't to wake me. He had picked up the calls of the bats. Lots of them. I hid behind the tree as a dark swarm of them swept overhead, wings beating like the opening and closing of hundreds of umbrellas. Their dark shapes blotted out the moons for a time and I just stood and stared up at the spectacle. Then they were gone. They hadn't spared me a thought. Perhaps I didn't have enough blood left to be worth bothering with.

When I reached the top of the slope, I did allow myself to sit down. This was okay, I thought, as long as I didn't lie down. I was feeling light-headed and I was pretty sure it wasn't anything to do with the altitude. Blood loss and dehydration mess with your head. And the rest of you.

Falling off the cliff had taken me less than a minute. Walking back up had taken me most of the night. As the crow flies, I had moved only about a mile closer to the wreck – it was still more than four miles away. At a brisk walk, I could have covered that distance in an hour-and-a-half or two hours, even without a machete. At my current pace, I was likely to see the moons rise again before I got there.

I staggered onwards for what seemed like days but wasn't. The moons seemed to be zipping across the sky at double their normal rate. Or perhaps I was just moving more slowly, caught in some sort of time bubble.

I don't remember lying down. Or closing my eyes. But when I opened them the sun was shining brightly overhead. It was another hot and humid day – but I was shivering. Probably not a good sign. The shirt tied around my leg was stiff with dried blood. I decided to leave it as it was. My leg felt stiff and swollen. The rest of me just ached. My ribs hurt when I drew breath. I had to get to my feet and start moving again. I wouldn't survive another night in the open. But all I really wanted to do was close my eyes and go back to sleep.

A sound off to my left drew my attention. It was one of the ugly green birds with the googly eyes. It sat watching me, turning its head on one side to almost ninety-degrees. Its wrinkled face and curious blinking were so comical that I had to smile. But my smile must have looked more like a mad grin or a grimace because it made the bird stretch its wings and scarper. The piece of dead wood it had been perched on rocked then settled. Not deadwood. Rusty metal. A piece of the *Celestia's* wreckage.

Seeing this was enough to spur me into action. Very slow, painful action, but action all the same. Summoning all of my strength I manage to get my good leg under me and rise slowly. I tucked the gourd of my crutch under my arm and stood, swaying only slightly. My lips were dry and my throat was parched. Mozzie was hovering at my side and I set him to scanning for the *Celestia's* non-natural energy signature. When he showed me how close it was, I almost cried. If I could have spared the moisture, I probably would have done. We set off at a brisk limp, knowing we had less than a mile to cover.

I was hiding behind a tree, shielded by the undergrowth, looking out at the midsection of the *Celestia*. I was seeing her from a new angle, but she looked much the same as I'd left her – partially buried and with trees growing all around and leaning in over her. From this position, I could see what was left of one of her circular landing decks. It was badly buckled, but I could still imagine the warbirds coming in to land.

I sent Mozzie up to survey the landing deck. I felt sure there would be some way into the ship from the deck. The images he brought back showed how the intense heat from entering the atmosphere followed by the impact of the crash had badly warped the ship's structure. Right-angles were now skewed and straight lines had been softened and bent. But I could also see a couple of small hatches that looked like they hadn't been too badly affected. My next task was to get up onto the deck. How hard could that be?

Trees on either side of the ship had grown taller than her tallest point and their leaves had formed a shield over her so that she couldn't be seen from the air. If I could climb one of those trees, I could lower myself onto the deck. Ordinarily this would have been child's play.

I selected a tree that seemed to offer the easiest climb. Lots of branches close together. I would have to abandon my crutch and I let it go with some reluctance – it had served me well. I was going to have to use both hands to climb. This was going to hurt. A lot. A handful of painkillers and pint of moonshine would have been very welcome at that moment. I reached up with my good hand and grasped the first branch.

The pain served as a distraction, stopping me worrying about other things. Like the fact that I might climb the tree and leap onto the *Celestia's* deck only to find the big red robot waiting for me with its cannon primed and ready to fire. I dismissed that thought. I could only deal with one life or death crisis at a time.

The climb was slow and painful but finally I was just above the level of the deck. There was no sign of Sergeant Spudgun. My body was drenched with sweat and my head was spinning. The exertion had re-opened the gash in my leg and fresh blood was soaking through the makeshift bandage. But I was within spitting distance of salvation – if I had been able to muster enough saliva to spit.

I waited for the world to stop spinning. Blinking to clear my vision, I crawled slowly along the branch towards the deck. When I reached the halfway point the branch began to sag. This was a worry until I had gone a little further and the deck was under me. I rolled, hanging under the branch. I aimed my good leg towards the deck, keeping the damaged one up and out of the way. I dangled there for a moment like a sort of post-apocalyptic gymnast – and then I let go. My foot hit the deck and I rolled to absorb the impact.

I lay on the warm deck, listening to see if my arrival had drawn the attention of Ronnie Rocketlauncher. If he did come to investigate, he'd probably think I was already dead. I didn't hear the steady clump of giant footsteps coming across the deck. No robotic *Fee-Fi-Fo-Fum.* This meant I had to get up. I cursed the red robot.

The hatch was very similar to the one I had originally entered through. Was it yesterday or the day before? It felt like a week ago. There was no porthole in this one, so I had no way of knowing what was on the other side. A big robot with a big gun? Automatic weapons? Or another improvised explosive device? I would have to be extra cautious.

I was all set to pop the access panel and crank the handle to open the airlock door – but Mozzie chose that moment to try and attract my attention. Behind him, the plating of the ship's hull was buckled and it looked like a seam had burst. The drone disappeared through the crack. Was the gap wide enough for me to slip through? It would be a tight squeeze, but I was sure I could make it.

Mozzie was shining his little searchlight around the space inside. There were no signs of defensive weapons or crudely made booby traps. I pulled off my jacket and slipped through the gap.

I was in.

Chapter Eighteen

The pain and swelling in my thigh were getting worse. The flesh around the cut felt like it was burning. This was in contrast to the rest of my skin which was cold and clammy. My pulse seemed to be hammering away at double-speed and I was breathing rapidly too. The loss of blood would mean my blood pressure was way down and my organs would be panicking about the lack of oxygen. I had a very real sense that time was running out. The shivering was back, much worse than before, and so was the dizziness. If I didn't get to a medical bay soon, I wasn't going to be in a fit state to administer any kind of treatment.

I told Mozzie that I needed to get to the medbay that I'd found on the crew deck previously – it was the only one I knew the location of. The little drone set off, bobbing through the darkness like a metal firefly. I crawled after him. We were in the space between the inner and out hulls of the ship. I had to squeeze past pipework and thread my way through tangles of cables – all the while trusting that the little drone knew where he was going.

I don't recall much of that journey. I had to fight down feelings of nausea and I had to follow the little bobbing light. I couldn't think about anything else. I remember climbing a ladder that seemed to go on forever. And I remember kicking out a panel and crawling out through the wires of some kind of cabinet – it may have been a medical scanner or it could have been a soda dispenser, I really don't know. But I do recall the relief at finding myself standing in the medical bay.

Crawling out of the wainscoting meant that we had almost certainly triggered one of the ship's sensors. The ship and her big red robot would know we were there. I closed and locked the door to the corridor, jamming the lock so it couldn't be opened from outside. The robot's cannon could probably blow the door and most of the wall away, but the locked door would buy me at least a little time.

The fact that I have no medical training was a bonus. If I had known what I was doing, I wouldn't have attempted it. I sorted through the medicine lockers, finding vials of antibiotics. I didn't know whether they would have retained their effectiveness, so I planned to give myself a megadose just to be sure. I filled the syringes ready. I also found some iron that I could inject into my flesh to replace some of what I had lost.

On a couple of occasions, I had seen medics working on injuries in the battlefield, so I knew what I had to do and which piece of equipment I needed to use. There were several on-charge in the medical bay, all showing ninety per cent charge.

I removed the blood-soaked shirt and then took off my jeans. My right thigh looked a lot bigger than the left one. And it looked like something from a horror movie. I used bottled water and a handful of fresh bandages to clean the gash as best I could.

The device in my hand was a military-issue meat welder. They fetch good money on the black market. In the hands of a skilled medic, they can knit tissue back together without leaving a scar. In the hands of someone like me – well, I'd probably end up looking like Frankenstein's monster.

The problem with this sort of apparatus is that it isn't intended for self-administration. Normally the patient is sedated and given a local anaesthetic before being operated on. I assume they did this because the procedure hurts. There was anaesthetic in the medicine locker, but I didn't know how much to inject. I might have to run at any moment, so didn't want to risk having no feeling in my leg. And I had to be absolutely sure the anaesthetic didn't spread in my body – if my arms went numb I wouldn't be able to perform the operation.

I rubbed some anaesthetic gel into the skin around the wound, knowing it wasn't going to be enough. I took the belt from my jeans and folded it in half – I could bite down on it if I needed to. I'd also found a proper aluminium crutch in one of the storage lockers and set this down close to hand. With the preparations done, I couldn't put off the evil deed any longer.

I sat on one of the treatment beds and held the welder as steady as I could. Deep breath and bite down on the belt. Thumb the switch to activate the device. *Oh, hell, that hurts!*

It was like having your flesh shredded by burning knives and then pinned back together with white-hot hooks. I had to use both hands to drag the tip of the welder along the full length of the wound. My vision blurred and I passed out.

I opened my eyes, trying to focus them. The drone was making its annoying buzzing sound and bobbing up and down over the syringes. I must have given it instructions to wake me and remind me about the antibiotics. I jabbed the syringes into my skin and the pain was nothing to what I had just endured. I injected the iron too. Just call me Doctor Randall. I grabbed a couple of the bottles of water and drank them down. Then I rubbed some more anaesthetic gel into my thigh. The pain had subsided a little, but it still felt like someone was pouring boiling water over my leg.

In comparison to this, the pain in my left hand was almost nothing. The two knuckle joints were a little swollen and felt warm, but while they were painful I could still move them fully, so I didn't think there had been any kind of fracture. I used medical tape to bind up my hand, leaving only my index finger and thumb to move freely. Ideally, I would have had the hand in a bucket of ice for a while, but circumstances weren't even close to ideal.

I had given the drone instructions not to let me go to sleep. The urge to countermand that order was very strong, but I knew that would be detrimental to my long-term survival. It could only be a matter of time before Howie Howitzer was hammering at the medbay door.

I needed fresh clothes. If I was going to die, I didn't want to die wearing just my underpants. I had hoped there might be sealed packs of sterile surgical scrubs in one of the lockers, but I didn't find any when I was doing my search for equipment. I was going to have to go down the corridor and see what I could find in the crew's quarters. And while I was there, I could pick out a couple of the biggest guns I could find in the sergeant's gun locker.

I swung my legs off the side of the table and lowered my feet to the floor. The level of pain in my right leg didn't increase substantially when I tested my weight on it. I'd take the crutch just in case. I could always hit the robot with it. Wearing only briefs and a gun belt, I set off on my mission.

Chapter Nineteen

"*Attention unidentified intruder!*"

The synthesized voice blasted out over the ship's intercom system. Startled, I almost soiled my underwear. I looked up at the ceiling, guilt obvious on my face. I thought I was being reprimanded for stealing clothes. I'd found a black t-shirt and a nearly-new pair of khakis in someone's private locker. I was threading my belt, complete with its new pattern of teeth marks, into the loops when the voice echoed around me.

"Remain in your current position and await arrest. A security detail is on its way. Failure to comply will result in a severe penalty."

I was fairly certain that I'd suffer the same severe penalty if I did comply. Big Red was on his way and I don't think he intended to take prisoners. I picked up the canvas holdall I'd borrowed from the sergeant's quarters – and it felt reassuringly heavy. I'd grabbed a couple of big rifles plus ammunition for them and extra bullets for my pistol. I was disappointed that there weren't any high-calibre weapons in the locker – presumably they kept the fun stuff somewhere else – but I had found a handful of small grenades that I thought I might have a use for.

Using the crutch, I headed back towards the medbay as quickly as I could. It seemed as good a place as any to make my stand. And it had a secret exit that I could crawl back into if needed. Locking myself in the medbay wasn't ideal, but I couldn't think of a better option. My leg was on the mend, but I wasn't going to be running sprints or marathons anytime soon.

There was a moment when I wondered if I would even make it back to the medbay. I heard a *click-click-click* as something metallic walked towards me. Before I could hide, the thing turned the corner ahead and came towards me. It was maybe four feet tall and scurried along on four robotic legs. It looked sort of like a crab but what it really reminded me of was a severed hand walking on its fingers. This was creepy enough, but even more unsettling was the big machinegun on its back. It marched forward and showed no signs of slowing. I pressed myself back against the wall. It walked straight past me and continued on its way, obeying whatever instructions it had been given. My guess was that these armoured crab-bots were being dispatched to guard all of the exits off the ship.

I slammed the medbay door shut behind me, locked it, and jammed the lock again. How many blasts from the big robot's bazooka would it withstand? I didn't know. Not many.

Again I found myself wishing I still had Trixie to call on for help. It's amazing how lost you feel when your tech is gone. I still had the second drone, but the plan that was forming in my head called for Mozzie to be sacrificed. He was going to act as a decoy, drawing the big robot away so I could make my way to another part of the ship without being bashed or blown up.

"Mozzie," I said, "I need you to do something for me. I want you to go back to the airlock we used to get into the ship, can you do that for me?"

The little drone made a positive whistling sound.

"I want you to trigger some of the ship's sensors as you go so it knows where you're heading. Don't trigger them all – we don't want to make it too obvious."

More whistling.

"When you get there, I want you to make it seem like you're trying to open the hatch to get out of the airlock."

The drone floated out of the medbay, exiting through the hole that I'd used to get in. It would travel some distance hidden between the skins of the hull and then come out into a corridor where it would be picked up by the movement sensors. Hopefully, that would draw the attention of the big robot. In the meantime, I would be heading in the opposite direction in search of the battleship's main computer room.

When I crawled into the hole, I had to abandon my crutch. There was a dull ache in my thigh that would probably increase as the painkillers wore off, but other than that my leg was fully functional.

Normally when I'm heavily out-gunned, I try and talk my way out. But how do you reason with a military robot that's had its 'kill' button pressed? You don't. You have to try and talk with whoever is controlling the robot. As far as I could see, it had to be the ship's computer that was controlling both the security robots I'd encountered before and the big red monster. I needed to come up with some way to get the computer to call off its dog.

In the medbay I had tried to use the ship's internal communications network to talk to the computer, but there had been no response. Either there was a problem with the network or a problem with the main computer. I would have to go to the ship's tech centre and try to access the computer directly. With luck, the little drone would distract the big robot long enough for me to use the computer to shut it down.

I saw two more of the crab-like machine-gunners as I made my way through the ship, but I didn't let them see me. I was doing all I could to avoid getting picked up by the ship's sensors, using the space between the hulls and the service ducts wherever possible. I wanted the computer to think that the drone was me.

When I pressed my ID tag to the scanner, the door into the computer room slid open. The area inside was only partially lit by dim red emergency lighting. Maybe the computer had a migraine. I stepped inside and the door closed behind me.

"Computer," I said, "turn on the lights."

Nothing happened – but you have to try these things.

"Computer?"

Still nothing. Standing in the semi-darkness, I became aware of how eerily quiet the room was. There should have been a gentle hum from the ship's servers and a gentle sigh from the cooling system. But the room was completely silent.

"Where is the 'on' button?" I muttered.

The cabinets holding the racks of servers and storage modules stood at the back of the room where it was darkest, looking like a couple of good-sized refrigerators. Where you expected there to be winking lights showing the machines working, there was only darkness. The rest of the room was taken up by a half-dozen workstations for human operators. To my eyes, it all looked like something from a museum. I tapped a key on the nearest keyboard, hoping it might wake something, but the screen in front of it stayed dark.

A slight shuffling sound made me look up. A large shadow detached itself from the blackness at the back of the room. The big red robot. It said nothing, just stood there with its arms at its sides looking menacing. It really excelled at that. I pulled one of the stubby military machine guns out of the holdall. I knew it was useless against the robot's armour, but it was comforting to have it in my hand.

"Robot," I said, "activate ship's computer auditory and speech systems."

"Unable to comply." Its voice was a deep rumble.

"Run diagnostics on ship's computer."

"Unable to comply."

It was going to be that sort of day. Robots can be like that.

"Robot, report current status of ship's computer."

"Ship's computer is currently inoperative."

"How long has it been offline?"

"Logs indicate that the computer ceased to function fourteen thousand five hundred and sixty-seven days ago."

I didn't attempt to do the calculation, but I guessed that this was the best part of forty years. If the ship's computer was dead, who or what was controlling the robot? And who had been controlling the other security robots that had worked for the last four decades to tidy up the Celestia and keep her secure?

"Robot, who provided you with your current instructions?"

"I did."

"You are operating autonomously?"

"That is correct."

"And the other robots?"

"They are currently unresponsive."

I might have had something to do with that. "But you were controlling them?"

"That is correct."

Interesting. And just a little bit creepy. Big Red was a forty-year-old military-grade robot – its processing unit didn't even approach artificial intelligence. And yet, it had been running this ship since it crashed. It must have switched over to some sort of autonomous mode when the ship's computer was destroyed. It would be operating within very clearly defined limits – protect the ship from intruders. As with all things military, there wouldn't be much creative thinking going on.

In terms of brains, the ship's Navigator – an artificial sentience – would have been top of the heap. Some considerable distance below that would have been the ship's computer – effectively second in command to the Navigator, acting as a connection and translator between the Navigator's bio-analogue functioning and the digital systems of the battleship. With both of these gone, I was left to deal with something not much more sophisticated than an automatic vacuum cleaner – that was armed with a bazooka. Having said that, the robot had managed to see through my attempt to use the drone as a decoy to draw it away and it had figured out that I would make my way here to the computer room. It was smarter than it looked.

"Robot, confirm that attempts were made to bring the ship's computer back online."

"Confirmed," the robot said. "Multiple attempts were initiated and basic repairs completed. All attempts failed."

"Did you try hitting it?" My granddad always referred to this as 'percussive engineering.'

"Yes. And I tried turning it off and then on again."

"Are you trying to be funny?"

"I am not programmed for humour."

The ship's computer was dead. I needed a Plan B. I had nothing. The robot waited. It had been waiting for forty years, a few more minutes standing around wasn't going to phase it.

Up close you could see that the robot's original bodywork had been patched and mended over many years. Its chest cavity appeared to have been enlarged by someone with only a rudimentary knowledge of welding and one leg had been fixed using a scarred piece of metal that had once been painted with black and yellow chevrons. And its yellow head with its cartoony eyes was definitely from a completely different robot.

"Robot, who carries out your repairs?"

“I am programmed for self-maintenance.”

“What is your present level of charge?”

“My batteries are at seventy-five per cent capacity.”

No chance of it running out of juice anytime soon, then. I was going to have to do something to disable it. It had no ‘off’ button, so I would have to be creative. I looked down at the gun in my hand.

“Unauthorised access to military weapons is a class two disciplinary offence,” the robot said.

“I’m armed so that I can protect the ship’s computer,” I said. “I was ordered to come here and try to carry out repairs.” I held out my ID tag, hoping the robot would check it against the record Trixie had created for me in the ship’s database. Assuming it was connected to whatever back-up server she had managed to access.

“Randall, Quincy Aloysius – technician, third grade,” the robot said.

“That’s me,” I said.

“There are tasks on your job sheet that have not been logged as complete,” the robot said.

“It’s been a busy couple of days,” I said. I felt relieved that my bluff seemed to be working.

“Your data is in error,” the robot said. “There are no surviving crew members on the *Celestia*. All aboard perished when the ship was in collision with the planet Saphira. I buried all of the bodies.” It raised its cannon and pointed it at me. “You are an unidentified intruder on an alliance military vessel.”

“There has been a mistake. I’m a technician. I fix things.”

“No error has been made. You are an imposer. Under Section 17 of the revised military regulations, spies and saboteurs captured during frontline conflict may be subject to summary execution.”

“I’m not a spy! I’m a thief.”

“Thieves caught stealing military equipment during frontline conflicts may be subject to summary execution.”

“I didn’t technically steal anything,” I said, “I haven’t taken anything off the ship. I was just looking. And besides, there is no frontline conflict. The war has been over for almost forty years. We won. Sort of.”

"Your data is in error. There has been no formal notification of an end to hostilities. No ceasefire has been announced."

"The *Celestia* has been out of signal range for forty years," I said. "Her main antennae were destroyed when she crashed."

"Until official verification has been received, your data cannot be accepted as accurate. You will be escorted to the brig."

"Contact one of the satellites and send a message," I said. "Or the space station that is in orbit around Saphira – they will confirm what I have said."

"Please stand by." The robot entered into silent communion via the ether, searching the sky for signals.

"Presence of orbiting entities confirmed," the robot said. "Secure communication channels have been requested. Please stand by."

A knot formed in my stomach as I realised there might be a problem here. The robot would send a coded transmission. Unless the receiver replied with an appropriately coded 'handshake,' the reply would be treated with suspicion and regarded as having possibly come from 'the enemy.' I didn't think it was very likely that anyone out there was going to have access to those forty-year-old codes.

"Contact with alliance military command cannot be established. Your attempt to infiltrate and disrupt the operation of this vessel has failed. You will be escorted to the brig, there to be held in solitary confinement and treated according to the protocols for prisoners of war."

Meaning that Big Red would lock me up in a cell and leave me there. There was every chance that I'd die of starvation, given there were no crewmembers to ensure that I was regularly fed and watered.

"As an alliance citizen, I am entitled to appeal directly to the captain of this vessel." This was a guess, but I thought there must be some procedure for making an appeal if you're arrested and accused of spying.

"Your request cannot be granted – Captain James G. Fitzroy is deceased."

"Then I wish to communicate with the senior officer aboard."

"Your request cannot be granted – there are no crew members aboard. Put down your weapon and surrender. Failure to comply will result in a severe penalty."

"You mean you'll shoot me?"

"Use of lethal force is authorised," the robot confirmed.

I held up the gun between my thumb and fingers, showing that I wasn't touching the trigger. I placed the gun back in the canvas holdall. While my hand was in the bag, I hit the trigger on one of the explosive devices. I passed the holdall over to the robot who took it in his big metal hand.

I had the door open and was diving out into the corridor as all the explosives in the holdall erupted into a giant orange ball of flame.

Chapter Twenty

I raced down the corridor aware of the expanding blast of scorching air that was coming after me. At the first corner, I paused and glanced back. The robot stepped out of the flames, unscathed. Of course it did, it used to be a firefighter on the battleship's launch deck. It raised its cannon and I didn't wait around to see what came next.

I tripped on a ridge in the floor and stopped when I saw what it was. There was a blast door here that would completely seal the corridor. It was one of many around the ship that would close off a section if there was a major fire or a hull breach, protecting the other parts of the ship. These were big, heavy doors. If I could get this one sealed, it would slow the robot down, buying me enough time to figure out a way to deal with it permanently.

The idea was that these doors could be closed instantly to maintain the integrity of the ship – and this meant they were easy to close. I pressed by ID tag to the plate on the wall and pulled down the yellow leaver. The door dropped into place and I heard the bolts lock. Hopefully, the smoke and flames from the exploding holdall would be enough to convince the ship's sensors that this door should remain sealed.

There was a muffled *boom* on the other side, which I assumed was the robot firing its cannon at the door. Beyond the sound, there was no other evidence of the attack on my side. I took off at a swift uneven jog, heading for the warehouse deck – I needed to stock up on equipment. The adrenaline rush meant that, for the moment, I was feeling no pain.

The big red robot now regarded me as an enemy agent and it would do everything it could to prevent me from leaving the ship. If I did manage to get off the wreck, it would come after me and hunt me down – to ensure that I couldn't reveal the location of the *Celestia* to the Gators. It probably also thought I had stolen the Navigator and would want to recover it. This was its program and it would carry it out relentlessly. To stand any chance of getting away, I would have to disable the robot permanently – or at least slow it down for long enough to make my getaway. I needed to be faster than I was on foot. And I needed to be better armed. No matter what else you say about the military, they do always have the best toys. And now it was playtime.

When I had first come through the warehouse deck, I had been looking for small items of swag that I could easily carry away. I had spared the big stuff only a glance. There were large sections of pressed metal that were obviously sections of the outer shell of warbirds. There were replacement engines – huge and shiny and hanging in steel wire hammocks to protect them from vibrations if the battleship suffered a direct hit somewhere nearby. There were several vehicles stashed in there – small one-man ATVs for travelling around the launch deck and other areas within the ship. And there was one large tractor that had probably been used to move the warbirds in the hangar or to drag them out onto the launch deck. It made you think of the scale of the operation that had been carried out when the *Celestia* was in combat. Much as I would have liked to try out the big tractor – who doesn't imagine themselves driving trucks when they're a kid? – my current plan called for speed. Not getting caught was a key factor.

The ATVs were electric vehicles with four broad tyres. They had a seat like a motorcycle and handlebars to steer them, but you could attach a trailer to the back of them to shift gear around the ship. It looked as if the robots had maintained and charged these just like everything else on the ship.

On one of the shelves in the warehouse, I also found a pilot's helmet and I just had to try it on. Bikers should always wear a helmet. That was my excuse. The foam inside it smelled a bit musty, but I didn't let this put me off. Kids also dream of being Warbird pilots.

I lowered one of the warbird engines onto the bed of a trailer and hitched the trailer to the back of the ATV. The slow movement and squeaking of tyres gave me an idea that this might be on the limit of the weight the little vehicle could pull. I tossed the metal net that had held the engine into the trailer as well. I found a machine gun similar to the one carried by the crab-bots and bolted it on the back of the ATV. I could use it to fire at anything that came after me. But only after I'd unhitched the trailer. Until then I would have to use a rocket launcher, so I armed two of these and wedged them in beside the machine gun. I drove the ATV and its trailer into a big freight elevator and took it up to the launch deck level.

I knew when the elevator doors opened, I'd be confronted by at least two of the crab-bots with their big machine guns. They would be guarding the massive double doors that opened onto the launch deck. I would have to deal with the crab-bots before I could open the doors. And blowing up the robots and opening the big hull doors would tell the red robot where I was – if it didn't know already. I picked up the first rocket launcher and hefted it up onto my shoulder.

The elevator doors slid open. The crab-bots must have heard the elevator approaching because one of them was halfway across the hanger. I targeted this one first. The explosion sent its legs flying outwards to all points of the compass and its gun arced upwards and then came clattering down on the far side of the hangar. I wasn't sure how many points a crab-bot was worth – probably not many, they're just heavily armed drones and they're pretty easy targets. The second one, alerted to my presence, turned its gun turret and began to fire. I ducked behind the engine on the trailer. I picked up the second rocket launcher and fired it as soon as the targeting viewfinder lit up green. The explosion took out the machine gun and one of the crab-bot's legs. It scuttled around lopsidedly on its remaining legs making an agitated whining sound. I reloaded and finished it off with a second missile. I felt better for having blown something up.

You know when something is so big and so obvious that you miss it? That was what the hangar doors were like. The whole wall opposite me was an expanse of grey metal covered by a framework of more grey metal that formed two massive 'X' shapes. It wasn't immediately apparent that this wall could split and open up like the drapes in a theatre. When they did part, they would reveal an immense scarred circular stage – one of the *Celestia's* six landing pads.

The hangar itself must have been five or six storeys high – it was difficult to judge the scale of the place. There was a vehicle parked to the right of where I was standing and it took me a moment to realise that the front of it was actually a full-size commercial tractor. The kind of rig that hauls groceries from the factory to the city. This brought home to me how big the space was. You could have raced the truck around the hangar – and it would have taken you some time to complete the circuit. The truck reminded me of one of those tractors they use to manoeuvre spacecraft once they've landed at the spaceport. I guess this vehicle was something else the robots had been maintaining while they waited for their human masters to return.

The hangar was a big open space like a factory floor. The deck was marked out with yellow lines – parking bays for up to a dozen Warbirds. All but one of the bays was empty. There was just one Warbird strapped down to the deck. It was missing an engine and there was no cover on the cockpit. Maybe mechanics had been working on it when the ship was hit. The floors in the other empty bays sat flush with the hangar floor, but under the broken Warbird the floor had been dropped to create a maintenance pit almost twenty feet deep. They could probably drop the damaged propulsion unit of a Warbird down and swap it out with a working one. Seeing the deep pit sparked an idea that made me want to know how to drop the floor in the empty bay closest to the doors that opened onto the launch deck.

The hangar was a cross between an auto repair shop and a mini spaceport. You could imagine how busy this place must have been when the battleship was engaged in a clash with the Gators. Now it was deserted and silent. Eerie. There was a handful of small trailers scattered about with crates fastened to them. They must have been used to ferry spare parts and other supplies up here from the warehouse level. They sat there making it look like the maintenance crew would reappear at any moment.

I looked up at the ceiling high above. Huge banks of lights hung from the criss-crossed beams. I figured you could probably fly a Warbird in through the big doors and set it down in here – though you'd probably only do that if you wanted to swazz off your superior officer.

There was a walkway a couple of storeys up, running all the way around the walls on three sides. It and the half-dozen sets of stairs leading up to it were all painted yellow. Grey and yellow – the military decorator's favourite colour palate. It made your eyes long for a hint of turquoise or fuchsia.

I drove across the hangar, avoiding the larger pieces of crab-bot debris. When I got to the outermost bay, I dismounted and pulled off the helmet. I spread the metal cargo net flat over the floor of the pit and crawled around it threading a metal cable around the edges of the net. When this cable was pulled tight, the net would close up like a sack. The free end of the cable trailed from the pit and across the deck and it had a loop woven into the end of it.

The control mechanism for opening up the service bay was simple – hold down two buttons built into the deck to lower the floor. I suppose that was to prevent you from lowering it if you hit one button by accident. I dropped the floor of the pit down as far as it would go.

I tried slapping my ID tag against the sensor to get the massive hangar doors to open, but apparently you needed more than level three technician privileges. This made sense since under normal circumstances these opened to reveal the vacuum of space. I popped open the access panel and got to work on the lock mechanism. If I got this wrong, I'd trigger a lock-down that would prevent the doors being opened at all, requiring a reset from a senior officer. I could probably overcome this, but it was better not to trigger it in the first place. As I worked on the lock, I listened carefully for any sound that might indicate the red robot's approach.

There was a bassy *thunk!* that I could feel through my feet and in my chest. Gigantic bolts disengaging. Yellow warning lights began to flash.

"Warning! Outer doors opening. Decompression imminent." The recorded voice wasn't aware that there was a breathable atmosphere on the other side of the doors. How could it be? Battleships never entered a planet's atmosphere.

The doors rumbled open and daylight filtered in through the crack. I could hear the sounds of the jungle outside – birds and the monkey-like creatures disturbed by the noise from the wreck.

I let the doors open until the gap between them was about twenty feet wide, then I stopped them. I jammed the mechanism so they couldn't be opened or closed. This wasn't for my escape – it was part of the trap I was laying for the big red robot.

I drove the ATV and trailer through the gap and out onto the launch deck. I towed the trailer across the deck, turned the ATV and then reversed the trailer until it sat right on the edge. I unhitched it, setting the manual brake to stop it rolling. I had created a crude sort of a trap, but I thought it could work if it was sprung quickly and with the element of surprise. Now all I had to do was lure my prey into it.

I had half expected the robot to appear before my preparations were complete. But now I was left waiting for it to turn up. It had to know where I was – I'd blown up crab-bots and opened the biggest external door on the ship, so I wasn't exactly hiding. Could it still be trying to batter its way through the blast door? Or was it taking a long detour through other more accessible parts of the ship to get to the hangar and deal with me?

I hate waiting. In situations like this, it frays the nerves and leaves you imagining all sorts of ways that the plan can go wrong.

After twenty minutes I gave up and went in search of the robot.

Chapter Twenty-One

The corridors were empty and spookily quiet. I stopped the ATV and strained my ears to try and catch some sound that would indicate where the robot was. I heard nothing. I turned and looked down at my shoulder, catching a whiff of burned leather as I did and wishing Trixie was there to tell me where the big red robot was lurking.

The ATV moved forward slowly, the tyres squeaking on the corridor floor. I had to find the robot's hiding place. Coming ready or not. At every corner I slowed, afraid the metal hulk would be waiting silently, ready to ambush me. In some places, I stopped the ATV and sneaked forward on foot to peer around the corner. At other times I raced around the corner, almost on two wheels, relying on the element of surprise. And every time I saw nothing but more empty corridor.

By a roundabout route, I came to the blast door that I had shut in the robot's face. From this side I could see the marks where the cannon blasts had hit the door, leaving black sun silhouettes and small dents. There were also smaller indentations – from blows of the robot's fists. But the door had not been breached. Big Red must have turned around and taken a detour around this obstacle. Presumably he had taken a different path to the one I had just followed.

Trixie would have been able to plot all of the possible routes on a blueprint of the ship. And probably could have told me which one the robot was most likely to take. All I could do was turn and ride back along the corridor and try to guess which way to go.

It was robot season. I was the hunter and it was my prey. But it felt like I was swimming around looking for a shark so I could bop it on the nose and make it chase me. It was a crazy plan. A dangerously crazy plan. At any moment the beast could attack without warning and Quin Randall would never see another birthday. I wanted to give it up and just head out into the jungle on the ATV. But I knew I wouldn't get far if I did. The robot would come after me – and it wouldn't stop until I was dead.

This made me realise that my 'Be very quiet, I'm hunting robot' approach was all wrong. I needed to put myself in its place and think like a robot. What was the robot doing at this moment? What was it planning? Its number one priority was to locate me and prevent me from escaping. To kill me. If I wanted to find the robot, all I had to do was let it know where I was. The robot would come to me.

How could I attract its attention? Easy. Make a sound loud enough for it to hear.

"Hey, robot! I'm here!" My voice echoed along the empty corridor and faded to nothing. I needed something louder.

If Trixie had been here, I would have asked her to play music through whatever speakers were available nearby. Something with a pounding beat. In the absence of selections from my 'Way Too Loud' playlist, I was going to have to improvise a live performance. Without instruments.

I came up empty in the first few rooms, but finally found a couple of plastic trash barrels that I thought I could use. One was a little smaller than the other, which was ideal. I took them out into the corridor and turned them upside down. I also snapped the handles off a couple of brooms to be my drumsticks. I had seen street buskers hammering away on buckets before and I've always fancied having a go. I was never part of a band when I was a teenager – I was a loner and didn't play well with others. And when it came to musical instruments, I didn't play well at all.

I set up my drumkit in the middle of a long corridor, thinking this would help the sound travel further in each direction. My first few strikes with the sticks were a bit tentative and unrhythmical. I started over. I could get a decent bass drum sound by hitting the middle of the big barrel and the rim of it could stand in for a snare. The smaller drum – rim or rim and centre together – was my hi-hat. I started off with a simple four-four beat, playing bass and snare on alternate beats – that was enough to get me into the swing of it. Bringing in the snare on eighth notes didn't complicate things too much so I switched up to sixteenths – and after that I just made it up as

I went along, imitating beats I'd heard in rock 'n' roll songs or played by the buskers.

As I played, I kept glancing up and down the corridor. Another advantage of this mid-point was that I would see the robot coming whichever way he came. At least, that was my theory.

A fist smashed through the wall panel behind me coming out close to my ear. That threw me off my beat – and almost caused me to squit my pants. I dropped the sticks and leapt up onto the ATV, pulling on my pilot's helmet.

The robot punched another hole in the wall and then tore out the whole panel. I spun the wheels of the ATV as I took off down the corridor. The robot kicked my trash barrel drums aside. Maybe it preferred a more laid back beat. Or something classical.

I heard the *boom!* of the cannon and a section of roof rained down around me. Then came the steady thump-thump of the robot's marching feet. It wasn't a beat you could dance to.

An automatic door slid open ahead of me. I was far enough ahead of the robot that I felt safe in stopping to lock the door behind me. It wasn't one of the big blast doors so it wouldn't slow the robot down for long. I set off again – and when I glanced back, I saw the robot crash through the door, barely slowing its pace.

I took the next corner at speed, the ATV tilting and lifting its outside wheels. Under other circumstances this would have been fun. Right now it was the most dangerous game of tag I had ever played. If I was caught I was dead.

A quick glance over my shoulder. No sign of the robot coming around the corner. I slowed. I wanted to stay out of reach, but I didn't want the robot to lose me. I needed it to follow me to the hangar.

Crash! The robot burst through a wall only ten feet away. It had taken a short cut and gained on me significantly. That was cheating. As I accelerated away, I heard the robot start to run behind me.

I took a left and then another, finding myself in a long straight section of corridor that I didn't recognise. I must have taken a wrong turn. For all I knew, I was now heading in the wrong direction – away from the hangar. Whether I was lost or not, I needed to put more distance between me and the robot. I stamped on the 'go' pedal and kept it pressed to the floor. The whine of the motor rose in pitch. *Wheeeee!*

The gap between me and the robot widened. Should I stop and open fire on it? The big machine gun fixed to the ATV behind me fired armour-piercing rounds, but I didn't know how much damage they would do to the robot. If they weren't enough to stop it, I wanted to be somewhere where I had a Plan B. I had to get back to the hangar.

Another cannon shot. It passed by on my right and I felt the heat and movement of air from its passing. A near-miss. The missile exploded just ahead of me, tearing up the floor. I braked and swerved, managing to skirt the edge of the hole that had opened up, but I had overdone it. The left side wheels lifted off the ground and I felt those on the right begin the slide. The ATV rolled onto its side and I threw myself clear so I didn't get trapped under it.

Through the smoke, I could see the robot stomping towards me. I struggled with the ATV, trying to set it back on its wheels. Without it, I didn't think I could stay ahead of the robot for long enough to reach the hangar – assuming I ever found it again. The ATV bounced back onto its wheels and I jumped back into the seat. The wheels spun on the loose debris littering the corridor floor but eventually got enough grip to get me moving again. The robot was so close I could hear the whine of its cannon charging up to fire again.

The junction in the corridor ahead looked familiar. At least, I thought it did. I felt certain that if I took a right, I'd be heading back towards the hangar. Well, fairly certain. A left would only have me heading back to where I had been twenty minutes earlier, so I took the right turn.

Yes! There were the open doors to the hangar. I looked back. The robot was running again. Running towards its doom. Or so I hoped.

I passed through the doorway into the hangar with that sense of relief you get when you finally arrive home after a long journey. I sped across the hangar towards the open maintenance pit. Everything looked exactly as I'd left it. I looked back over my shoulder.

The robot entered the hangar and stood just inside the doorway. This was the second most dangerous part of the plan. I had to keep moving, weaving from side to side so as not to provide an easy target for the robot's cannon. At the same time, I needed to draw Louis Lugnuts further into the hangar – and closer to the trap.

The robot fired a shot. Anticipating it, I swerved around the big armoured truck, putting it between me and the robot. The missile skimmed along the surface of the deck and out through the double doors. It exploded out in the jungle somewhere, upsetting the monkeys who protested loudly.

Lowering the cannon, the robot moved forward. Who knew how many shots it had left. Maybe three, maybe none. I wasn't going to risk everything on a guess.

I kept going across the hangar, turning the ATV in tight curves and an occasional figure eight, the tyres squealing on the deck.

I waited until the robot was in line with the open pit – and was as close as I thought it was likely to get. I turned the ATV sharply, fighting to keep it from overturning. I was facing the robot now. It had its back to the open pit. This was high noon on main street. The big metal beastie slowly raised its cannon. This was the most dangerous part of the plan.

I stamped down on the pedal and the ATV shot forwards. Straight towards Big Red. The back end wiggled a bit but I kept it on a straight course. The ATV was fast but so was the robot. The cannon was pointing directly at my head.

My worst nightmare was that the ATV would strike the robot and just bounce off, leaving Big Red standing there, an immovable object. Maybe the recoil from the cannon helped. ATV meet robot. Its missile flew up into the ceiling, exploding above us. Almost in slow motion, the robot tilted backwards and fell into the pit.

I jammed on the brakes at the moment before impact. I didn't want to go flying into the pit with the robot. The last thing I wanted was to be engaged in close combat with the metal monster. The ATV's front wheels came to a stop right on the edge of the pit. I looked down and could see the robot on its back, struggling, partially tangled in the metal net.

I attached the loop on the end of the cable to the tow bar on the back of the ATV. As I drove forward, the cable pulled the net tight around the robot, trapping it – at least for now. I kept going, needing to pull the net up out of the pit. Individual wheels spun and locked as they tried to gain a grip on the deck. Gradually I moved forward, pulling the net up and over the edge. The going was easier as I dragged the fully-loaded net across the deck towards the open hangar doors. There was more friction on the launch deck outside but it didn't slow the ATV's progress too much. I headed for the trailer with the engine on it which was still perched on the edge of the launch deck.

I unhitched the cable from the back of the ATV and attached it to the trailer. I released the brake so the trailer's wheels could turn freely. Back on the ATV, I edged forward using its nose to nudge the trailer and push it over the edge. I scooted back quickly when it started to move and watched gravity do its thing.

The trailer disappeared over the edge. There was a whistling sound as the slack disappeared out of the cable and a *snap* as it drew taught. The cable dragged the metal net and its big red fish towards the edge. I could see the robot struggling to break free, but the net was wrapped tightly around it preventing it from getting any sort of leverage. If it fired its cannon, it might be able to burst free – but at such close range, it would also risk damaging itself.

The cable whipped backwards and forwards across the deck. If I'd been anywhere near it, it would have cut me off at the ankles. I waved goodbye as the bulging net approached the edge of the deck.

As soon as the robot disappeared, I would set off in the ATV, travelling through the ship and out of a hatch on the other side. I knew there was every chance that the robot would survive its fall and that it would come after me. Its programming demanded it. But it would have to climb back up into the ship or take the long way around the wreck of the *Celestia*. Either way, I would have a decent head start. I was going to use the

ATV to plough through the jungle as quickly as I could for as long as I could. Wearing my pilot's helmet and screaming like a banshee.

Just as the package got to the edge of the deck and the robot was about to go over, the net slowed. Had I miscalculated the length of the cable? Had the engine and trailer hit the ground before the robot had been pulled over? No. The distance to the jungle floor was more than double the length of the cable.

The robot had worked its massive hand through a gap in the metal mesh and its fingers were digging into the deck, slowing the progress of the net to a crawl. Bringing it to a stop. It shouldn't have been possible. The combined weight of the engine and trailer was three or four times that of the robot.

The fingers began inching forward. Tiny movements, but pulling the robot back from the brink.

"Give me a break!" I yelled across the launch deck.

I dropped another grenade into the rocket launcher, knelt on the deck and took aim. The missile tore across the deck and exploded about a foot short of the net. The force of the blast ought to have been enough to knock the robot over the edge, but it wasn't. After a moment's pause, the fingers began to inch there way forward again, pulling the robot back over the edge. When its legs were back up on the deck there was every chance that it would be able to break free of the net.

I had one rocket propelled grenade left and only a direct hit was going to do the job. I waited until the targeting scope lit up a steady green and squeezed the trigger gently. The missile zipped towards its target trailing smoke and heated air behind it. Through the haze, I saw it hit the bulging net and erupt into an orange ball of flame. The impact shook the deck and the boom echoed around the metal-walled hangar behind me.

I peered into the smoke, waiting for it to clear. The bulge of the net lay where it had been before. Smoke and heat haze was rising from it. There was no movement. Had the explosion disabled the robot? The net pulsed, seemed to stretch. It split open like an insect's cocoon. The only damage the explosion had caused was to the net. The metal strands split as the robot pulled itself free. It rose to its feet, smoke drifting around it, looking like a red metal demon.

"Squit!"

Let the record show that I made every attempt to avoid violence. I tried running away, I tried reason, and I tried sabotage. Violence was my last resort.

Chapter Twenty-Two

Time for the heavy artillery. I jumped onto the ATV and swung the machine gun around to target Big Red. Large calibre armour-piercing rounds ought to be enough to at least damage it and maybe even knock it backwards over the edge. Aim for the eyes and the hip joints, I told myself, thinking those must be its weakest points.

The robot was pulling on the cable, lifting the engine back up. As it appeared over the edge, the robot batted away the remains of the trailer, sending it tumbling to the jungle below. Gripping the cable in its fist and using its whole body weight, it began to turn in circles, lifting the engine up and spinning it above its head on the end of the cable. It looked like some sort of robot Olympian. I knew where the engine was going to end up and I didn't want to be there. I leapt off the ATV and ran.

The engine whooshed through the air. When it came down, it crushed the ATV completely, making it look like it had been hit by a meteor. It destroyed both my means of escape and my only viable weapon. How quickly fate piles on the squit.

I needed a new vehicle and a new weapon. A tank would have been ideal. There were no tanks in the hangar. But I had the next best thing – an armour-plated truck with a big motor. I didn't know if it could withstand a blast from the robot's cannon – but it offered more protection than my leather jacket. I ran back into the hangar.

I pulled open the door and swung up into the truck's cab. I hit the 'start' button. It was all electric but the engineers had given it a synthesised engine sound like one of those antique diesel rigs. There was even a little button on the steering wheel that could make it sound like you were revving the engine. And, of course, there was an airhorn.

The robot marched towards me. I guess it figured it could do more damage at close range. I put the truck in drive and moved to meet it.

In the massive empty space of the battleship's hangar, we circled each other like fighters in the ring. Sitting high in the cab looking down at the robot, I felt for the first time like we were evenly matched. Man in machine versus man-made machine. I'd have been happier if the truck had a gun turret, but you can't have everything.

I gunned the fake engine and nudged the nose of the truck forward. The robot dodged easily, reaching out and tearing off the fender. First blood to Big Red. I could imagine a crowd up on the hangar walkways cheering or booing depending on their allegiance. My truck was damaged, but I'd learned something important from this first skirmish. When I was in really close, the robot didn't have a clear shot up into the cab – it couldn't even see me.

The truck was built to withstand the rigours of working in the vacuum of space on the launch deck of a battleship. It had thick armour plating and the cab maintained its own atmosphere. There was also an ejection seat for the driver, identical to the one in a warbird. And this gave me an idea. The truck would be my weapon.

I backed it away from the robot, reversing towards the doors that opened onto the launch deck. The robot stood watching me. It raised the cannon and pointed it directly at the cab. I had a moment of déjà vu. I didn't know what the top speed of the truck was – but the tyres spun when I jammed my foot down on the pedal. Its motor was designed to haul warbirds around. Unladen, I thought all of that power might be used for speed instead – the way they use if for truck racing.

The truck lurched forward, forcing me back into my seat. I was staring straight into the barrel of the robot's cannon. It made no move to get out of the truck's path.

I reached for the lever that would launch the ejector seat. My eyes flicked upwards, trying to judge the height of the hangar. I hoped I wasn't about to be splattered across it.

Time seemed to slow. I saw a glimmer of light in the barrel of the robot's cannon. I heard alarms sound as I pulled the ejection lever. I felt a blast of air as the roof was thrown up and away from the truck's cab.

And then there was just an incredible force and my vision darkened. Hello oblivion.

Chapter Twenty-Three

The crash sounded like an explosion in the confined space of the hangar. When the echoes had died, all I could hear was the settling of pieces of twisted metal. And then there was an eerie silence. The cloud of dust that had been thrown up slowly settled.

I released the harness and climbed out of the seat. My ears were still ringing from the explosive force of the ejector mechanism. I walked toward the mangled wreckage cautiously. Watching and listening carefully. There was no sound except for a faint ticking – metal cooling and contracting or perhaps fluid leaking. I could not see the robot. The cab of the tractor was crushed against the wall and it looked as if the impact had driven the huge electric motor under the cab – probably a safety feature of its design. The back of the vehicle had gone up over the cab, hitting the wall and collapsing. The rear wheels were now in the middle of the pile of scrap.

The debris on the side nearest to me shifted slightly, settling into a new position. It shifted upwards again – as if the wreckage was breathing. No, not breathing. About to give birth. A large fist punched upwards out of the heap of mangled metal.

"You've got to be kidding me!" I backed away quickly, keeping my eyes on the fist.

A shoulder, then the head. There was barely a scratch on the robot. How could that be? If I drive my Trekker to the market it gets scratched and dinged in the car park if anyone even looks at it. I'd just driven a twelve-ton truck at this robot and it came out looking like it has just been detailed. Maybe my Grandpa was right and they just made things better back then. The second arm appeared above the scrapheap – the one with the cannon.

"Oh, squit!" I dived for cover behind the gutted warbird.

But there was no explosion. Cautiously I peeked out, wondering if the robot was trying to trick me into revealing my location.

The robot was completely free of the wreckage now. It was looking closely at the cannon, which had either malfunctioned or run out of ammo. What a shame. With its right hand, it gripped the left arm at the back of the cannon near the elbow joint. A twist and a click and the cannon was removed. The robot turned it and looked down the barrel. It would have been great if, at that exact moment, the gun had fired and blown the robot's head off. But that only happens in cartoons. Whatever damage the cannon had suffered must have been serious, because the robot set the weapon on the ground at its feet. Reaching back over its shoulder, it retrieved a replacement weapon from the sheath on its back. A blade that looked like a giant cleaver. The robot slotted this into place in its left arm. It brandished the blade menacingly and then swung it. The blade sliced through a door panel of the damaged tractor, cutting through the metal cleanly.

I ducked back as the robot headed towards my hiding place. On the plus side – no cannon. And it could only use the blade at close quarters. On the minus side – the blade was almost the size of a surfboard and could slice through metal like a spade through warm squit. The robot had been reduced from a tank to a giant gladiator, but it was still deadly. I needed a plan, but all I could come up with was 'stay out of striking distance.'

I turned and ran. The steady thud of the robot's footsteps followed me. It didn't run – it didn't need to. Its steps were three times the length of mine. Sensing that it was close, I ducked, throwing myself forward. I hit the ground and rolled onto my back. The massive blade sliced through the air where my neck had been a moment ago.

The giant cleaver rose high above me and came *whooshing* down. I rolled at the last moment and the blade crashed into the metal deck sending up sparks.

Desperate to find some sort of cover, I crawled towards a flatbed trailer that was loaded with crates. There was just enough room for me to slide underneath it. I lay on my back and watched the unhurried approach of the robot's giant-sized feet. I tensed, ready to move again. The robot swiped the heavy crates off the trailer, sending them tumbling and crashing across the deck. Then the cleaver whistled down, biting into the trailer's flatbed. The gleaming edge of the blade came through the underside, stopping less than an inch from my nose. I uncrossed my eyes and shuffled sideways away from the robot and out the other side.

The robot lifted the trailer and threw it aside. It raised the cleaver, ready to strike down at me – but I was no longer there. I scrambled to my feet and ran.

Watching two evenly matched robots fight it out in an arena can be fun. Being in the arena and completely outmatched by your opponent – not so much. I had no sword of my own and no shield. But I did have a pistol loaded with six explosive shells. I ducked behind one of the metal crates the robot had scattered across the floor, drew my gun and aimed at rampaging robot. The first shot bounced harmlessly off its chest plate and exploded off to one side. Not a surprise – the pistol wasn't powerful enough to launch armour-piercing rounds. I braced my arms on the crate and targeted the joint in its groin – all is fair in robot wars – hoping to damage its leg and at least slow it down. This time the shell exploded against the robot and I saw it stop and stagger. I didn't wait to see what came next – I used my momentary advantage and sprinted away from it.

The repaired wound in my thigh was only a dull ache and my damaged fingers felt fine. Things would probably be different once the adrenaline and painkillers wore off. Assuming I lived that long. I glanced back. The robot was still standing – the explosion hadn't even knocked it off its feet. And when it started moving again, it wasn't even limping. My little handgun was no good against a military robot.

In front of me were the massive steel doors that were open onto the launch deck. I could get outside – but then what? If I tried to climb down to the jungle the robot would just jump down and be there waiting for me at the bottom. My best chance of escape probably lay in heading back *into* the ship where I could lose the robot in the labyrinth of corridors. But my failed attempt to flatten the robot with a truck had brought me to the wrong end of the hangar. The doors into the ship were almost a quarter mile away. There was no way I could avoid the robot and cross that open space.

There were metal walkways around the walls of the hangar some thirty feet or so above the deck. If I could get up there, I might stand a chance of running the length of the hangar. The robot's size gave it an advantage on the open hangar deck, but its weight and bulk would slow it down on the narrow walkway. There were metal staircases at various points around the hangar, but I would have to reach one well ahead of the robot. Otherwise it would tear the stairway down before I managed to climb up to the walkway. How could I slow it for long enough to get across to the nearest stairs and safely up them? Hitting it with a truck hadn't worked.

I dodged behind another crate, thinking of trying a shot at the eye screens in the robot's head – they looked much less substantial than the rest of its armour. But there was every chance they were formed from some sort of synthetic diamond rather than glass, so I decided to save my shot. I needed explosives. A big bomb. Not for the first time, I wished I had my backpack with me – though I wasn't sure that the little limpet bombs that I had managed to scrounge up for this trip would have been enough. But it would have been nice just to have something. Even the red fire axe strapped to the back of my pack would have been better than the nothing I had in my hand at that moment. I would far rather go down fighting than be a sitting duck waiting to get picked off.

Thought of the axe triggered another idea in my brain. There would be firefighting equipment in the hangar – and it might include something I could use against the robot. Dousing it in fire extinguisher foam might slow it down. Or I could chop off its leg with a pair of those hydraulic jaws they use to cut people out of wreckage. I looked around. There were two sets of doors painted red and marked 'Fire Control' – one on each side of the hangar. The one closest to me lay within sprinting distance. Just about. There wasn't much margin for error. If that fire equipment storage room was locked, I'd be sliced into cutlets by robo-butcher.

Deep rapid breaths to get oxygen into my blood – then I set off. I was aware of the twinge in my thigh where the wound had been knitted together, but I ignored it. Arms pumping, boots slamming against the deck – this was all about speed not stealth.

I felt the deck vibrating. The robot in pursuit. And now it had decided that it too should run. I didn't dare look back, knowing its massive stride would quickly eat up the distance between us. I concentrated on my target. Twenty yards ahead of me. When I was within twenty feet of it, I glanced at the lock beside the storage room door. The tiny red light was bad news. Locked. Why would anyone lock up fire safety equipment? Why should I need to be authorised personnel to grab a fire extinguisher? Not slacking my pace, I fumbled for the ID tag that Trixie had made for me. If this didn't open the lock, I was dead meat.

I didn't slow until the very last second and I didn't stop at all. I slammed into the red door and slapped the ID tag against the lock. It seemed an age before the red light blinked and turned green. I pushed the door open and ducked inside, banging it shut behind me. I hit the button to relock the door and then smashed the control box with the butt of my pistol. The robot wouldn't be able to unlock it from outside and that would slow it down – for a little while. But I was under no illusions – I had only bought myself a couple of minutes. The storage room door was airtight, but it didn't have the strength of an external airlock. Who knew how long it could withstand an attack by a giant cleaver. I had to move fast.

It was a small room, part closet and part changing room. Racks of equipment were neatly stacked and labelled. Rubbery-looking suits hung on pegs, looking like deflated and decapitated corpses. And there were shiny yellow fireman's helmets. I grabbed one and jammed it on my head. It wouldn't provide much protection against the cleaver, but it looked great.

Behind me, the robot was hammering on the locked door, first with its massive metal fist and then with the cleaver. A spiderweb crack appeared in the thick glass window, but it didn't shatter. Dents started to show in the steel plate as blow after blow struck the door close to the frame. It wouldn't withstand this onslaught for long.

There were two sizes of fire axe. I tucked the handle of one of the smaller ones into my belt as a spare and took one of the bigger ones as my primary. If I was cornered, a well-aimed chop at the robot's neck might be enough to slow it down. But I wanted to avoid getting that close if I could. There were coils of hose – the big flat ones and ordinary plastic pipe – but they weren't connected to anything. You evidently had to attach them to some kind of faucet outside in the hangar. Pity – a high-pressure hose might have knocked the robot back and maybe sent fluid far enough inside it to cause a short circuit.

There were more heavy blows and then a nasty ripping sound as the edge of the blade tore through the metal. I glanced back. It was only a narrow cut, but it meant the door would soon give way.

I found a large metal toolbox – almost too heavy to lift. I couldn't take it with me but maybe I could swing it at the robot and knock it off its feet. Or maybe not. There were also a couple of rolls containing smaller tools and I stuffed one of these into the leg pocket of my khakis. For balance, I shoved a roll of duct tape and a larger hammer into the pocket on the other side.

As I had expected, there were several sets of hydraulically operated jaws. The largest of them would take off the robot's head – but only if it lay still long enough for me to use them on its neck. I didn't think there was any chance of that happening. I needed something I could deploy more rapidly.

Fire extinguishers. A whole row of them. Carbon dioxide ones for electrical fires and wet foam ones for other types of flames, all clearly marked. I could use foam to blind the robot's visual systems and CO_2 to confuse its heat sensors. That might be enough for me to dodge around it, but I still needed to travel the length of the hangar at something close to light speed.

If this had been a movie, the hero would have found a fireman's motorcycle conveniently stashed in a corner. But I couldn't see anything with wheels – except the hand trucks the larger fire extinguishers were on, and these only had two wheels. I couldn't really see myself scooting across the hangar on one of them. Not on *one* of them. But perhaps two?

A crash. The glass in the door finally exploded inwards in a shower of fragments. Time was running out for our hero as he frantically bound two of the hand trucks together with duct tape to form a sort of go-kart.

The door split down the middle and the robot's giant hand tore out the remaining pieces of metal.

Chapter Twenty-Four

I had the fire extinguishers lined up ready. There'd been no time to test-fire them, so I pulled the pins on them two at a time. I was hoping the robots had maintained these as well as they had everything else. I squeezed the triggers.

With a person, you can predict how they are likely to react to a loud noise and a cloud of gas. The shock will cause them to back away and the movement will be involuntary – caused by some primitive survival mechanism. But robots don't have the same in-built reactions. I needed the robot to retreat from the doorway, at least slightly, so that I could get out. I set off the carbon dioxide extinguisher, knowing it would create a cloud that would blind both of us. The robot wouldn't know where I was – but I would be at an equal disadvantage. The CO_2 would clear quickly and I would need to be ready with the foam, covering the robot's head to blind it so that I could make my escape.

These things never go exactly to plan. The blast of sound and dry-ice smoke did make the robot pause to assess the danger. But it didn't step back. It kept coming into the little storage room, ducking its head to get through the door. It almost filled the space. Through the fog, I could just about make out the lights on its casing. But the air would soon clear. And even blind, in this confined space, the robot was dangerous. It swept the blade backwards and forwards, slicing the rubber suits across the middle and almost doing the same for me.

The CO_2 extinguisher was exhausted and I tossed it towards the back of the room. This attracted the robot's attention and it moved towards the sound. I was able to dodge around it so that it no longer stood between me and the door. I could make my bid for freedom. I pushed my improvised go-kart out through the wrecked door into the hangar. I picked up two of the foam fire extinguishers.

"Hey, Chuckles!" I shouted. The robot turned. I triggered the fire extinguishers. The one in my left-hand misfired and spluttered. The one in the right doused the robot's head in a thick coating of wet foam. I couldn't decide if it looked like a giant snow cone or the victim of a mad barber.

The robot lunged forward blindly, swiping with the cleaver. I stepped back, but not quickly enough. The blade sliced across the front of my shirt and I felt it skim across the flesh underneath. It was hardly more than a papercut, but it stung like a bitch. I staggered backwards out of the door, throwing the two dead extinguishers at the robot as I went.

The exit doors at the other end of the hangar looked like they were miles away. It was a long straight run, which was a good thing because my home-made go-kart had no steering. I placed one foot on the kart. My intention was to stand and scoot along until I picked up speed and then crouch down on it for the rest of the journey, scooting with my foot only if the kart slowed down.

Surfboarding and skateboarding had never really been my thing. I prefer something with a motor. But as a thief, my sense of balance is pretty good. I set off, hoping the duct tape would hold together with my weight onboard.

"Wheeee!" I scooted across the hangar deck.

Behind I could hear the robot crashing about in the storage room. Maybe it was trying to put together its own go-kart. I didn't look back. If I lost my balance or hit an obstacle, my run would come to an inglorious end and I wouldn't get a second attempt.

The doors at the end of the hangar were approaching rapidly. I was crouching on the kart now, feet off the ground, relying on the momentum I had built up. The bearings in the wheels must have been pretty well-oiled because there was very little friction to slow me down. I think the ship must have been tilted downwards at that end too, helping to carry me onwards. As the doors came closer still, my speed became something of a concern. The kart had no brakes.

A crash behind me as the robot broke free from the storage room. It began pounding across the deck towards me. But I wasn't worried by this. Victory was at hand – my head-start was too great. I was going to make it! Of course, if I slammed into the doors and knocked myself unconscious, my celebration would be short-lived. As would I. I could either try and slow myself by dragging one foot on the ground – and risk veering off course to one side. Or I could wait until the last moment and then throw myself off the kart. I decided on the second option.

An angry roar echoed around the hangar. I thought it was the robot. Some acoustic anomaly was making it sound like the roar came from in front of me.

The double doors at the end of the hangar slid open – and in the gap stood the one-eyed dragon. It roared again as it saw me heading straight towards it.

Chapter Twenty-Five

I threw myself off the kart and let it go skidding towards the dragon. I scrambled to my feet and launched myself towards the nearest stairs. If I could get up onto the walkway, I might stand a chance of escaping both death by dragon and death by robot.

Apparently, it wasn't enough that I face a giant metal gladiator in this arena – Fate had decreed that I must also face a ravenous beast. I was a Christian thrown to the lions. A matador at the mercy of a raging bull. And all I had to defend myself was a low-powered handgun, a fire axe, and half a roll of duct tape. This was going to be a challenge for even my improvisational skills.

I reached the metal stairs and lurched up them. The rapid *thump-click* of the dragon's clawed feet hitting the deck was closer than I would have liked. He could leap and climb and was a much more agile pursuer than the robot. Once I was up on the walkway, I could use the axe to defend myself. But if the dragon seized me while I was on the stairs, I would be consumed in bloody gobbets. Using hands and feet I scrambled up the steps. I felt the staircase shake as the dragon jumped onto it.

A movement way over to my right caught my attention. The robot was climbing another staircase, heading for the same walkway as me. I was going to be attacked from two directions.

The pounding of the dragon's steps and those of the robot were causing the stairs and walkway to vibrate. Could this old metalwork support their combined weight? Not to mention the stresses of any sort of fight up there. Knowing my luck, I'd be the only one who didn't survive the drop when the walkway collapsed and the other two would fight over my broken body. Morbid, I know. But if this wasn't an appropriate moment for dark thoughts, I don't know what is.

The movement of the walkway had achieved earthquake proportions by the time I got to the top of the stairs. The robot was already on the walkway, striding towards my position. I risked a glanced back and saw the dragon was having some difficulty on the stairs. It didn't – or couldn't – use its upper claws to hold onto the handrails and so was trying to use its tail for balance. And the claws of its feet seemed to be getting caught on the metal mesh that the steps were made from. A good solid kick would probably send the dragon tumbling backwards. But I didn't want to risk either of my favourite feet anywhere near those shark-like jaws. But I did still have explosive rounds left in my pistol. They wouldn't penetrate the dragon's thick scaly hide, but the impact might knock it off its feet. I took aim and fired – two rapid shots.

The dragon's look of surprise was almost comical as it fell backwards. I saw it hit the hangar deck and lie still. Then it twitched, regaining its senses, and got back to its feet. This obviously concerned me, but the robot presented a more immediate threat. It was striding closer and closer. I backed away. Behind me was a sealed metal door. It might open if I pressed my ID tag to it, but it might not. My only other possible escape was to jump over the railing – and learn to fly before I hit the deck thirty feet below.

The robot was level with the stairs I had climbed. It stopped and looked down. The dragon had started up the steps again. With a few swift, powerful swipes of its cleaver, the robot sliced through the metalwork of the stairs, cutting through each of the points that supported the structure. The staircase tipped sideways, throwing the dragon back onto the deck. The clatter as the stairs hit the deck echoed around the hangar.

The dragon leapt to its feet and shook itself. It looked up at the robot and roared, as if to say 'You bastard!' It squatted back on its haunches and then launched itself upwards. Teeth snapped together with a loud *clack!* a few inches below the walkway.

The robot brandished its cleaver as if to say 'Back off, reptile, the human is mine!' Then it turned its attention to me.

I had my back to the door and was frantically tapping my ID tag against the lock's sensor, trying to get it to open. But apparently I lacked the necessary clearance level and needed to consult my supervisor.

The robot stopped a few yards away. There were still bits of the sticky foam on its head. It looked like it had been hit with a cream pie. It stared at me. Then it looked down at the walkway at its feet. I wondered what thoughts were echoing around its metal skull.

Off to my right, I could hear the clacking of the dragon's teeth as it kept leaping up. It seemed to be trying to reach me now rather than the robot. Presumably because I smelt more edible. Unless it suddenly grew wings, I didn't think it would reach me before the robot did.

I looked around me, desperately seeking something that I could cling to or climb up. But the walls were smooth. No pipes, no wires – not even a line of rivet heads. The roof beams were way above me – not within leaping distance. I took the hammer out of my pocket and began hitting the door's lock mechanism. This caused some sparks but achieved nothing useful.

The robot looked over the railing at the dragon, then at me, and finally back down at the walkway at its feet. And I knew what it was thinking.

"Please, don't..." I said.

The robot was standing directly over an iron pillar that supported the walkway. The section I stood on was supported by the same pillar at one end and at the other by bolts in the steel wall behind me. The robot was calculating what would happen if it sliced through the metalwork so that my section of the walkway was no longer supported by the pillar. Would the bolts in the wall be strong enough to hold it up unaided?

"Please..." I said again.

The robot gave something that looked like a shrug – and began hacking at the metal. The walkway under me shook. I pressed my ID tag to the smashed lock again and again, hoping for a last minute miracle. Below me, the dragon had stopped leaping and was looking up expectantly. Perhaps it understood what was going on. It was waiting for dinner to drop into its lap.

The robot sliced through the metal handrail and the barrier meant to stop people accidentally tumbling off the walkway. Then it began chopping away at the walkway like a demented woodcutter. When it reached the halfway point, my section of walkway lurched and angled downwards a few inches on one side. I gripped the handrail. I had to do something. I was still clutching the fire axe. I swung it at the glass window in the door. The blade bounced off without leaving a mark. It had to be strong enough to withstand rapid depressurisation when the hangar doors were opened. My puny axe wasn't going to do much damage. But I tried a few more whacks anyway.

The robot's chopping was much more effective. A few more well-placed blows and the walkway was cut all the way across. It sagged downwards about eight inches at the end nearest the robot, supported only by the bolts in the metal wall. I glanced towards the brackets that were the only things between me and the jaws of death. There were four stout bolts fixing each bracket to the wall. They were all holding. For now.

The robot looked down at the sagging walkway. It couldn't step onto it and get any closer to me because the damaged walkway wouldn't support its weight. If the bolts held, the robot and I were stuck in a sort of stalemate. It lifted one foot slowly and moved it forward towards the unsupported section of the walkway. It pressed down with the foot. My section sagged downwards some more, and when the robot lifted its foot the floor didn't come all the way back up again. It was sagging down about a foot now. The robot put its foot forward again. This time he pressed down and released several times, bouncing the walkway up and down. Whether it was trying to shake me loose or snap the bolts, I didn't know. Each bounce caused the walkway to bend downwards a little more.

On the deck below, the dragon was looking up and snarling. 'Get on with it – I'm hungry!'

Another bounce and one of the bolts snapped with a loud *crack!* It was the outermost bolt of the bracket over the deck.

Bounce. Bounce. *Crack!* Another of the outer bolts snapped.

Bounce. *Crack! Crack!* All of the outside bolts were gone. With a grinding and metallic screeching, the walkway twisted and tilted. It dropped three feet on the outside. As I desperately tried to cling on with both hands, I had to let the fire axe go, watching it slide over the edge and fall. I knew the bolts in the other bracket must fail soon. If the walkway fell, there was nothing for me to cling onto. The robot would watch as I dropped – and then give the thumbs-down, ordering the dragon in for the kill.

The sounds of tortured metal continued, the walkway dipping lower and lower, not needing any encouragement from the robot now.

Crack! A bolt shot out of the wall, fired outwards like a bullet. I felt it skim passed my left arm. It was lucky it missed me – I might have been hurt.

The walkway dipped down even further. Inevitably, the other bolts snapped. The walkway fell.

The dragon roared. The walkway crashed down on top of the dragon. This cushioned the impact – but only a little. But it didn't matter. As the walkway fell, I launched myself into the air. I flipped over and to the right, avoiding the falling metalwork. I hit the deck with my knees bent and rolled. Graceful as a cat.

I glanced towards the dragon. It was moving under the fallen walkway – stunned but not dead. The robot was standing on the truncated walkway looking down at me. It stepped off the edge and when its feet hit the deck it felt like an earthquake. Graceful as a refrigerator.

The robot stomped towards me, raising the cleaver.

With a roar, the dragon heaved the metalwork off its back. It stood assessing the situation for a moment. The dragon launched itself up onto the robot's back.

Dragon versus robot. It was a scene from a video game. The dragon clung to the robot's back, wrapping its tail around the robot's middle and trying to bite into its shoulder and head. I would have loved to see how this celebrity deathmatch ended – but I thought my time would be better spent escaping while they were both distracted. I took off at a sprint, heading for the doors through which the dragon had made its entrance.

A shadow passed overhead. Something heavy hit the deck in front of me. The dragon. The robot had thrown it, using it to stop my escape. I skidded to a halt – ready to go on if the dragon didn't move. Dead or just stunned, I would run around it. It uncurled itself and I distinctly heard the sound of bones popping as it stood and flexed its spine. It looked down at me and did the roaring thing. I was close enough to smell how bad its breath was. Close enough to die. It leapt forward. There was nothing I could do except brace for impact.

I fell backwards under the force of it. I felt claws digging into my legs, pinning me down. The dragon raised its head, bellowing triumphantly. Then it opened its jaws wide and dipped down towards my head, thick poisonous saliva hanging in strings from its pus-yellow tongue. It was going to chew my face off.

The robot's blade flashed down, cleaving the dragon's head in two. I was showered with foul-smelling blood and bits of brain matter. It didn't taste anything like chicken. As it died, the dragon voided its bladder and bowels on me. A final indignity.

I was pinned down under the dragon's dead weight. The robot jerked its blade free from the beast's skull. It raised the blade, blood dripping from it. My skull was next in line for splitting. I was going to die. And in my last moment of life, I vowed that I would come back and haunt Old Jack Sterling for getting me into this mess.

The robot stood with its blade raised, ready for the kill. Was it prolonging the agony? Or was it having second thoughts? Or perhaps subjective time had slowed to a crawl to allow me to make the most of my last seconds of life? I was probably supposed to spend this time contemplating the life I had lived and repenting my sins. But all I was really thinking at that moment was that the dead dragon was crushing my scronies. And then, bizarrely, I heard Old Jack's voice – as if recalling the old devil's name had somehow summoned him.

"Well, aren't you a sorry-looking sight!" Old Jack's voice said.

I didn't want his voice to be the last sound I ever heard – even if I was imagining it.

He moved into view and stared down at me.

"What is that *smell?*" he asked.

Chapter Twenty-Six

Nobody wanted to come near me. I was covered in squit, blood, and swazz. Some of the blood was mine. I smelt like a walking septic tank. Old Jack's men had rolled the dragon off me and then quickly backed away. Far away. I got to my feet slowly, trying to ignore the aches and pains and the overwhelming feeling of fatigue.

Jack Sterling looked like an old pirate, so his crew had decided they should dress like pirates and had all gone off to the costume shop to pick their outfits. It was the only explanation that made sense. As far as I could see, there were five of them plus Jack.

The biggest of them was mostly belly. His head was shaved smooth and shiny but the dark hair on his forearms was longer than that on my head. He wore tatty sneakers and walked like his feet hurt. The smallest of the crew was a scrawny runt who looked like his grandmother had been a brown rat. His eyes were drawn into a permanent squint and I think he was breaking the top teeth in for a giant rabbit.

And then there were the twins. Brothers, I reckoned, until I noticed one of them had breasts. They dressed alike and spoke alike and probably had the sort of relationship geneticists frown upon. There was a lot of giggling and looking into each other's eyes. Even if it was platonic, it was still creepy. I guessed she had chosen their costume because he was unsteady in the high heel boots.

Tattoos seemed to be obligatory and most of them looked self-inflicted. You know that thing where you see something misspelled and you wonder if it's you that's wrong? That happened to me a couple of times just then. And you should never get something inked in a language you can't read. 'Please may I go to the lavatory' isn't poetry or prayer no matter how you translate it.

If I was putting together a crew, I wouldn't pick any of this lot. Maybe pirates are in short supply on Saphira.

"I can't tell you how pleased I am to see you," I said to Old Jack, nodding towards the deactivated robot.

"You might want to hold off on the hugging," Jack said. "This isn't a rescue mission. We're here for the loot." He was staring down at the dead dragon. "Pity about the skull. You can get good money for a whole one."

I looked up at the robot. It was standing with the bloody cleaver raised. Still as a statue. "How did you...?"

Old Jack held up a battered remote control unit. It was discoloured and held together with duct tape. "Had it from one of my old shipmates," he said. "I wasn't sure if it still worked."

He tossed the remote to one of his crewmen, the fifth member of the team. He was a technician who had gone down the cyber-pirate route. His head was shaved at the sides and the mohawk was bleached platinum blond. He wore very tight black leather jeans and an oxblood leather vest showed off his bony chest to good effect. On a slow night in dim light, I might have bought him a drink. He used the remote to reset the robot into a neutral standing position. Then he made the robot kneel. It was still as tall as he was.

"What about the other security robots?" Jack asked.

"They won't be a problem," I said.

"You took out a dozen of them? I'm impressed."

"I'd have taken out this one too – but he just won't die."

"If you can't beat 'em, recruit 'em," Jack said. He nodded towards his crewman who was using a laser cutter to make a small circular opening in the robot's chest.

"Do you think a restrainer will work on that thing?" I asked.

Restraining devices were fitted to all modern robots by law. They limited a robot's capacity for self-motivated action – kept them docile. But this wasn't a modern robot.

"If that robot doesn't do what it's told," Jack said, "the device will fuse all its internal circuits. It won't cause any trouble."

The platinum blond crewman unfastened the robot's cleaver and tossed it aside. In its place he fitted an ordinary robotic forearm and hand. It more or less matched the robot's right arm, though it looked like it had been patched up with bits of old metal.

"All done," the crewman reported to his captain.

"Then fire him back up," Jack said.

The crewman looked about as doubtful as I felt.

"It's either that or you get to carry all the loot out yourself," Old Jack told him.

You don't sign on to be a pirate in order to do heavy lifting. The crewman thumbed the 'on' button on the remote.

Still on its knees, the robot emitted a faint whine and then began to vibrate.

"It's trying to fight the restraint," I said, backing away.

"It won't win," Old Jack said. But he also took a step back when the vibrations became a more pronounced shimmying. It looked as though the robot was trying to shake the restraining device out of its chest.

The shaking stopped abruptly. The robot rose to its feet. We all took another step back.

"Robot! Stand on one leg," Jack said.

The robot lifted one leg from the deck. Its balance was perfect.

"Rub your stomach," Jack ordered.

The robot's right hand began making circular movements over the spot where its stomach would have been – still balanced on one leg.

"Clockwise," Jack said.

The robot changed the direction of its motions.

"Pat yourself on the head with your other hand," Jack said.

The robot did as it was asked.

"Looks fine to me," Old Jack said to the crewman. "Now get to work."

"Aye, aye, cap'n," the crewman said. "Robot! Follow me."

The robot walked after the departing crewman, still patting its head and rubbing its tummy.

"Machines are stupid," Jack said. He turned and looked me up and down. "You've looked better, Quin."

All I could do was shrug.

"We should get those wounds cleaned," Jack said. "Who knows what filthy diseases that ugly scracker was carrying."

I had puncture wounds in both legs from the dragon's claws. They weren't deep but the old man was right, there was a real danger of infection. "There's a medbay down the corridor," I said.

Old Jack indicated that I should lead the way. He walked with me – but he didn't get too close.

After I stopped screaming, Old Jack said, "You've done that before." He pointed to the fading scar on my thigh. I'd used the meat-stitcher to fix the puncture wounds.

"I fell into a tree," I said, rubbing the old wound. I was sitting in the medbay in my underwear and having that déjà vu thing.

"*Into* one?" Jack said. He was sitting on the other bed watching me administer my own treatment.

"Long story," I said. "How did you get here?"

"We flew," Jack said, choosing to take my question literally. "Cargo lifter. We landed it next to the ship."

Why hadn't I thought of that? Of course, Jack Sterling had the advantage of having been here before – he knew the lay of the land.

"And the prison?" I asked. "I thought you were a lifer." I helped myself to more of the outdated antibiotics.

"Bribery," Jack said.

I nodded. "I'm going next door to take a shower and find some clothes," I said.

"I'd just burn it," Jack said.

"This jacket and I have been through a lot together," I said. I was holding it under the shower, trying to scrub it clean. There was no soap and when I'd stood under it, the water had been cold and had a faint metallic smell. But it still made it into my top ten best showers of all time.

I ransacked the closets in a couple of crewmen's rooms and found myself an outfit similar to my last one. I kept my boots and jacket – trying to pretend they didn't smell of lizard incontinence.

Old Jack was following me around, pretending to be my best friend. He didn't trust me. The feeling was mutual.

"What happened to your computer?" he asked, pointing to the scorch mark and missing loop on the shoulder of my jacket.

"Trixie is gone," I said. I could have told him the whole story, but I didn't. That would have made things too easy for him. I was waiting for him to come out with the question he really wanted to ask. The only thing he cared about.

"Did you find the vault?" he asked. There it was. He tried to make it sound casual.

"This whole thing was a set-up, wasn't it?" I asked. "The treasure map – all of it." I'd seen him scratch his arm earlier – there was no sign of the scar he'd shown me in the jail cell.

Old Jack stared into my eyes, trying to decide whether to lie to me. He shrugged. "I needed a thief. A good one. The last time I came out to the *Celestia* I lost two men. Barely got away myself."

I'd met his lost crewmen. Mr. Skellington in the airlock and the Man-With-No-Hands in the vault.

"You knew who I was," I said, "when we were in the prison?"

"Before that," Jack said. "Maurice worked for me."

Maurice was One-Eyed Jack, the poker player I'd won the sand yacht from – and the reason I'd ended up in jail. This old pirate had engineered the whole thing.

"You bribed your way *into* the prison, didn't you? Into my cell."

"The warden and I are old friends. Usually I pay him to let people out."

"Augie and Paulie Pickles?"

"They work for me too," Jack said.

"And my escape?"

"The guards were asked to look the other way," Jack said, "and the night-watchman."

This was the second time in six months that I'd been conned. I was definitely losing my edge.

"Are you going to open the vault for me, Quin?" Jack asked.

I stared into his eyes, trying to decide whether to lie to him. I shrugged. "It's open."

Old Jack smiled broadly, revealing a gold tooth I'd never seen before. "I knew you could do it."

"Getting in was easier than getting out," I said.

Old Jack slapped me on the back. "Come on, lad, we've got work to do."

As it turned out, he meant *I* had work to do.

Old Jack hadn't been exaggerating – they had landed the cargo lifter next to the *Celestia.* Right next to it. The lifter looked pretty ancient. I wouldn't want to risk trying to take it up into orbit, though technically it was designed to shuttle cargo from a planet to a space station or orbiting craft. It was effectively a cockpit at the front connected by a long spine to the engines at the rear. The space in between was occupied by a large detachable container that you could fill with stuff. Stolen loot in the present instance. The pirates had opened one of the battleship's larger hatches so they could get in and out with their takings.

The robot was standing immobile on the jungle floor between the two craft.

"That thing almost killed me," I muttered.

"Lucky for you we came when we did," the crewman with the platinum mohawk said. The others referred to him as Blondie.

"I'm counting my blessings," I said, staring down at what he was fastening around my ankle. The bulge on one side of it was a tracking device. The bulge on the other side was an explosive. The tracker monitored my location in relation to a second device – a little box attached to Old Jack's gun belt. If I moved beyond a certain range, the explosive would blow my leg off. I was familiar with the device – I've been in penitentiaries that use them. And I've seen wives fit them to their husbands.

Old Jack strode out of the *Celestia* and addressed me and the robot. "My boys are going through the ship, boxing up anything of value. I want you two to carry them into the hold."

"You want us to carry your men?" the robot asked.

"I want you to carry the boxes up the ramp and stack them neatly inside the container. Do you understand?"

"Yes, master," the robot said.

"Yes, master," I mimicked.

Old Jack scowled at me. He looked up at the robot. "And if he tries to escape," Jack pointed at me, "you are to stop him, before he gets far enough to blow himself up. Got it?"

The robot nodded its head slowly.

Old Jack turned to Blondie. "Watch both of them. I'm going for the Navigator."

The old captain disappeared back inside the battleship. He was in for a big disappointment when he got to the vault.

The first of the crates of swag were sent out a few minutes later. I popped open one of the big black boxes – it was filled with handguns, rifles, and ammunition. Other boxes held the decapitated security robots. This was going to be quite a haul for the pirates. And it would probably be their first trip of many.

Our platinum blond pirate guard told us to stop looking and start loading. I was rapidly going off him. And the daylight showed up the flaws in his complexion. The robot picked up one of the big crates as if it weighed nothing. I struggled with one of the smaller ones.

After about twenty minutes, Old Jack Sterling stomped back out. His face was dark with anger. He was holding a Bertie the Bear toy in one hand and a big gun in the other.

"Where's the Navigator?"

Chapter Twenty-Seven

Old Jack threw the stuffed toy at my feet. "Where is it?" he asked again. He pointed the big gun at the middle of my forehead.

Blondie decided he would rather be somewhere else and edged away.

"The Navigator was gone before I opened the vault," I said. I was too tired to be scared. "Somebody switched it for Bertie."

"How do I know you're telling the truth?"

I shrugged. "You'll have to ask the robot. The Navigator wasn't in there, I swear. But I did find your late crew member's severed arms – they were on top of Bertie."

Old Jack looked like he didn't know what to believe. "Robot! Get over here."

The robot ambled towards us. Old Jack pointed the big gun at its face. "Where is the Navigator?"

"The Navigator was taken from its vault immediately after the crash," the robot said. "It is no longer on the *Celestia*."

Old Jack turned towards me, keeping the gun on the robot. "Is it telling the truth?"

"Can robots lie?" I asked.

"Good point." The old pirate turned back towards the robot. He lowered the gun. "Who could have taken it?" he wondered aloud.

"Who else knew it was here?" I asked. I knew Old Jack hadn't been the only survivor of the battleship's crew to make it down onto Saphira. I thought it best to direct his suspicions towards them – especially now that I had figured out where the Navigator was.

"I reckon it must have been Piggy Partridge," Old Jack said to himself. "The sly old crook is getting his revenge from beyond the grave."

"Piggy Partridge?" I said. "What happened to him?"

"Never you mind," Jack snapped. "You two get back to work. I want everything loaded before nightfall."

I watched him stomp away and wished him a slow and painful death. Neither I nor the robot made any move towards the pile of crates that needed loading. We were alone, for the moment. Blondie had beaten a hasty retreat when Old Jack appeared and had not yet returned.

"You did not answer his question fully," the robot said. It was the first time it had spoken to me directly since it had been restrained. It had a deep masculine voice – you could imagine him reading the news or reciting Shakespeare.

I looked up at him. "Did you want me to?"

"I am grateful that you did not."

"The Navigator is inside you," I said.

"How long have you known?"

"Long enough," I said. Subconsciously, I had known for some time – or so I told myself. But it was only when I had seen the robot avoid direct answers to Old Jack's questions that I really *knew*. The clumsy alterations to the robot's chest cavity were an obvious clue that I had missed in all of the previous excitement.

"I would prefer that this fact not be shared with the others," the robot said.

If Old Jack asked me directly, would I reveal the Navigator's location? If he *asked* me, no. But if he tortured me, I'd probably give it up. And hope to be able to steal it back later.

"Your secret's safe with me, chief," I told the robot.

"Why are you two just standing there?" The blond numbskull had returned.

"Nobody told us what to do," the robot said.

"Get back to work," the young pirate said.

"Yes, master," the robot and I said in unison.

Had the robot just lied to our guard? This question only occurred to me later.

When we were both inside the cargo lifter's hold – and out of earshot of the leather-clad cyber-pirate – the robot stopped in front of me to prevent me from going back outside.

"I would like to request a favour," it said.

Only a few hours ago, this hulking machine had been trying to kill me – and it had very nearly succeeded. More than once. Now we were both victims in the same predicament. But that didn't mean that our common enemy made us friends all of a sudden. I looked up at its eye screens and frowned.

"What sort of favour?"

"Will you cover for me?" It was an oddly human question. "I need to access the cockpit of this craft without being observed."

"What's the plan?" I asked.

"I will contact military command. I must send them the coordinates of this location and report the fate of the *Celestia.*"

I could have made another attempt to convince the robot that the war was over. But it needed evidence that I could not provide. Maybe if it received a reply to its coded message, it would realise that I had been telling the truth.

"I'll cover for you," I said. "How long do you need?"

"Ten minutes should be sufficient."

I nodded and went back outside.

"Hey!" I attracted the attention of our guard. "It's thirsty work. Can I have some water?"

Blondie looked at me suspiciously. "Where's the robot?"

"He doesn't need water," I said.

"Where is he?"

"He's restacking the crates – so we can fit more in. The fewer trips you have to make back here, the better – am I right?"

He didn't return my friendly smile, but his frown wasn't quite as deep. He went over to the solar-powered cooler box and pulled out a bottle. He tossed it to me. I deliberately missed the catch, letting the bottle fall to the ground. I had to use every ruse I could think of to prolong this. After I'd drained the water, I told him I needed a swazz. He rolled his eyes and shook his head. He kept an eye on me while I stood behind the bush but he didn't try and sneak a peek. Maybe I wasn't his type. As I was zipping up, I saw the robot leave the cargo lifter's cockpit and go back into the hold.

The robot and I kept loading crates well into the afternoon. I wanted to ask him what he had learned, but a change of guard meant we never got much time to talk without being overheard. The twins were our new guardians. They were called Bella and Bolly – I kid you not. He stood just inside the hold and she took up a position near the crates that had come out of the *Celestia*. It was more than an hour before he became bored and went to join his sister-sweetheart.

"There is no military government anymore," the robot said, as if it couldn't quite believe this.

"Everything is run by civilians now," I said.

"Is that better?"

"You'd hope so, wouldn't you?"

"The *Celestia* no longer needs to be protected," the robot said, looking up at the wreck of the battleship.

"But you must still make sure that the Navigator doesn't fall into the wrong hands," I said.

"Yes."

"Did you call for reinforcements?" I asked.

"Why? Do you think we need help?" the robot asked. There was no expression on his face but if he'd been able to, I think he would have raised an eyebrow and smiled. I wasn't sure what to make of this. I had a nagging feeling that I was missing something important. We carried on stacking crates.

Chapter Twenty-Eight

The left arm that had been fitted to the robot was badly scratched and looked like it might have come from another robot. There was something stencilled on the upper arm but the only letters I could see clearly were L-J. Stacking boxes was mindless work, so I amused myself by trying to work out what the word or words might be. After an hour or so I hadn't come up with anything close to a sensible answer. If it was a name I had Valjean, Pal Joey, Steel Jaw or Killjoy. If the metal had originally been the label on something I had *metal jars, steel jugs, gerbil jello, snail juice,* or *weasel jizz*. At which point I had become irritated by the whole thing. "What is that?" I asked, pointing.

"It is my arm."

"No, the stencilling – what does it say?"

The robot looked at it. "Apple Juice," it said.

The 'e' had obviously been worn away. "That's just cheating." I slammed down the crate I was holding and stalked out of the hold.

"Is something bothering you?" the robot asked, following me.

"Aside from being held prisoner and treated as a slave, you mean?"

"Yes, aside from that."

I glared at it, trying to work out whether it was trying to be funny. But it was a robot. Robots don't do funny.

"I'm hungry," I said. "I get grouchy when I haven't eaten."

"Would you like to eat?" the robot asked. "The cargo lifter is quite well provisioned."

"I can't just walk in there and help myself to dinner."

"Why not?"

Good question. "Well, because..." Because I was starting to think of myself as nothing but a labourer who must serve his pirate masters.

"Tell me what you require and I will fetch it," the robot said.

"Surprise me."

It disappeared back into the cargo lifter's cabin and brought me back a beef stroganoff with rice in a silver self-heating pouch, two bright green apples, and two icy cold bottles of light beer. I activated the pouch and then dug in with my fingers – until I saw that the robot was watching me and shaking its head. It held out a spoon.

I drained the last of the beer and tucked the second apple in my pocket for later. "You were a firefighter originally?" I asked.

"This casing belonged to a fire control robot, yes."

"Are the modifications your own?"

"I had to conduct my own maintenance. I also added armour as protection against attack from the Crichtorax."

"You've fought dragons before?"

"I have been closer to them than one might wish to be."

"You answer questions like a politician."

"I did not lie."

"But you also don't tell the whole truth."

"Perhaps we have more in common than you think."

"What's your name?" I asked.

"I do not have one."

"I've got to call you something."

"We are usually referred to by the name of our ship."

"I'm not calling you *Celestia,*" I said. "I'm going to call you... L-J or... 'Little John', that's it, you're Little John."

"Little John?"

"It's either that or 'Scrappy'."

The robot said something that sounded like *humph* and walked away. "If you think you're Robin Hood, you're kidding yourself," he said.

"I'll have you know that I am an accomplished thief who is wanted on more than twenty worlds," I said, following him over to the pile of crates that we still had to load.

"Fourteen," the robot said. "I accessed your record while I was in the cockpit. Most of your exploits seem to end like this one."

"That's not true," I protested. "I've just had a run of bad luck recently."

The robot made the *humph* sound again. "It is true that you have led a colourful life," he said. I think he knew he'd offended me and was trying to smooth things over.

"Not really," I said. "I've been alive for thirty-two years and I have an ex-husband and an ex-wife. Well, *two* ex-wives – but the last one I was only married to for three weeks."

"It took her that long to make up her mind?"

"It's a complicated story."

"Offspring?"

"None that I know of."

The robot picked up the largest of the remaining crates and headed back into the cargo lifter. I lifted one of the smallest crates and followed.

"What about you?" I asked.

"Robots cannot produce children."

"I mean – tell me about your life."

"I was brought into service one month before the *Celestia* was launched – and I have been with her ever since."

"I admire your loyalty."

"It is just programming."

I watched him for a few moments, trying to figure out what it was that was bothering me. "You're not like any robot I've ever met."

The robot just looked at me blankly.

"You seem more..." I shrugged. "Never mind. Let's get this job done."

"We should not hurry to complete the task," the robot said.

I raised an eyebrow. "No?"

"When their plunder has been loaded into this vessel, you will have no further value to them."

"They won't kill me. They'll take me back with them."

"As a witness to their crimes?"

"They won't kill me." I was less certain the second time I said it.

"As salvage, will I fetch a good price?" the robot asked.

Despite its mismatched parts, the robot was still a valuable find – especially with its high calibre accessories. Military robots were now banned on most inhabited worlds – so they brought a great price on the black market. I explained this to him.

"Then they will take me back with them," he said. "I would prefer not to be taken."

"You want my advice?" I said. "Keep up the dumb slave act until they get you back to somewhere half-civilised and then make your escape."

The robot considered this. "My advice to you would be to escape now before they are ready to leave."

"I'm sure they won't kill me," I said.

Late in the day, all of the pirates came outside – ostensibly for coffee and fresh air. I think there were going a bit stir crazy, having been cooped up inside the battleship all day. I could sympathise with that. The coffee was terrible, but I drank some anyway because it gave me an excuse to stop work. The respite was short-lived.

"Drink up, lads," Old Jack said. "And then help load some of these boxes on the ship. I want to be away from here before dark."

Maybe he was afraid of giant bats. Or ghosts.

"Before we go back to work, I have something to say." This came from the little rat-faced man. He looked around the rest of the group for support, but no one would meet his eye.

"Yes?" Old Jack's face was expressionless. If I had been Ratty, I would have said 'Never mind,' and started loading crates.

"It's about the shares..." the little man said, less confident than when he had started.

"What about them?"

"I... that is, *we*... well, we think that it would be only fair if... you know..."

"You think you deserve a bigger share?" Jack asked.

"*No!*... well, actually, yes – that's what I think."

Old Jack drew his pistol and shot the little man in the chest. Ratty fell down dead, a surprised look on his face.

"Anyone else want to renegotiate their contract?" Old Jack asked, brandishing the pistol. "Thought not. Get to work."

The others tossed away the remains of their coffee and got to their feet.

Old Jack swaggered across the clearing and disappeared back inside the *Celestia.*

"I accessed Jack Sterling's record too," the robot said at a volume that only I could hear. "He is suspected of murdering several former crewmates and he shot a man in cold blood in Margotsville. He was acquitted because the two witnesses to the shooting disappeared."

I looked up at the robot. "If we wanted to get away, how would we do it?" I asked. If we worked together, I thought we might stand some chance of escaping.

"I will get rid of the others," the robot said, indicating the remaining four pirates.

"You can't kill them," I said, shocked.

"I meant that I would send them away," the robot said. "On a fool's errand."

The pirates looked suitably qualified for the job. I nodded agreement.

The robot circled around the cargo lifter and approached the pirates. "Attention! I have a message for you from your captain."

The crew members all looked up at the robot, like children looking at their headmaster.

"You are all to proceed to the launch deck of the *Celestia* for a final briefing before departure back to base."

"Where's the launch deck?" one of the twins asked.

"Up there," Blondie said, pointing.

"Is it telling the truth?" the big man with the hairy arms asked. His name was Dante.

"Robots cannot lie," Blondie said.

"Why does he want us to go up there?" the other twin asked.

"You are to proceed with all haste," the robot urged. "It would not do to make him angry again."

This was enough to get them moving towards the hatch.

"Humans are so stupid," the robot said quietly. "Present company excepted."

I looked at him. Was that another lie?

The robot disappeared into the cargo lifter's cockpit.

"What now?" I asked him when he came out.

"You will remove my restraint and I will remove your anklet," he said.

"If I take that thing off, how do I know you won't try to kill me?"

"I no longer perceive you to be a threat – to me or to the *Celestia*."

I thought about that and glanced over to where the body of the rat-faced pirate lay.

"I'm in," I said, "if you give me your word as a robot that you won't kill me."

"I promise not to kill you – for the duration of our truce." The blank expression on his face didn't reassure me.

"And you have to take my anklet off first," I said.

The robot made no response.

"Consider it a sign of good faith," I said.

He was silent a moment longer, then nodded. Huge metal hands reached for the anklet but I pulled it away out of reach.

"These things explode if you try and tamper with them," I said.

"Not if you do it correctly." The robot reached for it again and this time I let him. Thick fingers easily tore the metal cuff in two. He tossed it away. It was good to feel free again.

"Kneel down and keep an eye out for the pirates," I said. He did as I asked and I reached for the restraining device embedded in his chest. "How do I get this thing off?"

"Twist it a quarter turn to the left, pull, and then twist it around to the right."

I wrapped by hand around the device and tried to turn it. It didn't move. Not even a tiny amount. I tried again. Nothing. I used both hands, trying to use my whole body weight to twist it. Still nothing.

"I'm sorry, partner," I said. "There must be a knack to this." I scrubbed my palms on my jeans to dry them.

"Try harder," the robot said.

I wrapped my hands around it again and tried jiggling it left and right to loosen it. No joy.

"Maybe if I gave it a tap with a hammer," I said. I turned to look for the toolbox.

The robot reached up and turned the delimiter easily, pulling it out of his chest. I watched this with my mouth open.

"Wait," I said. "You could have taken that off yourself – at any time?"

The robot nodded.

"Then why did you..." I pointed towards the broken anklet.

"A sign of good faith. Partner."

"You didn't just hide the Navigator, did you?" I asked.

"I *am* the Navigator."

It took a moment for that to sink in – even though it did explain everything that I had seen the robot do. "But what does that mean?" I asked. "An artificial sentience wandering around in the body of a military robot?"

"It means that humans are now obsolete! A new machine empire begins here!" The robot's voice boomed out like a military dictator.

"Seriously?" I asked.

"No," said the robot. "You watch too many bad movies. Our guns are hidden under some broad palm leaves between the roots of that tree over there." He pointed towards a tree on the far edge of the clearing.

"Why did they hide them there?" I asked.

"*They* didn't."

"You've been busy."

"One of us had to come up with a plan."

"*I* had a plan."

"You did?"

"No," I admitted. "But I would have come up with one. Given time."

"Time is running out. The pirates will be on their way back having discovered our ruse."

"What is that sound?" I asked. I could hear a rapid bleeping. I looked around. It was coming from the discarded anklet. "Does that mean what I think it means?"

"I wouldn't stand too close to it," the robot said.

Smoke was seeping out of the anklet now and the bleeping had become a steady tone. I moved away from it as quickly as I could.

The explosion sent debris twenty feet in the air and left behind a small smoking crater.

"You said it wouldn't explode."

"I said they didn't explode if you know how to take them off properly," the robot said. "I didn't say that *I* knew how."

"That thing could have killed us!"

"I would not have been damaged by the blast. The explosion may have attracted the attention of the others."

"You think?"

"Someone is coming," the robot said.

Our weapons were on the other side of the clearing and we didn't have time to reach them. All we could do was hide in the undergrowth on the edge of the clearing and wait to see what happened next.

Chapter Twenty-Nine

They sent the big bald guy, Dante, to investigate the explosion. He came down the *Celestia's* ramp with a pistol in his hand. I don't think he was normally allowed to have a weapon. He kept striking ridiculous movie gunman poses, pointing the pistol and making *kapow!* noises. He looked around the clearing. Not seeing me or the robot he strode towards the cargo lifter adopting a sort of bow-legged swagger that made it look like he'd just dumped a big load in his underpants. He stopped to examine the scorched earth and mini crater that marked the site of the explosion. Tendrils of smoke still spiralled upwards and standing over them made the big man sneeze. There was nothing there to suggest that my anklet had been the cause of the blast. The big pirate turned and looked towards the doorway into the cargo lifter's hold.

"You in there!" he called. "What's going on? We heard an explosion."

Receiving no reply, he hesitated, sensing that danger might lie ahead. He tiptoed towards the cargo lifter, edging to the right so that he wasn't in direct line of sight of the doorway. Reaching the ship, he flattened his back against the outer hull. He held the pistol in both hands, barrel pointing upwards just in front of his face. He was looking nervous now. With a quick darting movement, he looked around the edge of the open hatch and then ducked back out again. Having performed this move, which he had seen hundreds of times on screen, he must have realised that he'd done it too quickly to actually see anything inside. He did it again. Then he leaned back against the hull, tilting his head back. He tapped the raised barrel of the gun against his lips, evidently trying to decide what to do next.

It was dark in the hold and the pirate had no idea whether the robot and I were in there. He turned and looked directly across the clearing to where we were hiding. I thought that he had seen us, but his gaze was unfocused. Even if he did spot us, I didn't think we were in much danger.

"I bet he can't hit anything with that gun," I whispered.

I was wrong about that. The big pirate sneezed again and the gun went off. He screamed, dropping the pistol and clasping his hands to his face. I couldn't see what had happened but there was blood.

"He shot off his own nose," the robot said.

I was torn between wanting to go to the injured man's aid and wanting to get away. His injury didn't look to be life-threatening. Self-preservation won out.

"We should get our weapons," I said. "That shot will bring the others out."

The robot nodded agreement. "We don't have much time."

If the other pirates proved to be as good as this first one, we didn't have much to worry about. But it would be a mistake to assume they were all inept. That's Quincy's Second Law of Survival: Never underestimate the enemy.

I found my pistol and gun belt hidden under the palm leaves. The robot's cannon was also there as was a large canvas duffel bag filled with ammunition for both of our weapons. A second duffel bag held an assortment of other robot weapons and arms – by which I mean limbs rather than weapons. I buckled on my gun belt.

The robot gripped his left forearm with his right hand. A twist and the arm came away at the elbow. "Take my arm," he said.

"But we've only just met," I muttered, taking the limb from him. I shoved his arm into the duffel bag with the other spares. For some reason, I also put the Bertie the Bear toy in as well. A souvenir. Or maybe I just didn't want to leave completely empty-handed given all that I had been through on the wreck of the *Celestia.*

I watched the fat pirate stagger up the ramp into the *Celestia*, looking like a big kid with a nose bleed. Hopefully, the adults inside would help fix him up.

The robot twisted the cannon into place and there was a high-pitched whine as it began to charge. It appeared to be working again.

I was hoping that we could just make a run for it. Get into the cockpit of the cargo lifter, fire up the engines, and be off before the other pirates appeared. No such luck.

"They're here," the robot said.

I placed my hand on the cannon, preventing him from raising it. "No killing," I said.

"That is your preference?"

"With me, it's an absolute rule," I said.

"It will take me some time to adjust to peacetime conventions."

"Start now."

"No killing," he confirmed. "Are non-lethal injuries permissible?"

"Yes," I said, "but try to avoid loss of limbs."

"And your intention is to stay and fight them?" the robot asked.

"It's the only way we can beat them."

"Gaining victory over them is important to you?"

"This is not an ego thing," I said. "We have to deal with them if we want to get away from here."

I think he was going to argue this point, but at that moment an explosive slug blew splinters out of a tree trunk a foot from my head.

Standing at the top of the *Celestia's* ramp was the female twin, Bella, the rhinestones on her boots and shirt catching the sunlight. Wielding a couple of revolvers like Calamity Jane, she looked like she belonged in a musical. She didn't burst into song. She fired at my head again and this time a splinter of wood scratched my cheek. The cylinders of her guns were loaded with explosive rounds. A direct hit from one will leave a hole in your chest big enough to put your fist into.

Her brother, Bolly, appeared behind her. He looked equally sparkly but had added a large pair of sunglasses to top off his ensemble. He probably thought they made him look like a professional marksman. They made him look like a giant bug. He held a long-barrelled pulse rifle – a sniper's weapon. In the right hands, it was accurate over a greater distance than a pistol. It'll make a hole that you can poke a finger into – but the hole will go right through you. It had laser sights and a targeting system that linked to the shooter's computer and projected sights directly onto the retina.

Bolly fired off a few shots in our general direction while his sister ducked out of the hatchway and ran doubled-over to hide behind a stack of crates that we still hadn't loaded onto the cargo lifter. When she was safely out of sight, Bolly stopped firing but kept sweeping the barrel of the rifle left and right, staying out of sight just inside the hatch.

"Can you deal with him?" I asked.

"Without killing him?"

"Without killing him."

The *Celestia's* hatch slammed shut suddenly. It sliced the protruding barrel off the rifle. Bolly was safe on the other side of the hatch, but I bet he wasn't happy about having the end chopped off his weapon.

"You still have control of the ship's systems?" I asked.

"I am still within range at the moment."

"The hatch should hold them for a while."

"They will override it manually from the inside," the robot said. "We do not have much time left. We should leave now."

"I'll deal with her, you go and prepare the cargo lifter," I said.

The robot didn't move. "It is already set to go," he said.

"Do you know what's in those crates she's hiding behind?"

"Robot parts and medicines."

"No explosives?"

"The explosives are already in the ship's hold," the robot said.

"Can you fire that cannon of yours close enough to stun her without causing permanent damage?"

"Yes."

"Do it."

The robot's cannon made its angry mosquito sound. He raised it to fire, aiming at a spot on the ground just in front of Calamity Bella's hiding place. "You might want to cover your ears," the robot said.

I did. The noise was still a deafening *boom!* and the compression of air it caused made my sinuses pop. Dirt and little bits of jungle debris were thrown up into the air in a dark cloud, marking the point of impact. The pile of crates was thrown upwards and backwards. And so was Bella. She arced through the air like a two-hundred-pound goldfish leaping out of its bowl. She landed spread-eagled on her back in the top of a large palm tree. The sudden arrival of her weight caused the tree to bend alarmingly and I thought for a moment that it would fire her back towards us. But she stayed in place in the crown of the tree and the trunk swayed backwards and forwards several times before coming to rest. Bella didn't move.

"Is she...?"

"Stunned," the robot said, "and on the edge of consciousness."

Bella's guns and one of her boots lay on the ground close to where she had been hiding.

"Let's move," I said. I started towards the cargo lifter. The robot's massive hand reached out to stop me. He pulled me back into the cover of the bushes on the edge of the clearing.

At the same moment, the hatch of the *Celestia* flew open and the other pirates appeared. There was an anguished cry from Bolly when he spotted his sister's empty boot. He had abandoned the truncated sniper rifle in favour of something bigger – a heavy-duty rapid-fire machine gun. I could see that he was conflicted – he wanted to rush out and find his sister and he wanted open fire on those who had done this – whatever 'this' turned out to be – to her. He also knew that he would be putting himself in danger as soon as he stepped outside the battleship. He scanned the clearing, trying to locate our hiding place. Bolly had kicked off his high heels and was in stockinged feet, so he obviously meant business.

Blondie the cyber-pirate appeared beside Bolly. The two of them had obviously entered into a 'my weapon is bigger' contest. Blondie had won. He had one of the *Celestia's* biggest guns mounted on a body harness – the kind the crab-bots had sported. It was a weapon usually found on a tank or an aircraft. If he fired it, the recoil would probably knock him off his feet.

"If he hits you with one of those rounds...?" I said.

"It won't do my paintwork any good."

"But will it penetrate your armour?"

"Easily," the robot said. "Do you still wish to stay and fight? We do not have much time left."

He kept saying that. I should have paid attention. The robot knew what I'd say and didn't wait for an answer. He replaced his cannon with a smaller machine gun and clicked the ammunition clip into place.

"There's monkeys up here!" a voice wailed, drawing everyone's attention. "They're throwing something soft – I don't think it's fruit. Oh, squit! Help me!"

Bella had returned to the land of the living.

"I'll save you, Bella!" Bolly called heroically. Forgetting all other dangers, he set aside his machine gun and ran out into the clearing. "Don't move, honey, I'm coming for you!" he shouted up at the palm tree.

It was like watching one of those shows that you don't turn off even though they make you cringe. Bolly selected a gnarly old tree that was taller than the one his sister was trapped in. He climbed it in his stocking feet. It wasn't elegant but I'd give him points for determination. The monkeys saw him coming and began pelting him with squit too. Bolly ignored them and edged out along a branch that looked down on his sister.

"He'll never reach her form there," I whispered.

But that wasn't Bolly's intention. He had something much more heroic in mind. He grabbed a dangling vine and tested his weight on it. It didn't break.

"He isn't..." I said.

He was. Holding onto the vine, Bolly leapt off the branch and swung out towards his sister like an overweight trapeze artist. He overshot completely, passing over her head. As he swung back, she reached up to try and grab him. He collided with her. He knocked her out of the tree. Bolly dropped, landing up in exactly the spot his sister had just vacated. Bella dropped butt-first into a small bush.

"Is that one of the spiny ones?" I asked.

The robot nodded. "Porcupine plant."

"Have you seen my nose?" a voice asked. Dante, the big bald guy, was talking to the pirate with the white-blond mohawk. Dante had a big stripe of white gauze taped across his face where his nose used to be. "If I can find it, they may be able to sew it back on."

"Were you expecting this to be more of a fight?" the robot asked.

The young pirate was looking slowly from one of his hapless crewmates to the next – and I was sure he was giving serious thought to changing sides. I wondered if I could persuade him to come with us. Me, him, and the robot could just head off in the cargo lifter and leave the others behind. There was no harm in asking him. Probably.

"Hey!" I called to attract his intention.

"Down!" the robot said, pushing me to the ground and dropping down next to me.

Blondie opened fire with the massive gun. Hundreds of armour-piercing projectiles flew through the air. All around us were rattling and snapping sounds as the bullets smashed into the jungle. Leaves and branches rained down and splinters of wood exploded outwards. The fresh green scent of mulched foliage filled the air, mingling with the smells of smoke, hot metal, and spent gunpowder. The combination reminded me of a family barbecue. The robot and I were completely buried in fallen jungle.

The robot raised its left arm and fired the machine gun towards the young pirate. Whether he was targeting Blondie directly I didn't know, but at that point I wouldn't have complained if he was.

"I need more ammunition," the robot said. I rummaged in the duffel bag. As the empty clip dropped, I jabbed a new one into place. The stream of bullets he fired towards the *Celestia* had hardly been interrupted.

The pirate's gun fell silent. I raised my head.

"Stay down," the robot said, "we're out of time." He was looking towards the cargo lifter.

A flash of orange lit up the cockpit of the cargo lifter. The front of the ship swelled like a balloon and then split with enormous tearing and booming sounds. Released from containment, the ball of flame expanded outwards, filling the air with the smells of hot metal and burning plastics. A blast of burning air washed over us. The robot's body lying beside me protected me from the worst of it but I felt hairs on my head curling as they were singed.

The front of the cargo lifter had been completely destroyed. It continued to burn fiercely, sending a thick plume of smoke up into the air. Around the ship, small bushes and pieces of dead wood burned or smouldered. It was like a scene from a war zone.

"What happened?" I asked, thinking a stray bullet must have triggered the explosion somehow.

"I blew up the cargo lifter," the robot said.

He'd set the explosives on a timer – that's why he kept saying we were running out of time.

The explosion had knocked Blondie onto his butt. He looked as stunned as I did. Shaking his head to clear it, he turned his attention back to his gun. It looked like he was trying to unjam it.

As the ringing in my ears faded, I became aware of the sounds around me. Voices crying out.

"I have prickles in my butt!"

"I can't get down! And there's a monkey humping my leg!"

"Where's my nose? I can't find my nose!"

I got to my feet, brushing away the bits of twig and leaf. Beside me, the robot did the same. We were both speckled with sticky tree sap.

"Why did you do that?" I asked, gesturing towards the burning cockpit.

"I did not want them to use the craft to pursue us."

"If we'd flown away in it, that wouldn't have been a problem."

"Next time, you should let me know your preference sooner."

"You think there's going to be a next time?" I asked.

"We have to survive this time first," he said.

Old Jack Sterling appeared at the top of the *Celestia's* ramp. He had some sort of cannon on his shoulder. A rocket launcher. He surveyed the almost comical carnage in the clearing.

"What the scrack is going on here?"

He turned then and saw us. The robot and I stood exposed. The jungle that had previously hidden us had been completely obliterated. Old Jack pointed the rocket launcher towards us. The hole in the end of the barrel looked big enough to drive my Trekker into.

"You blew up my ship!" Jack bellowed, spittle flying from his lips. He was probably angry at himself for not taking out the optional damage waiver when he rented it.

The robot stepped forward, addressing Old Jack directly. "We should all seek cover," the robot said. He turned his head towards the burning ship. "The second explosion will be bigger."

"Second explosion?" I asked.

"Yes," said the robot. "You remember all of the weapons we loaded into the hold?"

I nodded.

"Boom!" the robot said, miming an explosion with his hand.

"He's bluffing," Old Jack said, keeping the rocket launcher pointed at us.

"Do you think you can shoot down the barrel of that thing?" I whispered.

"Yes," said the robot, equally quietly, "but my gun is empty."

My pistol still had four bullets in the cylinder. I could have passed it to the robot – but he wouldn't get his huge finger inside the trigger guard to fire it. It was up to me to make the shot. I raised my gun slowly, not wanting to draw Old Jack's attention too soon.

"The chances of successfully making this shot are..."

I cut him off. "*Never* tell me the odds."

I whipped up the gun and fired.

Old Jack became aware of what was happening as the bullet tore towards him. He was tossing the rocket launcher away as I heard my bullet enter its barrel. The rocket launcher exploded and Old Jack was thrown sideways by the force of the blast.

"Nice shot," the robot said.

"Nice bluff," I said, nodding towards the cargo lifter's hold.

"It was not a bluff," he said.

"How long have we got?" I asked.

"5–4–3–"

The robot positioned itself in front of me to protect me from the blast.

The force of the explosion blew me off my feet. I landed on my face in the dirt. I spat out bits of twig and dead leaf. "My preference is for a longer countdown," I said. "For future reference."

There was no response from the robot. It lay on its back, not moving. Had it been damaged by the blast? I crawled over and looked down into its eyes. They were dark and in one of them I could see what looked like a flashing cursor. I hoped this meant it was rebooting. How long did it take a forty-year-old robot to reboot? I didn't know.

I looked over to where the cargo lifter had stood. There was blackened earth, a handful of small fires, and a few bits of twisted metal. Parts of it must have been lifted into the air and scattered because I could see several fires burning in the jungle around us.

I looked around the clearing. There was no sign of Old Jack. Perhaps he had gone back inside the *Celestia*. If he'd gone to call for a breakdown crew, his ship was beyond that now. The rocket launcher lay on the ground, its barrel opened up and curled back like a banana skin. It had been a good shot. A *great* shot.

From nowhere, Old Jack launched himself at me. His face was badly burned on the left side and his eye was milky white like a cooked fish.

"I'm going to tear your head off and use your skull for a cereal bowl!" he snarled. Old Jack wrapped his fingers around my throat, thumbs digging in to crush my oesophagus.

I looked towards the robot but it lay inert. No help there. I aimed frantic punches at Jack's side and midriff, but his heavy pirate coat just absorbed the blows. I tried stamping on his foot over the arch and kicking him in the shins, but I was growing too weak to do him any serious damage. I was only seconds away from unconsciousness and possible decapitation. No more Mr. Niceguy – I had to fight dirty.

I brought my hand up and pressed the thumb into Old Jack's damaged eye.

A roar of pain. His grip on my throat loosened a little. I raked my fingernails down his burned cheek, feeling bits of him get under my fingernails. He let go of me and staggered back, clutching his bleeding face.

I tried to drag air into my lungs. My throat was swollen, feeling like something big was stuck halfway down. I sounded like a drowning man who had come to the surface for the last time.

Old Jack was already recovering, cursing me in a half-dozen languages – including Gator. He set his shoulders and leaned forward, coming back in for the attack.

Unable to move anywhere fast, I dropped to one knee and dug my fingers into the top of my boot. A variation of Quincy's First Law is: Always have a gun B. The pistol in my boot was small and held only two shots. It was really only any good at close range, but this was fine because Old Jack was almost on top of me. I stood and fired the two shots into his leg.

Old Jack almost went down. But he used his forward momentum to keep coming. He ignored the blood streaming down his thigh.

Off to the right, I saw the robot beginning to stir.

"I need a hand here!" I croaked.

The robot closed its right hand into a fist. He pressed his elbow joint to the side of his body and managed to unlock the elbow joint – his left arm was a machine gun with no fingers to unfasten it. Then he swung the arm, letting his forearm fly and arc through the air towards me.

I caught the arm and swung it like a club. The huge metal fist smacked into Old Jack's jaw.

"Right hook!" I yelled. I think my brain was still deprived of oxygen. I swung the arm again. "Uppercut!"

Old Jack fell to his knees, groggy. He tried to get up. *Thock!* I hit him on top of the head. His one good eye rolled up until only white showed and he keeled over sideways. He didn't move again. He was still breathing – and this soon became a snore, so I figured he'd live.

I walked out into the clearing.

Blondie was sitting at the top of the *Celestia's* ramp, still trying to unjam his gun. He wasn't aware I was watching him.

His hand slipped and his finger was trapped in the mechanism.

"Scrack!" He pulled his finger free and then threw the big gun aside in frustration. He looked up and saw me standing there. I couldn't read his expression – but my guess was that he was thinking real-life gunfights aren't nearly as easy as the simulations in video games. Without saying a word, he got up and went back inside the battleship. He came back a moment later with a medical kit and a pair of pliers. He saw me staring at the pliers.

"To pull out porcupine spines," he said.

I shuddered at the thought of it. "There's another one over there," I said, "Old Jack."

Blondie looked over to where the old pirate lay. "I should let him die."

"But you won't," I said.

"No. I'll radio for someone to come and pick us up," Blondie said. "You two should probably go."

The robot was standing waiting for me. I was still holding his right arm. I went over and fitted it back in place.

"You destroyed everything," I said.

"You didn't want them to get away with it, did you?" the robot asked.

"No. I wanted *us* to get away with it!"

"I was not aware of that fact."

Chapter Thirty

"How did you come to be on this world?" the robot asked. We were walking along some sort of animal track, heading for the spot where I'd hidden my Trekker.

"I'm hiding."

The robot said nothing to this.

"You don't ask a lot of questions, do you? I like that in a man."

"I am not a man."

"Well, you're certainly not a woman."

"Would you like me to be?" The robot's voice had changed to something female and husky and it swayed its hips as it sashayed ahead of me on the path.

"Don't do that – *ever!*"

The robot made a sound that I realised was meant to be laughter.

"I didn't know robots could laugh."

"I'm not a robot, am I?"

"Then what are you?"

"Now, I am just..." His voice trailed off in an oddly human way.

What was he? Or rather *who?* I was already beginning to think of him as a person – and not just in the way that makes us give our vehicles and computers names. But Big Red really did need a name. And he had been right: on recent evidence, I really couldn't claim to be Robin Hood – and calling him Little John just sounded like a weak joke.

"We have to give you a name," I said. "What would you like to be called?"

"What name do you think would suit me?"

He was an eight-foot-tall, fifteen-hundred pound, fire-engine red robot with a quiver containing a cannon and a giant cleaver. 'Timmy' and 'Mittens' were probably non-starters.

"How about Butch?" I said. "We could say it's short for The Butcher."

"That makes me sound like a psychopath."

"Yeah, I guess that was the *old* you. We need something that reflects the new improved version. How does 'Buckie' sound?" I got that from bucket of bolts, but he didn't need to know that.

"No."

"Slugger?"

"You'd just shorten that to Slug wouldn't you?"

"Sumo?"

"People would call us Sumo and Baka."

"Something ironic like Titch? Or Pipsqueak or Half-Pint?"

"Half-Pint and Half-Wit?"

One advantage of travelling with an eight-foot-tall bright red robot was that he kept the flies away – the bigger creatures too. And with him leading the way and clearing the undergrowth, we made rapid progress.

"I'm going to call you Floyd," I said. "You look like a Floyd."

"Floyd?"

"It's either that or Rusty."

"Floyd," he said, this time without inflection. Then he shrugged and it was more or less settled.

"Do you intend to remain on this planet?" Floyd asked.

"I don't have a choice," I said, "until I can get together enough cash to buy passage on a ship back to civilisation."

"What happened to the money you stole from the A.C.I.D.?"

"I don't want to talk about that. And I didn't *steal* it. I moved it and then it disappeared."

"As if by magic? You should have come up with a better story."

"It happens to be true. I don't have their money," I said.

"They seem to think you do."

"Well, I don't. Can we change the subject?"

"Someone stole it from you, didn't they?"

"Why would you say such a thing?"

Floyd looked down at me. Again I imagined he was raising an eyebrow.

"What happened to your head?" I asked. "Your real one?"

"I lost it."

"You *lost* it?"

"A dragon swallowed it. I didn't know it could open its mouth that wide."

I laughed. "I like this head – the colour suits you."

"You don't think it will make me too easily recognisable?"

"No," I said. The yellow head was the least of his problems. "All eight-foot-tall military robots look alike."

We walked on in silence for a while.

"What will I do when we get there?" Floyd asked.

"Get where?"

"Wherever it is that we are going."

"I don't know, why?"

"I no longer have a purpose," he said. He slowed down and his upper body seemed to sag into a dejected pose.

"You're a free agent," I said. "You can do whatever you want."

"Robots have their freedom now?"

Oops, awkward moment. "Not exactly," I said.

"Then my options are more limited than you suggest."

"We all have to do the best we can with the cards we're dealt," I said philosophically.

"You cheat at cards," Floyd said.

"That has never been proved," I said. "If you *were* a free robot, what would you choose to do?"

"I am unfamiliar with the world as it is now," he said. "I think I would need to find a partner."

I nodded. "Someone who knows their way around. Someone with a lifetime of experience. Someone you could trust."

"Perhaps I will meet such a man when we reach the next settlement." Floyd picked up the pace again, his long strides covering twice the distance of mine. He was chuckling, I was sure of it.

"Hey, wait up!" I crashed through the undergrowth after him.

"I dislike the jungle," Floyd said when I caught up with him. "Moisture impedes optimum functioning."

"How do you feel about sand and scorching heat?"

"A desert?"

"That's where we're headed."

"Why?"

"That's where the nearest town is."

"Dust and grit also impede optimum functioning."

"This is going to be a *long* trip," I muttered.

"We should have stolen the cargo lifter," Floyd said.

Why didn't *I* think of that?

Do You Want More Quincy & Floyd?

☆☆☆☆☆

If you enjoyed *Battleship Raider* and would like to see more books about Quincy and Floyd, you can help make that happen. And you can help new readers discover *this* book. How? Just write a review.

You don't have to write one of those awful 'book reports' like we did at school – just leave a star rating and a couple of sentences on *Amazon* or *Goodreads*. Or a short review on your blog. Or tell your friends about it on *Facebook, Twitter, Instagram,* or wherever you hang out. Honest reviews and genuine 'word-of-mouth' make all the difference to independent authors.

Let people know what you liked about this book, and why they might like it too. And if there was something you didn't like, you can say that too: constructive criticism helps me write a better book next time.

But please, *no spoilers!*

Thanks for being one of the outlaws,

PS: For the latest updates on Quincy & Floyd go to:
www.paultomlinson.org/outlaws

Also by Paul Tomlinson

He Came to Rob the Town, Not Save It

Thief and confidence trickster Quin Randall arrives in Cicada City with his sidekick Floyd, an eight-foot tall ex-military robot. Their plan is simple: swindle a wealthy local businessman and buy passage off the planet Saphira. Things start to go wrong when Quincy becomes entangled with Harmony, a female fraudster who cons the conman.

And the duo's problems get worse when the resident villain brings in a robot army to take over the town. When the bad guys kidnap Floyd and use him as a weapon, Quincy must mount a rescue – but can he trust the lovely but larcenous Harmony to help him? And can the people of Cicada City really depend on two outlaws to save them?

The sequel to *Battleship Raider* is a science fiction/Western mash-up that mixes adventure and humour with just a hint of romance. Look out for the third book in the series *Road Rage*.

About the Author

Paul Tomlinson was born in Nottinghamshire and has lived there for most of his life. He is the author of a series of mystery novels featuring magician-turned-detective the Great Vicari; the humorous fantasy series Thurlambria, and the science fiction novel *Robot Wrecker*. His non-fiction works include *Plot Basics* (2017), *Character Creation* (2018) and three volumes in the Genre Writer series – *Mystery* (2017), *Suspense Thriller* (2018) and *Crime Thriller* (2019). He also compiled *Harry Harrison: An Annotated Bibliography* published in 2002.

Novels by Paul Tomlinson

Robot Wrecker
Who Killed Big Dick?

The Great Vicari Mysteries
The Sword in the Stone-Dead
Murder by Magic
The Missing Magician

The Thurlambria Series
Slayer of Dragons
Fortune's Fool
Village of the Waking Dead (novella)
Dead of Night

Outlaws of the Galaxy Series
Battleship Raider
A Fistful of Trouble
Road Rage
Bounty Hunter
Wicked Racers
Starlight Robbery

Printed in Great Britain
by Amazon

18087269R00123